The Live Goat

Books by Cecil Dawkins

THE LIVE GOAT

THE QUIET ENEMY (short stories)

THE A NOVEL
LIVE
GOAT

Cecil Dawkins

HARPER & ROW PUBLISHERS

New York, Evanston, San Francisco, London

Part One

Duncan McElroy

They never would of thought him. They wouldn't of had the least idea who killed her if he hadn't run. It took a halfwit not to figure that out, same as it took a halfwit to steal the little red saddle mule belongs like a pet to Toliver Pullen's wife to run away on. Nobody lays eyes on that mule and forgets it. Might as well of left a marked trail for us.

He must of lit out right after he done it. They think likely around sunup because she left home just before, and she never got farther than the pasture spring. And Pa never found her lying there till he was done hunting and cut across the Jurdin place on his way back home for breakfast. I was at the barn trying to milk that pieded cyclone when here come Pa hightailing it with his gun and his dogs, a passel of small game swinging from his belt, one arm streaked to the elbow with rusted blood, though if he'd paused to skin I couldn't see at his belt what it was he'd skinned. I was studying that while he commenced telling Ma, and I got the blood on him, the skinning, and that about Eily Jurdin all mixed up together. He said he judged she'd been lying there beside the spring a couple hours then.

Pa went (me tailing him, over Ma's lament) and told Mister Hite, wanting him to tell Eustace Jurdin. But Mister Hite didn't want to neither. He hung back too, at first. He had to go look at her. He had to see for hisself before he would tell such a thing to Eustace. I wanted to go and I didn't want to go. I hadn't ever seen anybody dead before. So I trailed along, hanging behind them, still of two minds even when I crouched in the thicket and looked.

It's a pretty place any time of day. That early, it wasn't hardly real, the old oaks leaning down their heavy limbs, thick as trunks of ordinary trees, great big moss-feathered flat rocks the size of monuments, and soft grasses that will take the print of your foot and hold it. The spring is clear as air, and the bubbles don't seem to rise but hang like strings of beads from the surface to the depths where little peppercorn snails feast on the watercress. The birds that time of day sound hushed and secret. She just looked like a part of it, lying there, her basket beside her, like a girl in a tale. I saw that the dry blood on Pa's arm had to come from some squirrel he'd shot but hadn't killed. He must of had to pick it up and slam its head against a tree, and that's where the red on his hand come from, not from touching her. For there wasn't a sign that anything harsh had happened. No blood on her at all. You would of swore she was asleep. She still had her bonnet on.

Of course I never seen her up close. I hung back among the vines grown over the stark trunks and stumps and branches of the deadening where Eustace and Earl been girdling in the wintertime, to push back the forest and get more than the Indian old field for planting. The blighted wood, tree limbs bone-white under all that tangle of vines—like a wood being dragged under by a green

4

wavering sea. Pa and Mister Hite never touched her. They stood side by side, silent, looking down. Then the preacher commenced I reckon to pray to hisself, for he taken off his hat. After he finished, he put it back on and nodded to Pa and they come away, me falling in again and following.

Then they was a sight of commotion—folks gathering, the men bringing her home, the women wailing.

The sun was straight up before Tuttle come stalking like a sandhill crane down the path from Pullens'. Everybody had to tell him what had happened. And it was some time before he remembered he'd come to ask around if anybody'd laid eyes on Sidney's saddle mule. Sidney, she just thought it had broke out. The bar was down in the stall. Everybody knows the little mule is smart enough to count and to curtsy when asked, so we all supposed it could lower the bar if it took a notion. Nobody put the vanished mule together with Eily Jurdin dead. Everybody naturally thought some stranger passing through had done it. Then here she come, hands clutching at one another like two pups scrapping, beside herself because she couldn't find him nowheres. She never lets him out of her sight, the way a woman will hover over one of hers that ain't right, though he ain't hers, she ain't his ma.

How come him to get such a start on us—we never known he was gone till she come clutching at her hands that away. And even then we didn't know at once it was him done it. We were just struck by such untoward things happening all at once. We didn't see that they fit together, except I reckon Mister Hite, who doubtless thought we'd had the devil invade our midst, which was no more than he'd all his life expected. It took Eustace—looking like he'd had a stroke and couldn't change expressions, the way Min Hite's daddy got before he passed on (but he was going

5

on ninety and Eustace is a man in his prime) —it took Eustace to see it.

"We'll have to go after him, Loren, and bring him back," he said to Pa, not much different, but for the frozen look of him, than if he'd said, "We'll have to hope Tuttle roof his barn."

He never even said why. We just stood there on the porch and in the yard looking at him and slowly knowing as he said it why. And he said, "He won't be easy to over-take, riding the Pullens' mule." We all known that was right. By then he had a good ten-hour start on us that this whole month past he's kept on stretching out. We're slowed down, tracking, and none of us can match pace for steadiness with Sidney's little mule. Except I reckon Toli-ver on his Beth. But we've all kept together of course.

Toliver Pullen

Even if that settlement up ahead is the one they told us to be on the lookout for, even if it is him yonder, sitting dumb watch over the little mule, no way in the world we can get back in less than another month. I had to come though. Wouldn't have looked right if I hadn't. No good reason not to, with the corn and cotton both laid by. Shameful, a man so bounden to a woman.

No way any of us could have known it would take so long a time or lure us so far away. Nothing like what it has turned out to be ever even entered our heads. I wonder how many of them have wanted to turn back but wouldn't let on. Not a one of us had ever seen The Old Man. Now we've crossed it. Not a one laid eyes on a prairie that now have passed through grass as high as the horses' heads for miles at a stretch and heard the prairie wind speak a different tongue from wind in longleaf pine. Or been in a palmetto swamp that's like a stranger planet than this one. We have gone through wonders, and every one of us, even Loren's boy, trying to look as if all of it was nothing more than we've been used to. Even before we'd good left home, we found ourselves already in country we'd never seen before. We come down from the escarpment that is a bib of the plateau above the fall line, following, Loren says, old Creek trails, and after a few days' travel—first following easily the little red mule's dainty tracks, and a good bit of the time trusting Loren's hunting nose, helped by people all along telling us, "Eyuh, we seen him pass, that little mule"—we had sat silent before a salt lick, staring at what a man told us were old bison paths. Radiated knee deep like wheel spokes in all directions. Swore he'd seen with his own eyes the humped and shaggy beasts, both there and northward at Mussel Shoals, where the Natchez Trace crosses the Alabama, yes and herds of deer too, sixty strong, when he first come there in twenty-six.

Wonders I never would have dreamed, but every day I have wished myself back where I come from. I am uneasy away from her. I know she is happier alone. I know she will be all right. But I go on being anxious. Maybe after this long time she will think I'm dead, killed by a river or a savage, and that she is free to go back home again.

The mule was the first gift of mine to please her, but it was not the first gift I made her. Not by a long sight. I swapped my father's rifled long gun to a couple moving down the back country from Tennessee, their noses set toward the end of the rainbow where land, the latest rumor has it, sells for ten cents an acre. To hear tell, you don't have to work land out there, it just tills itself. From the look of him, it'd have to. I felt some pity for the woman. I swapped the long gun to them for a thing she had around her neck. A jewel. Looked like she hated to part with it, but he thought he'd need the gun. They offered me silver, but I'd spied the thing lying on her throat and held out for that. I wanted it for Sidney. I thought she ought to like it. If she did, she never let on. It was a good rifle.

I bought the saddle mule off a traveling planter that stopped to rest his horses at the gin. He got to talking about these mules he raised. Said he'd brought the pedigreed jack clear from the Old Dominion. Before I knew it I'd contracted to buy a yearling. To go after it, I had a two-day ride out of the hills and a two-day ride back in. I thought it ought to please her. It was an oddity. And just the thing for a female. The breed is supposed to be safe, sturdy, dependable, intelligent, not given to panic nor shying. Full-grown now, its hoofs are dainty as a deer's. And every bit as surefooted as a goat. It will hold its gait —we've had reason this month past to bemoan it—for hours on end and never tire. If the planter was right, and I think he's been borne out, these animals are endowed with a sense of proportion few of your human breed can claim. Even as a yearling, its coat was beginning to show a kind of polished chestnut hard to describe. I never saw nothing else just like it.

The mule wasn't my first gift to her, it was just the first to please her. Even so, it wasn't that it was my gift, it was the mule itself won her over, being so gentle and smart and comical you'd swear if it could talk it could tell you what wisdom is. Before it was big enough for breaking, it followed her around the place like a dog or a lamb. I would catch her talking to it, it with its long fine ears cupped toward her like flowers toward the sun. Whenever she saw me listening, she'd leave off. I have given her many a gift to try to win her away from herself.

The boy, riding alongside Earl, starts to lag, then waits up. As we come abreast, he looks at me strangely. He's caught me talking to myself. Keeps an eye on me, dogs tracks my when he's uneasy, and I can't shake him.

"You reckon it's going to be him up there?" he asks.

"How'll we tell? We've all of us a long ways back forgotten what he looks like."

Earl

Each of us hanging back, we come on the settlement single file. Lord knows why. They say you never see mounted Indians move except they go single file. Fatal to be mistook for Indians here.

They say use to be this here was part of Mexico, which I've heard of. But they had them a war not long ago and now, they say, it is the Republic of the Texies. How many countries can they be in all, I'd like to know. Maybe I will find some way to get it out of Eustace without letting on.

I would of thought crossing into another country the land, let alone the people, would be noticeably different. But so far I don't note this to be any more different than what we have already passed through was different. It is, if anything, less different than some of it has been.

I never known we would follow him this far. And I give up ever finding him back days ago when they knowed they'd lost his trail again. Not that *that* made any difference. For a long time then they'd seemed to forget what we come after and why. Ever day when we commenced to move I thought it unlikely we would ever stop, and ever night when we halted I thought it unlikely we would ever start again. We've come so far I suspicion we are lost. But they don't think of that.

And now looks like we've found him and it's as if they all knew all along that was going to happen, and knew we had for that reason to keep on going. A puzzle to me how they all just know a thing while I am always at a loss. How do they always know what is the thing to do and the way to be? Do they just know, the way a bird in spring-time knows to build a nest or the young bitch hardly more than a pup herself knows how to give birth—lick open the sack, lap the pup in the soft pink pocket of her tongue and make it breathe, bite the cord and swallow the mess to start her milk? Or is they some one overall thing they know that all the other knowing stems out of? Some one principal thing that, if you know it, points the choices you must make so that nothing at all is merely meeny-mo.

Sometimes I think they must be such a principal thing. And sometimes I think it is the thing meant in the Bible where it says "To him who hath shall be given and from him who hath not shall be taken away even that which he hath." For that is the way it has worked out in my life.

I am *him who hath not* this whatever it is I must get if I am ever to become *him who hath,* so that unto me, like unto them, shall be given.

Where did they all come by it, and what, exactly, is its nature? I could ask, but who would not think I was a fool? Eustace? Not no more. Eustace is a dead man now. Emile? That old Indiancountryman. He never come in a settler like the rest of us. Just living there already, like an Indian in his bark longhouse, and we heired him. Some say we rescued him and praise be he can live out his days among God-fearing civilized folk. Others say he would of gone with the Indians if he could of stood the trip. Look at him set that pony. If he could make this trip, he could of made that other, with the Creek. But he made this one because of the gal. He'd grown overfond of Eustace's Eily.

Still single file—except for Duncan and Toliver, lagging together—we commence to rise. Their settlement lies on a bench of plain looking out in all directions from some elevation. Must be it gives them a sense of safety, seeing all around. But in this checkerboard land of separated wood and prairie where we lie disclosed for miles, my skin puckers and pricks, the nape of my neck crying the need of a second set of eyes, and I have to curb myself from turning to look about.

Here, finally, I've got difference. The Dutchmen's settlement is like nothing I ever saw. They've built their houses in a clutch inside their gardens—not loghouses, houses of sawn lumber painted white and gaumed with color and trimmed with carving. Beyond the ring of gardens, what looks like a common herd.

They've sighted us at a distance and come out to welcome us. The late sun glints off gun barrels, off great hay forks could spit us four at a time. No wonder they eye us

11

like we might be predators. Stripped and tattered by river, thicket, wood, burnt by a sun with no more mercy than the Lord, the clothes on our backs rotting from our own salt sweat, hair overlong and tied with whang, some wearing rag turbans like the Cherokee, we no longer strike God-fearing folk as more of their own.

We halt, our horses milling where rail fences funnel us into the mouth of a wagon road. An old sickle-shaped grandpa shouts, "Are you Christian folk? Do you keep the Sabbath?"

A dandy in blue embroidered galluses says to the boy beside him, but loud enough for us to hear, "Yes, and everything else they can lay their hands on." The boy laughs nervously.

A little gal with a honey plait weaves thigh high among them to climb the fence where she can get a better look at something's caught her eye.

Mister Hite launches his set piece on how far we've come to capture a boy who strangled a virgin on her wedding day. Georgia Gem beside me says, "J.W.'ll talk till dark now he's got him a congregation." Though their closed, doubting faces are turned, listening, on the preacher, the young'un on the fence stops breathing to hear his daughter Gem. It's Georgia Gem Hite she's staring at. I reckon she's got her ways of sorting people but Gem has her stumped. No wonder—the size of her, lank black hair chopped off at cheekbone level, hollow-faced, lantern-jawed, man's hat, men's clothes. If I wasn't used to her, I'd look too.

Mister Hite's voice dies. A fat fair bullet-headed fellow, the prongs of his ugly fork now planted in the sand to give him a staff to lean on, points. "See them woods along the river? Where the birds are circling?" While we turn,

Tuttle, now the atmosphere's more friendly, lifts his leg over the mule's head and slides off to sidle up to one of the women. Over the woods, the birds high up float on air as easy as geese on a mill pond. The man adds, "I couldn't say if it's a mule."

"You can't miss it. You'll wisht you could. Just follow your nose," says the dandy. The boy beside him laughs. "I declare! All this way. She must of been someone you all was devoted to," a young girl says to Toliver. A tall spare woman with one milk eye says, "Vat is it herds men seasonally in droves and to and fro and always bent on filence, either doing it or avenging it with more?"

Eustace turns his horse and moves off. Emile turns to follow, but a plump lace-bonneted grandma steps up to his pony and taps out her words on his stirrup cover. "Dot's right. Ain't we chust been t'roo it? First Mexikins, den Merikins. Svarming over us! It's men! De women wouldn't do it! I'd feel chust like a fool!"

Emile removes his pipe and bends smiling over her. "Mary, there's meat in it but it's drowning in your sauce."

The old woman's head darts back away from him like a chicken's. The dandy laughs. But we're moving off. Tuttle lopes from the Dutchwoman's kitchen garden to mount his mule on the move. The little gal, still eyeing Gem, huddles closer to the fence as she passes. Their gaunt old grandpa lifts his quavery voice after us, "His plessing on you in dis year of our Lord . . ."

Gem snorts. "If this is still in the month of August the year of our Lord, it's because the Devil wouldn't have it."

I have the gift of divining the time of day from the thickness of yellow in the light. Deny me sight of sun and shade, I could nonetheless give you the time, by the thickness of yellow in the light. Shadows stretch fingers toward

13

us from the wood. High over the trees the shabby scavengers ride air shafts so thick with yellow, thick with stench, they needn't work their wings to stay aloft. A little further on, it blankets us, chokes us, blinds us, an obscenity that keeps us from meeting each other's eyes. The yellow is so thick as we enter that mortal jurisdiction—as if the journey took a day, now day and journey both draw to their end.

Duncan McElroy

One minute nothing between us and the copse but a little empty space, shadowed in the late light; the next minute, there sets a man on a horse. Not as if he's emerged from the woods, more like he just appeared. His pants are skin and so's his sleeveless jacket, both black with grease and age, and a skin hat covers all of his head above the ears. "Coming for him?" he hails us, jerking his head toward the wood.

Mister Hite, our spokesman, nods. "We come some ways to get him. Traveling?"

A white thread of scar, like a line drawn with a straightedge, lies at the least angle across the bridge of his nose and, running clear across his eyes, divides his face. His horse frisks, unsettled by the noxious air. He quiets it, glancing down, and I see whatever made the scar also relieved one eye of a sliver of its lid, giving it, lashless, a naked look. While one eye moves, the other stands still and draws its bead on us, giving him a fixed expression

14

that strikes me first as a little astonished smile till I see that the mouth don't join in or even lend itself, but stays out of it altogether.

Answering Mister Hite, he says he's going across the border east and if we're turning back, if we're picking up in them woods what we come out after, then he'd like to join with us. "Sensible in these times to swell your party big as you can get it," he points out.

Mister Hite bids him, "Sir, will you identify yourself?"

And he says, "Why, I was born a Tuckahoe."

Mister Hite puzzles, nods, commences to move again. The stranger backs his horse aside to stand like an entire honor guard for us to pass. Then I know without turning my head that he's fallen in to follow.

Inside the smoke-grey live oak grove, magnolias rise gigantic, eighty-some-odd feet, and laurel and bay and rhododendron. Do I dream—I must, in August—the sweet of blossoms mingling with the other thing? Something's come over me. Something besides the shade and the awful smell, nearer now, held in by the high leaflace canopy. The river out there silent. No shoals like ours at home. And lacking that and bird sounds you'd expect, the air is mighty still. Something begins to happen. Something I couldn't name. I don't want to go no farther, don't want to see, try not to let it in through eye or nostril. I don't want the shade of thought off there behind a tree in the landscape of my head to suddenly leap out at me where I can name it Eily. Inside me a cricket in a matchbox cage, battering and battering, sets off the drum inside my ear. And for no reason a-tall I close my eyes and think *Now I lay me* . . . and in my mind's eye didappers at a stream edge running, running, a blur of broomstraw legs. And after this month of pure adventure and pleasuring in it all, silent I'm screaming at myself: *I never should of come a-tall. I never should of never should of* never *should of done it.*

And all that long way back before us still.

Eustace Jurdin

Not her the mule. She is nothing. A gravel in my brainshoe. I'm aware. I know it's there. But nothing. A gravel.

Part of me that was, is not. Torn out of being. A gape, a hole, a breach, a ragged emptiness. Some knowing that shared my knowing thereby confirming me.

But *is not, gape, hole, breach, emptiness*—nothings. She's a nothing now. A gravel in my brainshoe.

No! Shy away shy away. It is the mule the mule. Nothing will I be spared? All right. Choke—smother—blind—stopper me with offal. Scourge me with the bloom of death. Torture me that I may not feel.

I wear blinders and still must shy away shy away.

I was a blindfolded boy touched, they told me, by the white-hot poker. And though I knew it was an ice dagger from the saltpeter cave, I felt the snakestrike of the sear.

They told me. And this time the telling itself blinded me. Though I knew this time it was the brand, I felt instead the ice. It numbed and froze me, keeping me in life for a time yet.

For this?

16

Loren McElroy

And there he is.

You got to be the thing you hunt. And then you got to bring that thing to earth if you want yourself back whole.

I know all about you, boy. It's been some time now since I parted your hide and said move over and stepped inside. I would of thought if you ain't just right why you'd make haphazard choices. If you had, I'd never of led them to you. But you made *same* choices, according to a peculiar light I had to learn to see by.

And I learned. I even come to see where, and why, you'd left the choice up to the little mule. The mule's choices were easy to read, being always humbly reasonable. Yours were a different matter altogether.

Indian trails all the way, and they say you can travel a thousand miles in any direction from any one of the branch paths I picture as wrinkles in an old skin map, and that parchment an ancient tracery of this whole country we don't yet even know. But I was always right and could always prove myself when we passed folks again. Somebody always remembered the little mule.

No matter how fast you went, looked like you wasn't running away a-tall, but to. Or else you'd no mind anybody might be following. But more like, you couldn't stop without something stopped you, like you was a rock a-rolling down a gully.

Any varmint will head for his home grounds when he's being run. You could of circled in the hills this long and led us as good a chase. But I seen early you was wanting to leave the woods, leave the hills, to get for yourself a wide clean plain, which is something you can't have ever seen but must of had to dream for yourself, some home ground from another life, held in your mindlessness the way they say some fish or turtles know to travel countless impossible miles to return to their birthing ground to die.

Well, I've been in my time fawn and doe and buck, and bear and bear cub both, and turkey, squirrel, vixen, wolf. Rabbit, possum, coon. Every kind of bird. I never thought I'd be called upon to turn part defective boy, part mule. But I have managed. And there you are. I know all about you. I been you for some time now. You got to be the thing you hunt. And then you got to bring that thing to earth if you want yourself back whole again.

The Tuckahoe

The dimwit they've surrounded, drawn knee to chest, cheek to knee, and pressed into the animal's putrescent belly like some outlandish foal, gives no sign of sentience till struck by a sound too slight for any ear but his and the horses'. Out of the ball he's made of himself his head pops up like a rabbit's. They watch him listen. Then, with another dart, he turns.

Blue-black thatch fits his head like fur and so crowds his

face that his features take out in length what they lose in breadth, a face you might imagine some elvish thing to have. And the center is not the tip of the nose but the decided node at the tip of his long upper lip that—swollen, softly vulnerable as a nursling's—seems to collect and condense all the light in the dim wood.

His eyes flit over them while they wait. Then the oddly fetching face splinters into—recognition? The deepening smile washes wave on wave over them—of pure joy in his deliverance by friends from a world so strange he's had to bury himself in and to clutch—apparently for days—the one thing here he knows, the one familiar thing, as a child I once heard of, alone left alive in a massacre, clung to the breast of its dam till it came off in his hand.

Emile

I must climb down off my pony now in a way to alarm neither Isaac nor the watching men. Everything I do must take the shape of the inevitable for my Celts.

Was it through instinct, Isaac, you made unerring choices —even now, giving yourself into the keeping of the little mule? Nothing could more surely render you untouchable.

Easy. Easy. Animals restive, wild-eyed, expressing what Isaac and the men must in their stillness feel. The mule lies on its side, pregnant with death as no one of its breed will ever be with life. Its stiff legs cage him. Peering out from his barricade, he watches me approach—sungrin smile, stung lip, child's neck a stem too slender for its bloom, eyes opaque now as a pool under a lead sky.

Tige Fargus erupts, snagging me midstride. "Hot damn! Get your fill, shit eater! Settin on his haunches laughing like The Mischief as much as to say 'what took you all so long!' We'll mischief you! Led us a chase I won't forget if I live to be a hunderd! Little bugger! Nothing but a left-over scrap of human that should a been drownded in its afterbirth!"

My old heart pounds as I hang there, poised. But not a movement, not another sound.

"Come, Isaac, take my hand."

He hesitates. "Come, Isaac." He is reaching. Now draw him smoothly away from the little mule. Now pluck the maggot from his eye and drop it back among its brothers in the shattered belly—torn, but no sign of how, or of how it died, worm-filled, the wormwhite all but covered by greenheads glutted and drunk, carousers in their doggery. My gorge wells, but "Come." I say it loud enough for them all to hear. "Come down with me to the river, Isaac."

I lead him between Duncan McElroy and the stranger. We walk to the edge of the clearing, enter the sparse brush, leave the wood. In the thickening dusk we venture down a gentle sidewise path along the bluff. The others emerge from the trees and follow single file along the crest above us.

"Isaac, we'll bathe ourselves," I say. "We are going in the river with our clothes on."

They say he doesn't hear, though the woman says that isn't so. She will put her hands up close to his head and smartly clap. He will always jump a little when she does it, and turn around. Out of her hearing they say he only feels the clap of air. But Eily's chatter rained on him sound or light, something he caught, if nowhere else, in the small cupped tip of his rosy infant lip.

I gave her the use of my pony. I'd sit in the morning sun and watch the lane till I'd see her come flying, her bonnet in her teeth, braids thick as cattails lying on the wind.

And Isaac, as if he's waited there, emerges from the wood.

She has news for us, leaping down before the pony stands still for her. "Oh, Aimyul! I'm going to marry! He came with his pa and spoke to Eustace. And Eustace hung back cranky and rude till Ma flew at him scolding. And now it's settled. I never saw anyone I like to look at more. He's Sidney's cousin, from the tidelands, and like her, soft and bonnie, not rough like us."

Isaac, bewitched, watches her range from door to pony to chopping block. "And hair like cornsilk." She sighs enormously. Isaac pumps his silent laughter. "Scoff all you like, it's true, you know. And hands like a lady's. Nary a corn on him that I could see. And the soothingest talk you ever heard. I could hardly tend what he said for listening to the sound of him." Throwing herself onto the chopping block, hugs her knees. "I daredn't move I felt so big and clumsy." And laughing, "Then I couldn't *wait* for them to leave so I could run tell you."

With her curious awkward grace, falls greedily upon the flowers she's planted by my door and cannot leave alone. "And I shall have babies, lots of them, because—bother!"— has she pricked her finger, or is it for the ingrate babies? —"the bad things will grow up and must be replaced every year." Shoves her face into her ragged nosegay. "Only—one

21

thing I dasn't think about." Her eyes look at me over the phlox. "I'll have to go away." (I wish I'd looked at Isaac then.) But her smile returns, turned inward. Absently she touches larkspur, peers at the rabbithead in its ruff. "He said he'll give me anything I want."

Something clouds her face. She spins around. "Isaac? Isaac! Now where has he run off to? Isaac!"

I lean downstream, gag, vomit a little. The current carries it away. He waits, watching me with those grey eyes. The world rights itself. We wade farther out. The water is warm and clear. One hand in my hand, trusting as a child, he bends to lay his other palm just on the surface and lets it follow along beside him like a toy pirogue. Where the depth drops into the channel, I thrust him under all the way and hold him. He begins to struggle. Have I the strength?

I once complained to her, "It's awful to grow old."

She laughed at me. "Oh but worse, Aimyul, not to."

I have to let him go. He bobs up coughing, strangling, gulping air. He climbs my galluses, my arm, clings to my trunk to steady himself, and gasping, opens his eyes and flies at me with both fists. I catch him by the wrists. "I'm old and clumsy, Isaac. You're all right." He studies me, then brings down his heavy brow like a visor over those pale, so vulnerable eyes. I tell him, "I can't save you, Isaac. But I'm here. You won't have to be alone."

But he's floating his pirogue again, not minding me. Spread out along the blufftop like roofless pediments of some old ruin, they wait. We wade heavy-legged back to the shallows where I scour him rough and pink with sand. Last, he offers his upturned face, eyes for a moment watchful. Then eyes and lips both firmly shut and he's waiting with pure trust for me to wash his face.

22

Toliver Pullen

No telling how it died. Likely he never thought to feed it, then tied it up too short at night to graze. Had to nibble what branches it could reach, what grass it could snatch at on the move. No doubt he stove it up too but kept on going. Rode it plumb to death.

Eyes swimming from the stink, mouth filling and refilling, I sit eyeing Sidney's bridle which I must reclaim from that rotten jaw. He chose this wood so like a church—those spires, this slanting colored light. You'd always see him around the church, once we got it up, and the graveyard next to it, which holds all the dead we've had since settling —Mrs. J. W. Hite, her ninety-year-old pa, the pitiful thing Hedy McElroy come nigh dying to birth. Her screams leeched all the blood from Sidney's face till I prayed they'd stop one way or the other, after a little I couldn't care which. Hung around the church and the graveyard, whose very permanent population he's now swelled by one. They said he talked with the dead. With Min Hite he wouldn't have got a word in edgeways, and her pa'd long lost his hearing, and babies don't converse. People will say anything.

Eustace probably guessed it. Said he was waiting on Sunday. He liked to sit with folks. Had some way of knowing when on an evening we'd happen to gather on one gallery or another. He'd show up if he had to cross the valley to do it and sit too like he could hear the talk. Then when Eustace's gal and old Emile made their own congregation, they say he forsook the church to join with them. But looks like he picked in this wood a church again and waited on Sunday. And here we come to humor him.

Step down off Beth, try to touch the buckle. "A terrible thing," I rehearse for her. "Terrible. But never mind, I'll bring a brute to Beth in the spring and you'll have a foal to raise."

"A terrible thing," dragging the fancy bridle out from under the cheek, which shreds a little, and feeling light-headed. Then return to Beth. This minute we are turning home. The miles we travel will no longer stretch the distance out but pull it in. Poor little mule, you're dead. I had to sell Eustace a field to buy you. And you were Sidney's prize. But I feel what I feel. Rein Beth around, head out of the wood after the others.

When I first came on Sidney with it loose in the well yard, tagging after her like a pet, outdone I made my belt a halter. "It's no place for a mule. I'll get you a kitten or a pup."

She only looked at me.

"What do you want it *here* for?"

"Toliver, it's so dear."

She never says it, says my name. That's why I let her keep it. Because she said my name. But the mule following her lamblike disgruntled me. Her talking to it disgruntled me. Put me out of sorts. Played on my nerves. It's not that it was my gift, it was the mule itself that won her.

Now it's dead and gone.

The Tuckahoe

I'd surmise when I said I was born a Tuckahoe one thought I'd said I'm some sort of an Indian, another that it meant "a kind of barrister," and another that I'd claimed to be victim of some strange malady, as though I'd said "I'm an asthmatic." The others were sure I'd said I belong to a mysterious religious sect. But, as many diseases have the same symptoms, because there are, after all, such a multitude of maladies and at the same time such a meager number of ways by which they may show themselves, and in fact even at times choose the very signs we take for health (so that a rich sanguinity, which we take as a sign of ruddy well-being, might just as likely presage a fever), just so, they chose the very sign by which so often wisdom shows itself—that is, silence—to do the very opposite of *show,* that is, to hide, the very opposite of wisdom, that is, ignorance.

Who can they be? Where have they come from? Why do they prize this little Isaac loon? Watching Old Grandfather bathe him tenderly in the river, I think perhaps for love. He might be the lost flawed son of one of them. But when he leads him out, the sand-colored man gets down off his horse and, wearing a lavish necklace of coiled hemp, awaits them like a priest in ceremony. Soft sandy hair on head and arm, sand stubble on lightly tannened cheek, he picks up the little loon's delicate wrists

25

and binds them together while the captive, looking down, gives courteous attention to each loop of the clean ceremonious knot, as if he might be receiving a gift, or an honor. Then, lifting the rope coils over his own head, the sandman dròps one loop—first halo, then crown, then garland—upon the little loon's.

Old Grandfather stands small and alone, having reluctantly given the boy over to the sandy man, who, one end of the hemp in hand, steps into his stirrup. Then the old man mounts with a groan his handsome round-loined pony and we move again, the boy walking at the rope's full length behind the sandman's horse. What pageant can this be?

We spend the frugal remaining light in an amble along the southeast-flowing river. Well beyond the mule's effluvium, they pick wordlessly and as a man the stopping place —a cluster of trees in a riverbend. They dismount. Sandcast Loren points with the length of his arm and hand and finger, and the loonboy drops where he's told and from his place against a treetrunk watches everything. One they call Tige builds a fire. One called Tuttle—so tall he seems to have lost in so much growing his life's allotment of energy, shoulders so narrow and sloping you'd think he'd been taken in two hands at an early age and stretched like pully candy—this wordless Tuttle cooks for all of them. He's found a flat rock in the shallows to tilt toward the fire. Upon it he bakes a cake of ground corn, which the men devour with eye and fancy long before it's done. One by one, as they wait, they modestly move off to the river and bathe and return with dampened hair that, catching the firelight, glistens.

Tuttle goes last. Not to bathe, to retrieve the plump skin bucket he's suspended from a branch into the stream.

What has he cooled in the evening-cool water? Their prophet Mister Hite follows and remains behind. Returning, Tuttle puts a sausage the size of Goliath's member upon a table stone.

A grin spreads Tige's face. "Whatchoo feeding us now, Tuttle?"

Earl takes it up. "What'd you do with the rest a the brute?"

Tige says, "Tuttle he hid behind a bush when he seen the bull coming and stuck out his hand to see what part he could catch a holt of. Thetere was the handiest."

Earl says, "I wisht he'd a laid hold of its rump roast instead."

Tige says, "Tuttle, you swaller some inches a thetere, it'll kill you or cure you one."

Eustace lifts his eye and just perceptibly nods in the direction of the woman. Tige flushes black. Earl grins in confusion. Georgia Gem, sitting with her arms balanced loosely on her knees, throws a look at them and snorts. Tuttle ignores it all, though his peaked eyebrows sharpen their apexes, pointing some impersonal sadness, some long stoical mourning for the race that in no way interferes with his cooking. The sausage done, he marks the division with his knife then counts with his slow finger to make sure. Eleven. I'm excluded? No. He hands me a share like the rest. It's churned butter-flecked milk they pass in the bladder skin from mouth to mouth. I see it's the loonie Tuttle has excluded. No one appears to note that ravenous eye. Rolled up on hands and knees, he moves like a calf on a tether, short-staked, chafing at the imagined constriction of the circle made real by Sandloren's pointing finger.

Old Emile rises, hitches his pantaloons, and steps over to Isaac, holding out a morsel of bread. Loren's hand, with a freight of sausage, stops midway to his mouth. It's him Emile looks at as he says softly, "Come, Isaac, be our slop pail. We don't want to be pestered tonight by scavengers."

The boy lurches, grabs with his bound-together hands. The morsel vanishes. Another moment is gone forever before Loren carries his own bite to his lips. Why does the captive belong to this sandman?

I suspect it's for distraction that Emile asks me, "Sir, how do you represent yourself?"

"Why," I say, "I am the younger son of a younger son, which is a way of saying *nothing*." They look stolidly into the flames, one sucking his pipe, another nursing his quid in his cheek. I elaborate: "What's any man? To his father a son, to his son a father, to his man a master, to God a servant, a scoundrel to his wife, and a mystery to himself." Silence. "Well, I can tell you a great deal more of who I am, if you've the inclination." But as no one lays claim to such an inclination, I ask, "Where do you hail from?"

The old man chuckles. "A place they style Culloden, which lately did not exist. In its place was the Creek Confederacy—the land of the Upper Creek, of the Talladega and Kiamulgee, the Natche and Eufaula, the Coosa, the Tallepoosa, a paradise of booming pine and crystal waters and dripping springs and blue fogs and cloud castles—a place the Spanish predator named Eden."

"Are you a Spaniard, sir?"

"No by God, a Frenchman. An Indiancountryman."

"The place is a slave state, out of the Mississippi Territory?"

He shrugs.

I light my Indian weed. "The drinking water of this freedom land carries in it the chemistry of opposites. Now you take my grandsire—a poor man with no hope of betterment

—sold himself as a bondslave to pay his passage. When the seven years were up, still a pauper he sold himself for a longer time to another master, to get money to buy land. And then, when he'd got set up, why he bought a slave himself. Now his son, my father, judged the institution unfeasible. He gave the man his manumission to see how he would fare. Fared well indeed. Sold himself promptly for a time till he had enough money to buy a man himself. And so it goes and each thing's wed to its opposite."

Toliver Pullen says, "The bondslave's different. He sells himself. Which implies he belongs to himself to sell."

"Splendid! We include in our number one philosopher."

Old Emile says, "My Celts are not friends to the peculiar institution."

"Well," I say, "the leagues against it harbor queer bed-fellows. Some froth against it because they hold it means living too close with men of color."

Emile laughs. "My Celts have their reasons."

"Some are wrong ones," says the philosopher.

Old Emile grunts. "Better against it for wrong reasons than for it for any reason."

I say, "By what yardstick do you derive your better and your worse? Where is your standard measure? Let me tell you, it is one you have either taken by arbitrary choice from among a number available, or have made up for yourself. And so might another man either choose or invent quite another standard. And any idea, if it's more than a mere acceptance of the slogans of the day, is born like the egg out of the stuff of the chicken hatching it. And there's no absolute way of ascribing your better or your worse except to make this arbitrary choice or invention. And so I say to you it's all the same, all the same. It's really all the same."

Toliver says, "I don't accept that because it must be an invention, good don't exist. I believe we're suited to such enterprise."

"My dear fellow, look around you. Then if you hold to that opinion, I can only think there's some cleavage between your senses and your sense."

"Pain, sir, can be said to be bad for the simple reason that it is painful."

" 'Can be said to be' I suppose. But there are both creeds and tempers that deny it. Purgatory is held in all of Mexico to be good just because it's reputed painful as Hell. Some say we know through love, but others say only through suffering. Through suffering the Holy Man showed his love and brotherhood." I extend a dry twig into the embers till it writhes, then hold it for Loren to renew his flagging pipe. And watching his eye: "Why I've seen men for whom pleasure and pain, a happily wedded pair, may not be separated."

Toliver shakes his head.

But, "Nosir" I say, "you cannot have your better or your worse except by choosing, which is to say that you are free. So are we all—though most freely choose slavery. And hence it follows—it's really all the same."

Tige Fargus erupts. "How you know all that? You talk like you know something! Howcome you think you know anything? Everything we need to know is in the Book and it's all a mystery. Take any parable. Take, howcome the prodigal to be favored when he done all wrong? It's written that the banquet was for him. Don't tell me you know why. It makes no sense just *because* we ain't to know. So howcome you talking, you Tuckahoe?"

Emile offers his tobacco pouch to Tige and the gift mollifies him. "My Celts," Emile says to me, "are Presbyterians of a sort." And to Fargus, "I don't find it so mysterious. If I had two sons—and I've had many more than that—and they both grew to manhood, but one of them stayed at home, content to remain a boy in his father's house, on his father's land, obeying his father, eating his father's bread, I'd favor, I know, the other one, who dared to go where he pleased and investigate the world and returned to me a man like myself. *I'd* give that son the banquet."

Tige eyes him, suspicious. "How you know that's what it means, old man? You don't know! If He had of wanted us to know what He meant, He would of told us!"

"Howcome you think He was talking?" bursts from laconic Earl.

Tige registers that. Then: "Talking has got more uses than telling!"

Earl says, "Name some."

Tige casts about, discovers: "Song singing!"

The woman laughs.

Earl says, "All Emile's doing is telling what he's made it out to mean."

"I don't have to know what it means! I liked it better the other way!"

"Well, you don't have to listen to him. You want it fi-fo-fum, why have it. Me, I like to listen to him."

Hiking my thumb toward their gentle captive, "What pleasure has he committed?"

The woman answers. "He kilt a girl, sixteen, on the morn of her wedding day."

I search their faces. No new expressions. Nothing to be learned. I shrug. "What man here has not put an end to a virgin?"

I see no movement, hear no sound. No warning of any kind, but I am lifted, suspended by the throat in the hungry hands of brindle-headed Eustace, who, till now, has looked so stiff and still you'd swear a whittler made him. His eyes insane, spume on his beard, trembling all over, the shudders throbbing into me through those fingers at my throat. Then I'm dropped. Unaware that my hand quite on its own has unsheathed my knife, I am hurt and bewildered why young Pullen is mauling my wrist so.

Eustace Jurdin, collapsed beside the fire, marbled as a drawn carcass, murmurs, "I beg your pardon, Tuckahoe. The girl was my daughter, Eily."

I look at him. I turn and look at the loonboy. He's fallen asleep tilted over, his forehead on the sand, his buttocks resting on his heels, his hands spread, shielding his skull.

"What will you do with him?"

One, then another, they look at me. Tige Fargus expresses an eloquent string of tobacco juice into the fire. A hiss. A puff of smoke. "Take im back five hunderd miles to Culloden and hang im."

Myron Tuttle

She wouldn't take nothing for it. I would even of took sweet milk had she offered. But she never. I wouldn't be beholding for my own sake, but I got to provide. If it's against anyone's dignity, ain't it mine? They don't know it was give, the souse meat and the milk. So it can't hurt them in their pride, can it? They got to eat. And the Dutchmen never laid eyes on them before and won't again. So their dignity can't be injured much if it's in the eye of strangers seen for a few minutes, can it?

It will be all right. It will nag me for a spell, then be all right.

Now what about tomorrow. One day follows another. Loren might kill some meat. Fowl would be good. Or fish.

If I rise early. They'll bite at first light if they's any there to bite. Bait. What about bait.

Naw. They wouldn't keep. Lessen alive, in water. No way to manage that, traveling. It will have to be bird.

He don't take care of hisself. Still wet clear to the skin, I allow, from taking Isaac in the river with his clothes on. And not sitting up to the fire particular either. Just won't take care of hisself.

I'll take Eustace's india rubber coat his Kate sent along with me. I'll spread it on the ground there before Emile's saddle. He'll either nod, grateful, or, ignoring it, go ahead and lay on it anyways, or kick it toward the bushes grumbling, "Damn you, Tuttle, don't fuss over me," not mad at me, mad at being old. All you can do is try. Then wait till he's asleep and drop a saddle blanket over him. He's apt to take a chill. And a chill might take him off. All this talk excites him. He'll catch a fever if I don't look out.

Baked in river mud for breakfast though, they'd be a treat. And bless sweet Jesus, she give me a thimbleful of salt. I'll do it. I'll set my mind for first light.

They'll sleep in the morning, if Toliver'll let them. They'll sleep except he worries them awake. He'll herd them on now, and drive hisself. He won't be wanting to stop a-tall. I could tell you this: you are better off away from her. You are a man apt to lose yourself. Living on the place, I have to see it day by day. What does a woman want with a man once she's relieved him of his manliness? What do they do it for?

They don't all. Kate Jurdin didn't. Though they's trouble there. Has been four-five years. Back beyond them four-five years, now there was two people pleasured theirselves in one another. But something went wrong. Though still she's a likely wife. Takes care of him. Pressed in my hands his india rubber coat (which, mind, I must spread out for Emile).

It's all in the bed. They say it can be blessed. Well I've not seen it.

Sidney is beautiful and cruel. But how can that be, when she's also gentle and kind? A lady. Gentle and kind and quiet like, eyes that smile before her lips. I look for that. It's seldom enough you find it. Easy to see why Toliver dotes on her. All that dark-brown hair. Them grey eyes with their black curled lashes. The cousin has them too. Strange to see that in a man. He stayed on the place whenever he come to call on his betrothed, now dead. He is like Sidney Pullen. Womanly graces and yet is manly. I never saw a brawler any manlier. The men respected him from the first. With all his soft-curling bright sorrel hair and uncalloused hands and his eyelashes, that's to his credit. Harder for a man looking like he looks to win their liking. He'd be here now, except we left before the bridegroom come.

Warm to others, cold to him. Kind to others, cruel to him. Free to others her quiet charm and grace and wit

34

but withholding them all from him. Give her affection to a mule! That's it, I guess. She'll mule him yet. Then how will she be satisfied? Why? She married him. Nobody forced her. She must a wanted to. And him who could of married any woman had to marry this one. Craves her too much. No telling where it'll end.

Perch, I reckon. Crappie.

When she come to him a bride, I seen them talking, or rather it was already and always him who talked. She in her flowers or in her salad, gardening, while he—who ought to been in his fields—standing in the row with his hands in his back pockets, talking talking. Or sitting on the verandah in the evening as the light was going, talking. I would hear the low voice of him who seldom talked now talking and my heart, like it'd fed on green persimmon, shrank, for I seen it in her face, her eye, in the very line of her form—she didn't want it, wasn't accepting it, *taking* it. Clothed herself in a duck-feathered will to shed it, to be shut of it. Then for a while he'd start to say something and couldn't finish it. And then he didn't talk no more, leastways not out.

Perch and crappie and maybe sunfish. Even if just a taste to go around, a savory, it'll be welcome. All this meat. You tire of meat. They're used to eating well. It goes hard with them not to. You do what you can do.

Still talking. What's it all for?

Well, I'll go and spread the india rubber coat. He'll take it or he won't. You do what you can do. I'll set my mind for first light then get some sleep.

Worms. Or, wanting that, some crickets. Are there dropworms in this place? If there's any here, I'll see the webs on the trees in the morning, when the wet in the air lays on them. Silver seines that catch the light. I can always try a little passel of downy underwing. You can usually come on some such trash in the flood line outside the riverbank, even if it's last year's flood and trash and line. But of course it takes a fish that will rise and strike for that. First light.

Jaw jaw jaw.

Fire dying and a little chill off the water and very late. They ought to be dead men. But jaw jaw jaw.

Eustace Jurdin

Alone in the woods. Lost. Light goes to its boneyard west. Night rises in the east. Moss and thick bark mark the north side of the tree. Soon look for Orion.

The hunter. Armed with knife and tomahawk. "When I was a lad," my father said, "we had to hunt with the tomahawk. Shoot a gun, the Indians were sure to hear. Then the hunter would be the prey."

A wolf howl. But is it a wolf that howls? Wolf or not-wolf, it's between the wind and me. Safe. "When I was a lad and lost," my father said, "I slept all night in cane. You're safe in cane. It will sound an alarm. They can't take you by surprise. It was after the frost, for the cane was that dyed, unnatural green. I remember toward morning a wind sprang up."

Then as if trapped. Not in a trap or caught, but trapped some way, made some mistake—taken a wrong direction, or trusted foolishly, or perhaps caught through carelessness in some self-set snare. But deathly beguiling, like falling asleep in snow. As if forced to something you want but dare not have unless you're forced and can think *through no fault of my own oh Lord.*

A sound startles me awake. I spring up.

"Shhh." Tuttle. "Not yet. Go back to sleep. It was your own self moaning." What's the man doing, in the middle of the night?

She is calling, calling, but I can't move, can't get to her. Then know it's my voice calling, and angry because *she* won't come to *me,* the fox not in his lair but in his snare. *Help. Save me.* Someone coming. Transfixed, horror. (*"I remember toward morning a wind sprang up."*) Now who can be coming—only the wind?—who that I daren't see?

An animal moans in terror or pain. But I am a child crying for his mother. She comes, not my mother. My wife, my bride. It is she not I who cries, and not in sorrow but in her ecstasy. *I thought it would be ugly but it's lovely, lovely.* Only a girl.

Only a girl lies after first frost in the dyed unnatural green. Her death stalks toward her in the springing wind. But I am tired and cannot wake, snared and cannot move. I cannot open my eyes for who knows what they'll see?

"Get up."

No.

"Eustace!"

"No!"

Smell fish frying. Open my eyes. Toliver is shaking me.

Part Two

Toliver Pullen

Used to be, I could go for time out of mind and never turn out what you'd properly call a thought. I would see something, hear something, smell something —all my mind had to do was know it. I must have been happy because I never once wondered was I happy. Now I'm forever wondering. But happy or not, I look upon that time before I ever saw her as being empty as the Garden always struck me when some circuit rider, meaning to entice, took the notion to describe it. Now my own youth is to my memory just such a soft and pretty-colored thing. Now, without knowing when or how, I have partaken of that tree, and my mind churns without direction from me. Through prairie, across rivers, into the dim bayou light I have blundered, the Lord—or the mare— taking care I don't stray from the others, while my mind turns endlessly as a water wheel dredging up the same matter from the same dark pool. And thoughts I could not have thought before now hold me more than the marvelous landscapes we have passed.

I have all my life been mistaken in every single took-for-granted thing. I have come to believe, for instance, that it is impossible for one human being ever to step into another consciousness, impossible for another to stand where I stand, at the hub of my world, and see as I see, understand as I understand, feel as I feel. It is not possible. For if it were, then that other person would leave off being himself (*herself*) and be me. And that is not possible.

I explain it precisely over and over, as if speaking to an assembled congregation who need to understand my exact meanings, carefully choosing each word, carefully stressing one and not another. "In place of the person I took for granted I knew inside out, like, say, my own late father, or like Eustace—in place of that other person stood my own dream. And if so, then no other human being has ever existed for me, but has only embodied some part of myself. I have denied him (*her*) a separate existence; that is, his (*her*) own being."

"But,"—a learned gentleman stands up to address the echoing amphitheater of my head—"But sir, may we not assume that one can enter another consciousness by two means: the poet's by means of his poem? and the beloved's by means of the singular sympathy dispensed alone to the lover?"

And while the wheels thus churn in this thick matter, Beth Pullen speeds up of her own accord to her most comfortable gait, a light running walk that sets her head bobbing. At times she knows who is in charge and, like the good mare she is, obeys the will of the hand, knee, heel of her philosopher. But now he might be napping, only his weight is there. The snaffle sits so loose in her mouth she could not only take it in her teeth but shove it out altogether with a flick of her tongue. If she happened to feel capricious, she might take him fording this shallow river to the opposite bank and he'd go on sitting her light and loose as a bareback boy.

But she is not capricious. Though this flat land in August is very hot, putting a frill on her saddle skirt, she does not want to take a swim, she wants to catch up with the others. She is jealous of his stature and her own and does not like to lag. Some ride plow horses, some white-muzzled mules. Of the few real horses among them, not one is her match, not even the old man's Chickasaw pony, and she knows it. So she speeds up to her little light running walk, head bobbing so that the yellow flies singing about her pole strap are frustrated in their attempts to settle. But a few of them manage, and draw blood. She swivels her ears, not so much to dislodge them—futile to try once they've settled—as to twitch the little muscles where the itching is and to plead for a branch to be thrust under her pole strap to shoo the flies away. But getting no response she snorts, like a sigh, and quickens her gait without changing it, for his impatience has become her own.

The gentleman has asked his question. Toliver Pullen, are you prepared to answer?

No. So reach for a branch, already near stripped by the hands of the riders up ahead, and pull off a meager switch to thrust under the pole strap of her bridle. She lifts her head gratefully with a whinny of thanks to her absent-minded friend whose consciousness she enters and leaves at will with her natural ease and grace.

Duncan McElroy

Along about sundown we come upon the house. Tuttle sends me with the skin bucket to see can I get some milk. Keyed up as a fiddle string, I can hardly hold still while he hands me tobacco, which has served him well in bartering, and instructs me. ("Sweet milk if they will spare us some.") Then I'm to catch up with them. Wanting to put my heel into old Maud, I wait instead and watch them move past, Pa last, holding one end of the rope that at its other end loops Isaac's head. He's kept up with the horses pretty good all day. As the two of them pass on by, I feel the least touch of lonesomeness. I recall the time Pa beat me. He wasn't in the lead then, but bringing up the rear, marching me before him to the barn. He only beat me once. It could a been enough. He like to killed me. Lashed me with the plowlines and, done with that, cuffed me till the blood run out my ears.

Eager to be somewhere else for a spell, alone or with some folks in a house or barn or yard, I wheel old Maud and cluck her into a trot. I know they've sent me because a boy might be more like to win a woman's favor and get the milk, but also because, with Isaac on the rope, they want to move wide around people, houses, questions.

Still two hundred yards off, I pick up the hum of a spinning wheel. I touch my heel right smart to Maudie's ribs. She jerks up her head to plunge into her rocking-horse galumph. As I near, the hum rises to a keen.

The door stands wide, without a porch to shadow it. I see right into a room full of women. They ain't exactly watching me, but they ain't avoiding watching me neither. As I tie Maud to their papaw tree, first one then another glances up.

Shy, I step up on the stoop. One of them nods to me as much as to say "enter and welcome," though nobody can really say anything over the spinning wheel. None smiles but they look right pleasant.

I stoop in the low door. It's a broad light-filled room, the shutters open. One of them touches the shoulder of the woman at the wheel. Startled, she stops the wheel abruptly, so that one minute the air is filled with sound, the next minute not. She sees me. Her old hand flies to her lips then collapses beside the other in her lap.

"Travelin?" asks one about the shape and age of Ma but minus her haunted look. "Go get your plunder and lay it inside the door and we'll rustle you up some vittles."

I stand dreamstruck at the thought of just settling in here, in this house, this room, with them. If I was to do it, I might never get up the gumption to leave come morning. I fetch a sigh. "Nome, thank you. I druther stay than not, but I'm with a party I'll have to catch up to."

They watch, waiting for me to explain who I am, how I come to be standing in their door, what I'm after. I can't think how to put it all. They go right on with what they're doing, all but the spinner. Two are carding with hand carders. Another is forming it into rolls as big around as a man's thumb and maybe a foot long and laying them beside the spinning wheel. Another is running the thread up on the broach.

"I see you're out to make yourself some cloth," I say.

A dimpled carder smiles. "Once we've dyed and sized the thread."

"And warped and beamed and harnessed."

"And sleyed it and plied the loom."

I find I'm smiling too. I stand there fixed to the doorsill, wanting the sun to balance and nap right where it is, perched like the egg on the westward wall of trees, and nothing to move at all. I want to look at it like a picture.

I clear my throat—though that won't help my voice from bounding treble to bass. Where are their menfolk? I show them the bladder bucket. "I wonder can you spare a bucketful of milk?"

All of them look at the spinner, the eldest, a straight, stern white-haired lady. Seeing them turn to her, she bends over and rustles in her black skirts and brings up a steer horn sheared off at both ends and holds it to her ear. One of them shouts into it. "He asks can we spare him milk."

She frowns. The other repeats herself. Then she searches my face, making her decision. I haven't forgotten the tobacco, but the house smells sweet and not a jaw working. The most I see is a dainty snuffbox on a table. So I'm shy at mentioning tobacco. I feel my face begin to raddle, but it mustn't seem I'm begging.

I hold out the bundle. "For your menfolk, in exchange for a bucketful of milk, if you'll oblige me. It's tobacco. A good light leaf."

The old lady ignores the tobacco. "Are there children in his party?" she wants to know, looking around at the others, then at me. "Children!" she shouts. My head pulls in a little. "Are there children?" I shake my head, despairing of the milk. But instantly she shouts, "No more'n a child yourself! Out back of the house—can you hear me?" I could not fail to hear her. The others bend smiles toward their laps. I nod. "Out back of the house a little way and listen for her bell! Her bell! You can let the calf out of the shed to get the milk down. Only, mind, put it back! Or there'll be none left!" And she shouts to the lady at her elbow, "Get him a proper bucket! I say *a proper bucket!*"

I stand half a minute longer, waiting for the bucket and loath to leave even when it's swinging from my hand. But she's turning to her wheel. So I back out and go in search of the cow.

Takes me a spell to find her and would of taken longer but she give herself away. She's standing in a thicket, hiding from the flies. I would a passed her by, but her female curiosity got the best of her and she turned for a look at me. That tinkled her little bell. You'd think she'd be covered with ticks—ours would, back home—but she's clean as a whistle.

I lead her into the barn and tie her to a crossbar. The calf gambols a lick or two, then butts its head up under her and lays to, thirsty. I let it get a good long draught before I shove it off and squat to the milking.

I'm just finishing when the door creaks. I all but knock over the half-full bucket. It's a tall man in blue cotton clothes. "Did she say you could have the milk?"

I can't find my tongue. I nod.

He throws some harness over the side of a stall. "Travelin?"

"Yessir."

"Whur to?"

"Home."

He turns for a look at me. "Wail, I don't reckon I'd know whur that would be."

In confusion I explain, "A place called Culloden."

"Your name ain't Charles? Bonnie Prince Charles?"

"Nosir."

"Wail, I reckon that's all right then."

I laugh. It's so pleasant in this barn, joshing with the man, the bubbles popping on the fresh-drawn milk.

Then a boy comes in leading a horse—not like our horses, a dray. "All watered," he says, eyeing me.

"My son," the man says. I study his face and listen to the sound of that echoing in my head. Beyond the man's head, out the door, the sun has disappeared and twilight's purpling. I tell the boy, "Hold open the mouth of thisere bladder whilst I pour," surprised at the sassiness in my voice.

He takes hold of the bladder.

"Get a good holt or it'll get away from you."

He nods, adjusts his hold, and when I'm satisfied I pour.

"Much obliged." But it don't sound obliged. I take and knot the bladdermouth.

"That's your horse yonder by the house," he tells me. I reckon he'll make a professor. "She's got small little hoofs on her."

"She's a riding horse, not none a your drays. We wouldn't have none a thesere drays. We'd sooner have a mule." I'm ashamed to sound so peeved, and feeling ashamed makes me mad.

He studies me, uncertain. "She got one brown eye and one blue."

"Oh," I say, "she's fancy."

In answer to his pa's question, I tell them I'm traveling in company, just come up to the house to fetch milk. "I'll overtake them now," I say.

"Pa," the boy says, "could I th'ow a blanket on Pigeon and ride with im a ways?"

I can see the man about to nod. But, "Naw," I say. "You couldn't keep up with me. I got to move."

The man watches me curiously, still friendly. The boy's cheeks flush. But I'm rounding the house before I remember I ain't thanked a one of them for the milk.

"Hold still, dang you," fussing even at Maud when she ain't moved a muscle. Setting the skinbag over her withers like a hen over biddies, I step in the stirrup and ease on up. She's swung her head around to eye me with her blue one, then cranes farther, trying to see what the bladder is. Whatever she makes it out to be don't ease her mind. She swivels her ear to pick up what sound it might let out. "It ain't alive," I tell her.

We head down the meadow to pick up their tracks. They're farther away from the house than I remembered. What if they've just disappeared, every last track and horse and man of them? The sun's fell backward off its wall and it won't bounce.

I pick up their tracks and—reins in one hand, the other hugging the bladder—let Maud rock in her good old palfry galumph till the track takes me into a wood where I slow her to make sure of their trail. Darker now. The wing of uneasiness brushes me. I peer into the trees to see can I catch the light from their fire. Instead I make out, stalking toward me with a staff, a figure cut out against the white sand of the footpath. I rein Maud to an amble and, drawing near the figure who draws near me, see a toothless old man with a chin like a cucumber. He waves his staff around his head and shouts, "Ey-there! Is it you?"

Maud presents him her broadside. I coax her straight.

"Answer me! Is it you?"

Surely it is me. Still the question's not the easiest to answer. "Stop!" he commands, hurrying up. "Don't go no farther! I seen the phantom horsemen up ahead. I stepped off the path and they passed me by. I dasn't breathe, they were that close. And I swear they wasn't a sound. Not a hoof a they horses touched the ground! And got a mortal boy at the end of a rope. Don't go no farther. It'll be your life!"

"They're not phantoms, sir," I say. "They're kin and neighbors of mine. The boy with his hands tied murdered someone. We come all this long way to bring him to justice." His face half turns till he's eyeing me with one eye, like a chicken. "We followed him all the way to that next river west of here." He lifts his hand, fluttering it and jiggling his head as if to quiet me. But I finish ". . . past a German settlement. And found him in a wood on the river bluff."

"Oh-oh-oh." His voice sets up a thin song. " I know the spot, the very spot. I tell you it was there in April of thirty-six, the very spot, and six hundred Mexikin dead littered the plain south of the river and the scoundrel Santa Ana wandering dazed in the open, the very spot, till a Texian, not knowing who he was, took him prisoner next day. And on the Potomac King Andy had stood up to his map and touched the tip of his finger to a spot and prophesied: 'If he knows what's good for him here's where he'll turn and stand.' And that was it! The San Jacinto!"

I don't know no Santa Ana or San Jacinto or King Andy. "I'll be getting on," I tell him. "It's a long ways back to Culloden."

"Culloden!" He lays hold of the bridle. "What's your name, son?"

"Duncan. Duncan McElroy."

"Duncan! McElroy! I known your grandsir; 'E died at Culloden!"

I see he's a lunatic. "Let go my horse. It's getting dark."

"Yes and I tell you this—I wasn't sorry. 'E was as proud as 'e was brave. A blessing 'e died in the heat of battle. They slaughtered the wounded Highlanders after. I know what I'm saying. I was there!"

"That was a hundred years ago."

"Like yesterday!"

I lean out and loosen his fingers from the bridle. He grasps my hand and says, "A kinsman of the laird! And like him! Oh, I see it in the eye."

I laugh. My McElroy grandsire took his long gun to King's Mountain but died at home in bed. I leave him standing in the path. He calls out after me in a voice surprisingly strong, "Duncan McElroy died at Culloden!"

Something—the dark—livens the hair at my nape. I can't see tracks any longer, but the sand of the footpath's white. Then something comes gliding down the tunnel the path makes through the wood. My heart tries to fly out my open hatch and I fall on the bladder bucket. It passes over me—an owl with a wingspread wide as my armspread, having to tilt down the narrow way.

I sit up ready to bawl. Because I'm tired, I tell myself.

I grumble at Maud, "Howcome you can't find their camp, you're older than I am." Then see up ahead a fire's glow split by treetrunks. Cursing the old man and this wood and the owl for putting fear in me, I amble closer. I'm deciding to stop, get down off Maud, and creep up to check is it our fire when beside me a shadow moves. I yank Maud till, snorting, she all but squats.

A chuckle, and "About time." It's Toliver.

I can't talk. I'm windless. Like I been walloped on the back. I hand down the bladder. "You done well," he says, hefting it. I slide off Maud and walk alongside him. "I was feared we might lose time out looking for you in the morning."

I hobble Maud where she can graze and lap herself some dew, then I join the men. They're passing the sweet milk I've brought, those who're still awake. Tuttle hands me a pone and a wing of a bird Pa shot. Emile moans in his sleep. Pa studies the fire and don't once look up. The Tuckahoe sits with a light in his eye, smoking the Indian weed. There's Isaac, asleep as he fell, any old whichaway. His mouth's open and spit's run down his jaw and wet the sand. I think first because he ain't right, then remember I've woke in the night myself to find that little line of spit down my own jaw, wet on the pillow. It must be that he's so wore out. Walked twenty miles today if he walked a yard.

I polish off my pone. I wonder did they let him have a bite. I think of what waits on him back home and hear the old man shouting after me again. Tuttle hands me the milk and I drink long draughts of it, can't get enough. It ain't me, it's Isaac will die at Culloden.

Georgia Gem Hite

. . . prissing and a-sissing—howcome he don't put on skirts? Next time he hands me the least of the breakfast pones I'll priss him! Right on top of the fire where he can siss in earnest! Stingy! In his fingers a pinch of salt would scream for mercy. I can't abide a womanish man.

Ay-goddes, I'm about to split. If ever I get me any trousers not hand-me-down from J. W. I might set comfortable in a saddle. I am longer bodied than he is.

Try and tell him that.

"Gem!" There he goes. "Tarry a minute and swap with me. This mule is th'owing my kneebone out."

He groans off Rufus and I have to swing down off the horse.

"You'd think on such a trip, he'd a lost some poundage. I'd put him right at half a ton! Never saw such a mule. I can't hardly straddle him."

But expects me to.

"Ride 'im sidesaddle. Curl your knee over his hump and you'll set up there like on the kitchen table."

Please don't instruct me how to ride no mule.

"Whoo-ee!" Fanning himself with his hat. "I know you're up there." A spoilt child whining at the Lord. "I don't doubt you hear me. Where at's your boundless

53

mercy? It's hot down here as the other place." Waiting, looking around the sky as if expecting a thunderclap and a cool shower out of the blue, then puts his hat back on and wags his head and grumbles, "Ast and ye shall receive. . . . Gem?"

"Yessir."

"Is they a pinch a that sweet leaf left?" He's asked me that every day for going on two weeks now.

"Nosir."

"I don't know what I wouldn't give for me a little sugar." He heaves a sigh. "We all need a little, to sweeten our thoughts and put us in touch with Him."

If I didn't know him, I wouldn't believe him.

The rope rides loose over Loren's arm. Pa and me fell back switching mounts, so I'm behind to see the defective come to a halt and stand there till up ahead the rope slithers off Loren's still-moving arm and off the rump of his Eagle and hits the sand. And Isaac is running. Not starting up and gathering speed, but running full tilt at first spring, like some animals can. I come to myself and wallop Rufus. The elephant like to shot out from under me, but we're gaining on him till he hits the brush. Then nothing to do but leap off and take out after him afoot. We bust into a little clearing in the head-high stuff and I know he will leave me if we hit that bush again, so nothing to do but launch myself at him, levitating. I strike him around the kidneys and we go down, him under me—I'd a thought I'd broke his back—and wrestling. He is slight, wore out, half starved, and you'd think spirit-broke, but I can't hold him. Another minute and he's rolled on top of me and got me fixed to the ground. I snap and turtle-like close my teeth in his wrist. That little suffering grin of his comes close and closer and he's at my throat with them tushes, white as any man-eater's. So I open my jaw and yank my head away and try rolling him off. Nothing doing. But here they come through the brush, and though they say he can't hear he leaps off me and runs again.

I lie there arm over eyes while they swarm after him, overcome by feeling I been in this place before. I hear a sound break out of me, feel the eyeball sting and know what it is—that the likes of Isaac could a bested me. Slight, wore out, half starved, he is still stronger than I am in the muscle. I'd forgot.

Picking myself up, I follow through the thicket till I come upon them standing baffled in a clump. They turn on me. "Whichaway'd he go?"

"It was you all after him, not me."

"Gem," Pa says, "I'd a thought you could a held him till the men got there."

Then weeds crackle and there stands Isaac—his whole front dark with wet, face wet too, and blue hair wet.

Emile says, "He wasn't trying to get away, he was trying to get to water!"

They must of forgot to water him. But how'd he know it was there?

"Smelled it, I reckon," Toliver says, though I never asked it out. And says to Earl, "Let's find it. We can water the horses."

Duncan and Earl and Tige and Toliver beat the brush and hunted, but only found it after they'd come back to where they started and set to dogging Isaac's track. Never would of found it otherwise. A little old weed-fringed sump.

Myron Tuttle

A mile or so after the stop, I note Beth Pullen's thrown a shoe. I call to Toliver and we rein up. He walks back a ways afoot, looking for it, but of course not finding it, then stands and studies the long way we've come.

They advise him he'd best turn back and search them bushes. No telling where he'll find her a shoe in this unsettled wilderness. But just looking at the set of his back, I see he can't. He knows it's only wise, but just can't bring himself to go back any way at all.

"Might as well stop here," Tige grunts. "He could get up at first light and go back then, give us a little longer rest. We got to find us some game or go hungry tonight." That's true. We won't get no farther today.

But Toliver looks hungry only for the road ahead. Not only can't he go back, he can't stop neither. I knew we'd have this trouble. So he tells us the least likely plan of all. He'll keep going till good dark or longer for, he says, there's after all a moon. He'll follow this dim trace, which "of course" he says must lead him to some settlement, and there, at this *of course* settlement, he'll "no doubt" find a smith.

"It'll put me ahead of you," he says. "That way, getting her shod won't hold all of us up."

Eustace, I see, has the sense not to like it. But Eustace ain't been saying much. "You'll keep to the trace?" That's all.

Toliver nods. I hand him a cold leftover breakfast pone, and he drops it in his pocket.

"If the trace gives out, or if you leave it?" I put to him myself.

"I'll leave a little cairn of stones. Look for that," he says.

Tige snorts, angry. "And then what?"

"I could go with you," Duncan McElroy says.

Toliver, already lost to us, don't even hear. We stand there watching him get smaller down the trace, till Tige says, "Hand over your prize, Loren, and let's go scare us up some meat."

"I could go with you," Duncan says.

But they're already gone.

"You can go hunt me up some firewood, that's what you can do," I tell him, gruff so it'll seem like something else. "Get on about it now." But the moon's up and there's thunder in the distance by the time we've eat. Then jaw some more.

The Tuckahoe studies first Duncan, setting there, arms hung on his knees, studying his hands, then Georgia, nose resting on her laced fingers, staring at the fire like it was reading matter.

"Is it this sad adventure, or are they never cheerful?" asks Tuckahoe.

Emile says, "Sometimes wild, sometimes morose. But never happy. Excepting," he says, "Eily. And excepting Isaac there."

"Never?"

He shakes his head. "It's the racial strain and nothing to be done about it. Unreasonable as it may seem, I've studied it all my life and concluded that if you're happy, you're happy. If you have nothing you're happy, and if you have something, you're happy. More happy if you have something and less happy if you have nothing. But happy all the same, if you're happy.

"And the same if you're unhappy. It's in the blood, happiness or unhappiness, and you're born with it, like the shape of your nose."

"You sound like a Scot yourself, old man. The shape of the nose can be changed."

"Yes, if a tree falls on it. So I suppose can these Celts be changed, if a tree falls on them. But a tree falling on them could not make them happy."

Just listening to it fans Tige's ire. "Don't gull us with this Latin."

Earl he's bent on following the talk and baffled when that's all. The Tuckahoe is nodding. I see he and Emile are agreed. But what it is they're agreed on I can't for the life of me make out. I wonder could Tige be right? But the Frenchman ain't unkind. I reckon it's that they're learned. I say, "I'm a man admires learning. You take, Toliver hisself is a man owns thirty books."

Tuckahoe says, "Toliver's in a hurry."

I can nod to that.

He says, "Who grabs comes away with a cracked hand. And sometimes not a hand." He sucks his Indian weed and smiles. "An old Indian saw."

Emile chuckles, tamping his pipe. "I think I know that Indian."

The Tuckahoe throws back his head and laughs. That's too much for Tige. "You bray like an ass," he spits at Tuck.

Tuck says, "I have always admired the proud and humble ass and would be glad to be more like him than I am."

Emile

    . . . smoking and staring absently across the fire at Georgia Gem, at the bold wing of her upper lip. But I've got to sleep or die. And too weary for either, lie back with my arms cradling my head, looking into constellations.

And find I am lying with my second wife, my mustee. Across a span of fifty years, my sure hand traces the long line from the young armpit down her side, dips its heel to catch the soft waist ditch, repeats that ditch, and repeats, then rises to the crescent of her hip that moves toward me, becomes her thigh, her smooth leg. And then she is a whole landscape, and I, grown big enough, cover the Indian field of her, the planting hillocks of breasts and belly and mound where I'll put my melon seed. And when I'm sheathed, I find her waiting bold-winged lips.

Across fifty years those constellations witnessed it. You are resurrected, young, across fifty years to comfort me in my age. This instant I love you as I loved you.

All those stars. Sky like a threshing floor. But lightning shudders in the distance. Well what's a little rain.

And what is time that in passing kills us all.

Earl

Gone to sleep. I'd never of thought he could make this journey. No guessing his age. To hear him tell it, even he don't know it. That old Indiancountryman, a friend to the Creek and says he known Alexander McGillivray. That red Indian had a whole name while I, white as ere man of them, never had more than *Earl*. But it can't be that, can it? That what *him who hath* has got is no more than his own last name? Just a word, ain't it? Not even a word. A sound. I could make one up. But they'd laugh. Though they don't laugh at Mister Hite and they all know he as much as made up his own name. But his case is different. The name J. W. was given him as a babe by his own folks, only the J. W. didn't stand for nothing, just meant for his calling name. He must of found it give him, too, a sense of lack, for he learned to write for the sole purpose of signing hisself Jay Dubya Hite instead.

But don't nobody call him nothing but Mister Hite. Not even his wife of forty-odd years up to the day she died. Is it because they're afraid if they call him that he won't know if they're saying Jay Dubya or J. W. and might take offense, or is it that they refuse to say a made name because to make your own name yourself is a thing you ought not under any circumstance undertake to do? Face hanging off his head, eyes on the ground like he knows he done something wrong, deep triangle hollows above his eyes. I've heard it said that's how you can tell the depth of a man's soul, by the depth of the hollows over his eyes. I've heard it argued that is one sure sign the Chinaman is and ever shall be heathen.

The old Indiancountryman has never owned up to more than just *Emile*. And none the worse off for it. Something about him—maybe age. No. More. But I wouldn't know what to call it. Big men all have it without lifting voice or finger. But he is a small shrunken man. Even allowing for some shrinkage with age, he could never have been imposing. But he has whatever it is anyway. Maybe he got it from the red Indians. Others say they're a sorry lot, but the old man only smiles and smokes his calumet and won't let on.

Though he tires easy walking, he can set his Chickasaw pony all day long and show it only as much as the rest of us. He once bet it could outrun Beth Pullen in a quarter. Nobody seen how, but down in Jurdin's bottom Toliver lost by a neck to Duncan McElroy on the pony. Of course if it had a been one-tenth of a mile farther, the mare would of pulled ahead and kept her lead. But nothing can beat these little Chickasaw horses at the quarter. Ain't many left. Now the Chickasaw have gone and taken all the brute males off with them, you can't hardly trade for one around Culloden.

He scoffs at the name. Says the place had got its own name already that even the Creeks inherited untold years ago from tribes they warred with over it. We've asked him what it was, but he says we've done give it our own and no need of more confusion. He says each time the valley's changed hands the people run out were more advanced than the ones come in. He says the valley itself must have some elevating effect. He says it might even someday civilize "these wild Celts, these tobacco eaters" as he styles us. I love to hear him talk. I could listen the livelong day.

Strange, when you come to think of it—all of us, way out here. Maybe it's thinking about it makes it strange. Of course we know why we're here, but thinking about it, it can seem strange.

Take, even if we known how we come, first, to be in Carolina, which not all of us do know, let alone knowing how all of us come to be in the new place—what's it mean? We come for our separate reasons. But what do they mean? What's it mean if Eustace come because, over a boundary-stone dispute, a man named McLeod thought to found with him a feud, so Eustace divided up his land among his grown boys—and after he'd give over in the dispute too (said, "If they's one thing a man finds it hard to forgive you it's a wrong he's done you")—and picked up and migrated? That Toliver come because Eustace come? His pa'd died and left just him and his brother. He never bore no love for that bully and, besides, the brother'd took a wife and wanted to buy him out. That Tuttle, who mothered them otherwise motherless boys, had to follow Toliver, whom he favored? Always farmed land belonged to Toliver's pa, and with Toliver kept up that arrangement.

They say they was getting to be too many people in Carolina for Loren McElroy. He's got to hunt or go wild, so he come for the game. That's what I've heard. I once asked Tuttle about him. "Why, he's a dependable man," Tuttle allowed. "A venerated hunter. After his older brother died, shot out in the woods, as a boy no more'n fifteen Loren McElroy sustained the whole clan of old men and women and childurn by the sheer rapacity of that gun of his. Ain't he sustained us way out here?"

The Hites come because, truth to tell, Mister Hite's a poor farmer and couldn't eke out a living except for Eustace, whose neighbor he's always been, and except for Gem, who knows right smart of farming. With Eustace going, he naturally found good reasons to go too, reasons besides all the debts he left behind. It was for our ever-lasting souls he shepherded us to a place we would call Culloden, while Georgia shepherded an ailing complaining Min Hite and her pleasant senile ninety-year-old pa—Mister Meanness himself, that Rufus mule, pulling their entire kit and caboodle.

Tige never come with us at all. On the road, we tangled up with some crackers with their booming long whips, droving cattle, and before they could unsort their animals from ourn dark had come, so we sat down together and built our fires. In the morning seemed like Tige just got with the wrong group going the wrong direction. Taken a regular allegiance to Loren McElroy.

Such a migration of people moving to and fro. Why moving, where going, with noses set in such purposeful—and opposite—directions?

Her and Isaac is some roundabout kin of Loren's Hedy. When we known them two was packing to come along, some grumbled about who'd raise her house for her. But she just claimed an old Indian log house empty for some time. Ramshackle, run-down old place. But she's a handy carpenter and ain't once been beholden.

Me, I never thought *not* to go, with Eustace going—working for him from an early age, living on his place since the Colvins left Carolina for the government lands. They wasn't any kin. I was just left behind in their barn one summer night by some traveling folks took refuge out of a summer rain. I wonder was I left on purpose or by accident overlooked? The Colvins didn't know what to do but to raise me. When they was ready to set out—I was already working for Eustace then, often just sleeping in his barn, taking my breakfast warm from his cow, bathing in his creek, him never even knowing (nor Kate neither, though you'd think she'd a felt the wear of my eyes upon her as she hunted for eggs, leaned to her milking) —Mister Colvin told me, "Ast Eustace can he keep you on and maybe you could eat at his table and sleep in his barn for your wages." So nothing to do but ask. And Eustace asked me what I wanted. I said, "Why to stay on with you, I reckon." So he let me. I was eleven year old, a big boy for my age and, Eustace said, a good worker, he would hate to lose me.

I never thought not to leave. I asked Eustace, "Where'll we go?" He said, "We'll just drop on down the back country till we find us a place like this one" and I said, "Not look for better soil? Howcome like thisun?" And Eustace he said, "Why so we can change our place without we change our habit, and make out right well using the furnishings of our minds, doing as we've always done."

I seen he was right. So we dropped on down the back country, all of us, and found some ridge and valley land, with longleaf pine and friable soil and freestone water, and called it Culloden, not on account of no prince named Charlie but because Eustace's pa come from Invernessshire. Arriving, Eustace advised me to take up some land of my own, adjoining. So I done it.

Does that answer it?

Toliver Pullen

It's partly that she's cultivated. Not that she's not natural, but in addition to being natural she has cultivated in herself all that is not just there, like weed and tree, but has to be cultivated. That is, she's part of nature as a garden is. Herself both garden and gardener. She cultivates herself. It's partly that.

Thunder rolls down the sky. The dusk yellows like before a rain. Then the thunder rolls over the mare and me, coming on louder and tumbling about our heads while my good Beth keeps her pace in spite of it, just perking her little ears.

As it rolls away, comes another sound—slow, rhythmic, followed without interval by its echo. I take it for a broadax some way off. But, the trace bending around a marshy pond, I come upon the manufacturer of the rhythmic strokes.

I would have drawn in my reins, but Beth, with that soft, abrupt, descending whinny of outrage, comes to a halt of her own accord and I feel the annoyance of one who, engrossed in the wish of his own life, is forced to stop and take account of some accident befallen a stranger. The maker of the rhythmic strokes is not a broadax but a hide whip, and the victim of the whip is not a tree but a man.

A dozen or so pairs of eyes turn on me and the lashing stops. I slouch in the saddle, confused by the embarrassment that replaces my annoyance. And yet not whipper nor whipped nor audience that squats alongside the trace shows any embarrassment at all. It's peculiar to me alone, a phenomenon distressingly familiar. And that knowledge increases the embarrassment, as if *they* have come upon *me,* as if I, not they, have some unsavory business in this place. I open and close my mouth and might even have apologized for my intrusion. But the eyes upon me are clearly neither curious nor amazed. One pair alone shows any emotion whatsoever. They belong to a boy sitting on a grey lop-eared mule with a shotgun resting across the pommel in front of him. The left eye stares at me; the right eye stares at the bridge of the boy's own nose. Is that look of rage meant for me? It's fierce enough to have drawn the eye into its predicament, like some powerful magnetic field housed inside his head.

"Hoo-ee. Ain't it hot."

Startled, I look for the speaker and find him squatting in the obscuring shade of a live oak on the opposite side of the trace from the others, fanning himself with a black felt hat held in his left and only hand, his right arm below the elbow being no longer a member of this company.

"Don't know what I wouldn't give for a little breeze. Travelin?" But he doesn't wait for an answer. "We don't genly meet folks along thisere trace. Name's Bullard. Thetere's my boy Tom," pointing to the one with the whip, "and thetere on the mule's his little brother Jole. 'Light and set."

It could be a command. Tom, just perceptible at the corner of my eye, coils his whip and moves toward Beth and me. But when I turn, he stops and stands, a rawbone youth with a high complexion but for the pale pate his dry black tonsure circles, aging him beyond his years. And

66

though the youngster's shotgun rests as it did before, the mule seems to have turned and thereby aimed it nicely.

I summon my voice, only dimly familiar. "Whose people are these?" with a gesture toward the squatting audience.

Bullard looks at them as if he'd forgotten they were there. Then he chuckles. "Tell me if I ain't reading your mind. You're thinking I might could be a trader breaking the law, bringing them in for sale. I ain't. Just a drover taking them to the cottonfields to a man who went and bought em." He brings out of his shirt a packet of papers folded and tied with whang and without rising holds them out. "If it'll put your mind at ease, you're welcome to look."

To refuse to dismount might by suggesting my fears embolden him. So I climb down and take the sheaf and set to worrying loose the leather string while Jole hisses at his father, "You durn fool, thisun maught kin read."

The thong gives and I find myself staring at a printed notice of a land auction. I make my eyes follow the lines without show of surprise. The drover watches minutely.

"Uster be a horse trader," he says, still fanning, eyeing Beth. "Yessir and let me tell you it's a sight better occupation. How I come down to my present perfession I never will understand."

He watches me turn to the second of the irrelevant documents he's doubtless harvested from tree trunks along the trace, this one an advertisement for a runaway named Ovid.

The voice commences again. "You look to me like a right prosperous feller, judging from your horse. I didn't catch your name." But I'm too engrossed in the printed page to hear. "Maybe you'll give Jole here a hint how to get ahead in thisere world. I ain't in a position to tell the boy myself." A sigh. "I had a hard fate all a my days. I can't account for it, how one feller'll feather his nest and another—th'own hither and yon, pillar to post—has to roost where the dark catches him."

I shift up a second auction notice, the settlement of an estate, and continue to pretend to pretend to read.

"I had adventures more'n my share," he drones, "but I never once't had the impression that the reins of my fate was in my own hands. Enough to make a man a Presbyterian. What's your persuasion?"

I give no evidence of hearing, but Jole makes a sound squeezed thin by the constriction of his outrage. "To hear him tell it, he never done a thing. But he's done shot down three men."

"That one there's my conscience. Sticks to me like a burr. I can't deny I shot three men. But the fust was an accident, the second self-defense, and the thu'd I was driven to. Besides, I never kilt a one. You ought to tell that too."

"That don't say nothing about his heart, just something about his shooting."

"Might as well go to hell for happiness as look to that boy for filial love."

"Spent six months in a Kentucky jail!"

"Sentenced for forgery when I can't neither read nor write."

"How'd you lose 'atere arm? Got drunk and went to sleep in snow till it froze! They had to cut it off im."

The drover clucks. "I was drugged by thieves and left for dead. A Christian come on me and as nothing was left in my pockets sold my carcass to a surgeon. The surgeon stole my arm for turble experiments and would of stole all the rest of me if I hadn't of woke in time."

"Left Ma and seven young-uns without a fare-you-well!"

"Or a drop of malice in my heart, though she whelped like a lady rabbit and made a hell of my homelife till I was forced out in the wide world alone, except for Tom and my conscience here. I ain't one to argue with fate, but I sometimes marvel at all I had to endure." He has narrowed critical eyes on my pretense at pretense. "Yessir, I shiver to think what I might be forced to next." He nods to Tom, who moves in closer. "I always admire a feller as kin read."

I refold the printed matter carefully, as if it might be valuable, and hand it back. The three Bullards study me silently. "I see you've got a bad actor on your hands." I nod toward the whipped man, who, arms drawn around the tree, wrists tied together, sags in a lewd embrace.

The drover smiles and stows the papers back inside his shirt. "They sell off the wust of um. Send um south to serve ol' king cotton to get rid of um. You take this un, he's a runaway by perfession. They couldn't do a thing with him, couldn't get no work out of him, couldn't save his soul, and he led um a merry chase. So they made up their mind to sell im south. That away, they'll get back their investment."

Tom shouts, "They'll have to go back to huntin possum stead a coon. Me, I'd a kept him for the sport!"

Jole whoops with laughter.

"Hushup your ugly mouth," the drover says.

"I doubt they got much for him in that condition," I say. "Unless they sold him with his shirt on."

"Eyuh, that back was rurnt fore ever I got aholt of him. He don't give it a chance to heal neither. He's broke aloose so many times already I've lost a day's travelin out looking for im. Them arns don't hardly slow him down. He's already like to goaded me into killing him. Maught yet."

"You'd do better to look the other way and let him go."

The drover's eye narrows cannily. "Wail, I reckon I cain't do that. Daid, he ain't wuth a blessit cent, alive he's right dear." He pauses to suck a tooth clean. "That's a mighty nice filly you're mounted on."

I reach for the reins just under my mare's chin.

The drover smiles. "Wail, Tom, give him a little more a your attention, then we'll be getting on."

Tom coils the whip. The drover is patting Beth Pullen's graceful neck. "Sho is some filly," he says wistfully. "No telling what I wouldn't give for me a filly like thisere filly." Shifting his cud to the other cheek, he turns courteously aside to spit. "As it is, me an that boy been sharing that old white mule."

My sweatband tightens.

"Our horse stove in about two days back and we sold her to a blacksmith."

"Hell," Tom says, "you know the smith was white."

Jole whoops again. The drover scourges them with a hurt, disapproving eye.

Tom starts leisurely toward the man tied to the tree, letting his whip trail out to its full length, ready behind him.

I lurch across the wagon track after him. The shotgun explodes in my ears. The pellets kick up dust in front of me. I stop, cast into confusion, perhaps I'm hit, turn, astonished, and look at Jole, who sits holding the smoking shotgun.

"He ain't tole you to move yet," he says, nodding in his father's direction.

70

My knees collapse and I kneel in the middle of the track, facing the hooded eyes of the lined-up audience silent as a frieze.

Bullard stoops and runs a loving hand over Beth's straight pastern then, rising, daintily lifts her lip to examine the length of tooth. She flings her head up and backs away from him. He laughs softly. "I'd sho admire to have me a filly like thisere filly."

If my learned gentlemen are looking down, in the moonlight they see a fool afoot. Who's lost his horse becomes a horse. And to a slave! A leveling.

Bent, staggering under the burden thrown like a sack of meal over his shoulder, he wavers drunkenly. A small incline, and his momentum carries him headlong down to trip on a hummock of grass and, like the angry horse he is, to buck his unwanted rider into the bayou, from which, breathing aloud, he must labor him out again to drop him on the muddy bank. Then headlong into the stream, and the water revives him.

After a time, he drags himself up, shivering, and builds a meager fire. At the bayou bank he tears up clumps of fern to heap on the flogged back of his companion. He claws silt from the bayou bed and smears this poultice atop the thick fern layer. Then lies back with ragged exhausted sobs.

The learned gentlemen will note: he nurses a frustrate rage. For he has lost his horse, and, circling, lost his way, and when the others find him—if they find him—they'll taunt him for a fool. Loathing the peculiar institution, yet trading the loveliest thing he owns to buy a slave, compelled by his principles to do what he was in principle

71

loath to do. Loving the mare he's sacrificed. And for what? A figment. A nothing. An idea. Certainly not that stranger lying there.

"And how get home without my horse?"

Fixing resentful eyes upon the inert form, gradually I see the muddy stuff heaped on his back. I stare at it. Then shout with laughter. Purposeful as a learned physician, nervously compelled to do something, I've done this! Invented this outlandish treatment! My foolish poultice assuages *me*.

I scurry to him on hands and knees and would have scraped it off again. But he heaves up an anguished moan, as if beseeching me to spare him further ministrations. Still, squatting beside him, it's all I can do to leave the poor devil alone.

I remember Tuttle's pone in my pocket. I dredge the soggy thing out and hunt, like Tuttle, for a flat stone to tilt against the fire. I'll see can I dry it out. Then, certain of eyes upon me, I spring around and peer into the surrounding trees. I remember my companion. But when I spin back to look, the flickering shadow light obscures his eyes.

"*Now* you wake up, after I've carried you half a mile. Don't roll over. I put a poultice on your back."

No answer.

"You're welcome. What's your name?"

No name.

"Well, then, Wiley, I told myself surely you could do one thing my mare couldn't, that's talk to me."

Nothing.

"Glad to be borne out on that." Silence. "I'll never see a better mare." The pone's still cold and wet. "A little appreciation might console me in my loss."

Only the crickets answer. I settle against a rotting log. "I hope all this idle conversation don't tax your strength."

I abandon my log, lie down, wriggle but can't get comfortable. I sit up, scoop out hollows for shoulders and butt, and try again, working to avoid the thought of Beth and to deny the resentment I feel toward Wiley.

What to do with you? But no need for me to solve that. You'll solve it for me by daylight. You're a runaway by profession.

"I have turned down twelve hundred dollars for the mare. What would a strong young able-bodied man bring on a good market?"

Throw myself onto my side. I have freed one lonely slave in the middle of this wilderness. And eleven others go in chains. Christ! I open an eye and see him. Go, Wiley. Please steal yourself.

I sit up and test the pone again. The bayou oozes out of it. With the flat of my hand, I press and send rivulets down the stone. Then I lie back. There's Orion rising and the Dipper to grant me purer detachment. Beth Pullen is after all a horse. (But I don't believe it! But I will.) Does he watch me across the fire? Waiting for me to fall asleep so he can run? They always pick them up again and call them runaways. Is letting him run reasonable? Wouldn't he be better off my slave?

Christ!

But he'll either have to turn wild and starve or allow himself to be taken. Then it'll be the block again for him. Hadn't he better belong to me than to the likes of a Bullard?

Dear God. He is by all rights his own man, regardless of law or practices. Inviolable, his own. So go to sleep. I sigh, relieved.

But isn't that awful? Under these awful circumstances? I throw myself onto my other side. Let him choose! A man must be free even to hang himself.

I roll onto my back and cross my arms over my face and wait, tense, for a long time, listening. But hear no stealthy step, no twig snap.

When I wake, with a start, it seems only a moment later, but Orion has stalked the field of heaven. So, he's gone. Relieved, no matter what my reasons, I roll over to rejoice at sight of the empty sand.

Not empty. There lies Wiley still. I hear his soft snore, watch the just perceptible rise and fall of his round chest. You wiley thing. Leg irons don't stop you running from Bullard but free as a worm you will not crawl from me.

Too worn out to keep yourself awake? I pick up a fistful of sand and toss it over him. He snorts. The snoring stops. I listen for the stealthy step, twig snap, whisper of parting brush.

Nothing.

Then that faint snore again.

I fight tears of exasperation with the man.

Then hear it. A branch brushing over his hide, a twig breaking underfoot. I lie perfectly still, relief elevating my chest, watched by a still form pausing to make sure. I wait, then—carefully, carefully—open an eye to indulge myself in the sight of his absence.

And see the eye of a red fox at the edge of the wood, attracted no doubt by the fire.

Cursing, I hurl a rock. The fox vanishes. The stone tears into the tangle of leaves, and thumps. And Wiley remains. He moves. I catch his eye on me, but instantly it shuts. Now I know we lie listening to each other's breathing. Those tremors of expectancy that run over a red squirrel's tail run over me. I listen. I strain. But daren't look.

All the long night I hear nothing of Wiley, not the slightest stir. All night long till dawn. I haven't caught a wink of sleep. My eyes sting. My head is a honeycomb riddled by exhaustion. Mounting all that sleepless night, my anger has peaked and I open my eyes, ready to shout the man awake.

And the sand is empty. Surely I've neither slept nor dozed. But now my dreams come back to me. So many confused dreams.

I'm suddenly so pleased with Wiley that I'm sorry to lose his company. I stretch and rise and move into the sun to yawn. The surface of the tilted stone is bare.

Damn you, Wiley! Without an instant's hesitation I sacrifice Beth Pullen for your likes and what do you do but steal my pone? A curse on your nappy head.

Hungry, horseless, compelled to advance backward like a crab, I hike out of the bayou and squint into the sunlight. And see, heading properly east, sun-colored Loren. I recognize first his Eagle's high-held muzzle, bald face flat out on the wind. I halt and strain my eyes. Three of them. But only one other rider—Duncan. But a third horse.

My mare. Saddled and led by the rein. They stop and wait while I limp up, Loren wearing his slight, unreadable smile, ignoring the insistent bobbing of his bad-tempered horse. "When we seen they had your mare we was sure they'd kilt you."

My face to her silk muzzle, I swallow an embarrassment of tears.

"He claimed you'd swapped her for a slave," Duncan

says. "Then a course we known he was lying. Pa taken her away from them."

Loren says, "I don't see no slave. Did you just let them take her away from you?"

Duncan eyes me critically.

Loren says, "I reckon if you can't take care of yourself, Toliver, you'd do well to stay with the rest of us."

"Thank you, Loren," I have to say. "I'm grateful you got me back my horse."

Beth's eye seems fixed someplace beyond my temple. I put my face in line with it, but just perceptibly she shifts, refusing to look at me.

I step into the stirrup. Though Loren and Duncan start away, she does not move but waits my lead as she would a stranger's, giving nothing. I touch her gently. Instantly obedient but without pleasure, she bobs into her running walk. I hang behind in shame and confusion. Wiley gone, Beth recovered, the whole of it somehow erased, as if the incidents themselves mock my unworthiness. Less than a failure, a mistake. As if the trial's been undone, withdrawn from me. As if I'm judged not man enough for it.

Part Three

Duncan McElroy

We've left the month of August.

Seasonal skies and the torment of a horizontal wind with nothing to break or hinder it over a whole expanse of prairie. Then, inside a minute, the grasses raked by the claws of a gale that howls like a spirit from the bad place. Tuckahoe shouts, "Norther!" A blue norther can hit so sudden they say a frog will freeze solid midleap and thunk on a frozen pond.

We press to gain the spine of a gorge only to look down upon a sheer-faced bluff no goat would hazard. Pa herds us into a shallow ditch along its perimeter and twists his Eagle by the head till down it goes, then crawls among us, putting the other animals down—except Toliver's mare (Toliver is doing it) and Emile's pony, who falls of its own accord, and Mister Hite's Rufus, too big or too dumb for even that wind to bother. And we huddle in the shallow, gasping after that onslaught. The sky, the earth, the air itself is blue.

Then Tige, pointing, shouts a curse. We look up and see Isaac out there on the rim, his rope whipping like a struck snake. We see it catch on a lone stunted cedar and him wheeling toward the gorge. Then he's over the edge and surely hanged.

Pa's up, wading through wind thick as water that tears at his clothes and smears his face. Gaining the tree, he hangs on for a second before he disappears. Tige's out of the ditch, crawling against the wind, me after him.

On our knees, we reach the rim together and, clinging to that little cedar, peer over the edge. Ten feet below, Pa lets himself hand over hand down the rope. At the end of it, Isaac spins slowly, looking up, eyes and mouth wide in terror. Is he screaming? Not I, not anybody, ever heard him utter a sound. And no sound now over that baying wind. He's caught hold of the rope above his head with his tied-together hands, saving himself for a little. I look at the knot—the size of a baby's fist, no farther from my eye than the length of my forearm—straining into the crotch of the little tree now bent along the ground. Cedars have tap roots clear to China but the knot is squeezing deeper into that crotch where the tree's once been broke, and might squeeze through. I watch that knot, can't take my eyes off it, till I hear Tige's voice, Pa's answer, and turn to see Pa haul him over the rim then pick him up and, carrying him like a baby, stagger back toward the ditch.

Panting, shuddering with cold, I collapse among the others and lie there spinning my wheels. Saved him for hanging from hanging and risked his own neck doing it.

After a time the norther itself falls still. It's cold, blue cold, the hair in my nostril splinter-stiff with it. The temperature must a dropped fifty degrees since that mad wind sprang at us out of nowhere. The horses surround us, downed in a ring. Inside the circle all of us, Isaac too, huddle together under the saddle blankets and that away —while the blue of the norther becomes the blue of the night of a cold moon—with our own body heat and the animals', keep life in us the night.

Toliver Pullen

From a distance it looks like the field of a bee-keeper. Closer, it might be hog hutches, though you'd expect hogs to be simpler housed out here. Then I think an Indian village but have to wonder at such a tribe of warren borers. For this is a community of earth dwellings. Not sod houses. Low clay mounds. Oblong anthills.

These flat expanses distort perspective. We lose sight of the community. Then, topping what looks no more than an undulation but comes to be a height, we look down on it and halt one behind another till we're bunched.

Each of us has already breathed it to himself when Tige has to say it out: "Graves." Out here in nowhere. And the graveyard exists in isolation—no church, no people, no settlement of any kind. Alone, deserted, a community of the dead. And more singular yet. Not all of the mounds are fresh-filled graves. Many of the score or more are fresh castings beside rectangles still open, receptive, waiting in the otherwise empty plain.

While we sit on the undulation in this landsea, amazed at the sight, we catch a movement. Lazarus rises out of one of the chambers and throws down—a shovel? His single cry reaches us, multiplied by its echo: "Chol-chol-era-ra!" Insistently, with fear or anger, he waves us off.

"Have mercy," breathes Mister Hite.

"Where at's the settlement?"

"They want to set some distance between theirselves and their corpses. That's the only *settlement* interests them. Cain't blame them, poor devils."

"Indians?"

"Most like a village over that away. There."

"He means to warn us off."

"Afraid of plague-bearing strangers."

"And the dead not yet named who'll fill them graves."

Then a crack and the echo of a crack. No gun with a range to reach us. But anyway we set his mind at rest by circling wide around him. He won't let us out of his sight. Stands there turning like the hub of a wheel that has us bound upon its rim and, by virtue of his turning, turning too. We keep an eye on the mayor and his orderly community. Jay Dubya speaks to God: "If you mean to scourge us, do it at home, not way out cheer."

Tige and Tuttle and Georgia: "Amen."

Tuttle says, "Don't hardly seem right to keep on going. They must need nursing. Who'll care for the childurn? Who'll do the cooking?" Nobody answers. He studies awhile, then sighs. "Reckon he's got the governorship of that gun. You do what you can do."

Duncan edges closer to me. "Isaac's looking. You reckon he knows what they are?" And answers himself, "I'd judge not. The women always said how sad that he ain't right. But as it turns out, he's lucky not to have no sense." Then, first looking around for Eustace and lowering his voice, "But if he hadn't a been that away he'd a knowed better than to kill her, wouldn't he?" And getting no answer, "Looks to me like things could a been worked out better, if you're God."

"I ain't," I tell him, thinking *We'll one day lie side by side in our graves. It'll be peaceful then we'll lie together. If man and woman ever.*

Tige's voice carries. "You reckon we're taken, like they say, at some proper time for it, when you've finished all your business? That away, a man might could relax and forget about it. But I reckon it's like everything else and no rhyme or reason or justice or even a say in it."

Loren says, "What wouldn't I give for me a squaw right now," and stretching himself, sings out, "A soft spring husk for this horny old August ear."

I don't look at Duncan. I don't have to. I can feel the heat off him.

Eustace, riding next to Earl: "Like beds turned down for the night. We may ride on by, but those are a vision of our already turned-down beds."

No thought of your dead gal, Eustace? No. To think her dead is to render her dead. And to render her dead is to kill her. This way do you think to keep her alive? By the power of your will? Are you after all a superstitious man? Yes, unless you know there are things in your power and things not in your power. And know the difference.

My learned gentleman: "Tell yourself that, Toliver."

Earl comes out of his study. "Makes you wonder what it's all for anyway."

Tuckahoe laughs. "You think it has any other end but this?"

Emile, letting his reins hang on his pony's neck, takes out his pipe and tobacco pouch and arranges a smoke. "I mind when the Creeks went west. My old wife watched them go—a trickle, then a Mississippi. I didn't say nothing. I watched her pulled. I thought she'd easier give up the habit of me than the habit of her Creeks. But me, I'd already built the last lodge I'll ever build, the house I mean, if I'm able, to die in. So I watched her pulled and she was pulled apart. She couldn't choose either way. Only way she could escape the choice was to die. That's what she did." Pipe into mouth and out again. "That was the year of the starfall. Thirty-three."

Rufus Pachydermus noses into the gap beside me. "Puts me in mind of a closed-off room, a grave," says Gem. "Some kind of a closet. All shut off, boarded. Takes your breath to think of it. And shrinking and drawing in on you. No door. No window. Can't get in or out. And suffocating. I heard a traveling preacher tell it once't—that was back in Carolina when I was a child—how in olden times they were liable to mistake and bury you alive—say if you was to have the sleeping sickness. They know because they had some call to open up a crypt and found she'd wore her fingers to nubs trying to claw out a there, and finally commenced to eater own flesh. Trying to stay alive. But died, a course."

Of course.

She spoke to her mother, who spoke to her father, who spoke to me. Of course I would wait till her time was past. For, in the language her pa appropriated from the Bible, her days of flower were unduly upon her. From all the excitement, her mother told her father, who told me.

But she came to me on our marriage night with a healthy lust, trembling in a silence filled with words I never thought these lips could say. Never knew fierce could be so tender. And all night long, till at dawn I slept and woke to find us murdered alongside Hymen, in the prodigy of gore and musk that was our marriage bed.

They were her mother's sheets, she said. *And in her mother's house.*

And wouldn't look at me. And then I could not look at her, having caught her shame—not for myself, for her, because she is the woman. I have heard men commonly feel that after. Could she have seen it in my face and hated me? But people recover from everything short of death.

Laughs one of the learned gentlemen: "Except, perhaps, such pleasure."

Eustace Jurdin

Going to fetch tobacco from my saddlebag, I happen on him where he's wandered to the end of his tether, fumbling for his cock, to pee. That childish hand, with long blackened squared-off nails still shaped by the cut of her scissors, takes hold of himself so gently that has so cruelly taken hold of her. The head wakes and snakes out of its skin a way as that hand steals a little pleasure that has taken at her throat such cruel satisfaction. The same hand moves, while hers—shy away shy away. That very hand—so childish and incongruous. I put out my own and stare at it. Hold still. Now there's a killer, when I let it loose.

Catching my movement, he starts, turns. Immediately his eye is hooded by a skin, like a fowl's.

—Ignat! Can I be satisfied, dispatching an Ignat?

—You'd have her killed by a dignitary?

—Yes. Then taking his life I'd rob him of something. But not this thing.

Earl

It come up a drizzle at daybreak, while we was still sleeping. To wake in rain like that, only the sky for roof, then to know better, it ain't no roof at all. Awful, the forlornness of waking uncovered, the rain indifferent to the difference between a bird or squirrel and me.

No breakfast. Even if we could scare up a fire, too dreary to set around waiting in rain. Still full of sleep, we saddle up, the leather slick, soft, smelly wet, and we walk.

And it rains. Never a downpour, though any change might a been welcome, but just like the air itself has turned into that drizzle-mist fine as fog closing around us, holding us together and apart, this whole landscape and all in it—tree, hill, horse and rider.

No use to stop. Worse to stop and just be still in it without shelter. Silent, hair slicked down, clothes pasted to us, we've turned from men to statues of men. Rain in my eyes. Rain like tears on Isaac's face. Head down, brow pulled, eyes hid, he stumbles. But before the rope is taut, he's clambered to his feet. Some of us hear a noise in his throat, but he's up and moving. Loren don't even see it.

Through a broad meadow with standing water over the

horses' pasterns, grass like seaweed waving in it. Once out of that, we come across wheel tracks and congregate in the drizzle, staring down, trying to read their familiar language. But somewhere along the way we have lost the knowledge of all such simple signs. The chill shudders through me. What are they? Wheel tracks. What could they tell us? Wheels passed north here, south here. What more?

We move on through slick, then soft, then mud into an afternoon like morning as morning was like the grey dawn. And me still marveling at us huddled together like sailors in a ship on this otherwise empty sea. Why these sailors, this ship, this sea? Is they some pattern holding from the beginning on? What an intricate thing must be the mind of God. But try to think *beginning*, I can't think it. Take, Mister Hite said some thinker fixed the beginning at four-aught-four B.C. Think a that. But can't think a that. Give myself up to it for days once, trying. Just couldn't do it. So one day when he was strolling down the lane and I was in a turnrow, plowing, I made up my mind and said, "I have tried and tried, but I can't think of endlessness and beginninglessness," and, hot-faced, asked could he hope me to understand how to think a them. He stood staring past my temple, shocked I reckon at such ignorance. I told him, "I reckon I let my attention lapse in church. I'd be much obliged if you was to tell it again, how."

And he recovered and said, "Well, take—a wheel rim! Think a that. It ain't got no beginning nor no end, has it? Think of it like a wheel hoop. Just let one finger of your mind run round and round a wheel hoop and you'll have it."

And I thought *Of course*, flushing till my ears rung at my thickheadedness.

And that was easy. I just kept on running my mind's finger around and around that wheel rim. But then after a little, I closed my mind's hand over that wheel rim till my fingers met and overlapped and I grasped it in my mind's fist. And seemed like to me it certainly was not by sideways measure endless. Seemed like it ended enough for me to close my fingers around it. And I spun that wheel in my mind's loose fist all day, trying to see could I get the hang of some endlessness, but only got more and more the certainty of its limitations. Seemed like it had more boundaries to it than I could of imagined before I held it in my mind's hand. I was as stupid again as I'd been at the beginning. Looklike, stretch my mind till I could feel it pulled—the way my eyes would pull when as a child I'd cross them to get a new perspective—I still could not think *without end, without beginning*. I known I wan't thinking nothing but *wheel rim*.

Surely others ain't so stumped, else surely we could not have the words to say so easily *endless, beginningless,* which can't no way be thought or conceived of. Could we? That wouldn't be conceivable either, would it? How understand that we could have words to say what we can't for dear life think? Think a that! Looklike every question I come upon, if I just stare at it, has kits.

So I come back to some hard fact—like this here drizzle —and careful not to question, I marvel at it, and still asking no questions, marvel at us, together, in it.

I reckon it wouldn't occurred to me to worry it to pieces but for this rain running colors together into grey. I was abandoned, they told me, in a summer rain.

You'd think slowed down like this he'd have an easier walk this day. But no. For one thing, the mud. He don't take one step that ain't lost and buried, requiring strength and skill to retrieve again within the Eagle's rhythm, which has become Isaac's necessity. And retrieves it only to slide and all but lose it again. To keep up he has to put hisself into a little stumbling trot, slanting off-balance toward the rope, holding out his hands, like he's running after us begging us for something. But a course he's holding out his hands to grab the rope and keep a little slack between his neck and Loren's horse. The slack keeps getting used up, for his feet in them clumsy brogans slide backwards as well as forwards, making him lose ground even as he gains it. You can see him panting, fighting to keep up, keep aholt of the rope so he's got that foot of slack.

After managing right well all morning, in the afternoon when he's wore out his foot hits a clay slick and the smear sprouts a three-foot shoot before he goes down. No sound out of him as he slides on his stomach like a child belly-sledding down a winter hill. Only they ain't no hill and he's being dragged and fighting to hold that rope and keep the pull of it off his neck. Seems like all of us watch for the longest, while Loren keeps walking, not looking back.

Then, like he's the one strangling, Emile hollers. Loren twists in the saddle and comes to a stop, but not in any hurry. Isaac slides to a halt then scrambles to his feet to grab himself more slack before the horse moves off. He is coughing, breathing out sounds closer to words than I've ever heard him make. He's gotten to be an expert on that rope and his connection to it, to the horse, to the ground under his feet. It takes his total concentration. Watching him calculate the rope, the gait, the texture of the mud, you could almost envy him because you know ain't nothing of hisself left over to register the grey, the mist, the belly gnawing its own linings, the lonesomeness, the spirit-damp, and on top of all, the exhaustion that is more than itself, is some kind of skin that holds all the rest. He can't register nothing of all that. He's too busy working all the aspects off against each other to keep his balance, keep moving—finally, keep alive.

In the mist we don't note how the country has commenced to change till it forces our attention and we are brought up short to set looking, knowing outside a nightmare we never before seen nothing like it. It's closed around us in front, on both sides, and behind. Not like something we moved into—like something that before we knew it moved in on us. The trees don't look like trees but like spindly giants so old their flesh sags on their limbs toward tea-colored water which, in the grey light, reflects them upside down. Then I see that this aged grey flesh is actually a moss greybeard. The trunks swell above the water line as if some sort of talus has worn off them in their aging to pile up at their feet.

Can't go no farther. We've run out of land. So we turn aside on what looks to be higher ground, but pretty soon it plays out too and we've got to turn again. Looklike with every turn our circle's getting tighter. We stop and set while Loren hands his rope to Tige and splashes off a ways. Soon as he disappears I'm sure either he is lost or we are, one, and we might all wander and sicken and die before we find our way out.

Then Loren fades back into sight, and motions. We follow, Isaac up to his calves in water, brows drawn so in a frown that his eyes look out from separate caves. Looking straight down, I see another horse growing out of my horse's hoofs, it's head toward China, ridden by a shaggy, saucer-eyed fellow looking up at me, brows so soft and furry they seem to curl. We've come to a stop again. Here we set, surrounded on all sides again save the one we come from, when across in front of us between the hairy trees, scared up by our splashing, rises a long-legged bird. "Egret," says Emile. No more life anywheres to be seen, though we hear it plain enough near at hand, slipping into the water or rippling its surface—flap of a wing, skirr in the reed. On we go in the shallow water till we come onto an open marsh and behold a flock of egrets stalking on their handy stilts, picking edibles from the matted grass. Again we find wheel tracks, two parallel depressions in the mossy turf. We follow them to a swollen stream that looks to have no definite banks, though the least bit of current moves.

Halfway across, Isaac falls. Looklike it had gotten easy for him again—or not easy, but as though he'd got so expert at a hard thing he gave you confidence it was easy. The splash stops Loren. You'd think nothing would be simpler than for him to get up again, to find his footing in that foot of buoyant water with hardly a current. But he's lying down.

We all watch, bewildered. He's floating, face up, looking for a sky hidden by mist or fog or cloud so low-lying it mingles with the tops of the spirit trees. Like a boat at its mooring, at the end of his rope Isaac rests.

Loren lets loose a curse and jabs his Eagle. Isaac has let go of the rope, so he's dragged by the neck, pulled across the stream, eyes wild, bound hands clutching for the rope, not able to get a hold before he tumbles face down in the shallows, and Loren moving straight ahead, not even watching over his shoulder.

Emile finds his voice and yells. Loren stops without turning and sets waiting. Isaac don't get up. We circle him. Tige leaps into the stream and drags him toward the soggy bank, hollering, "Hod damn you, stand up on your feet." But every time Tige stands him up Isaac lets his knees sag and sinks back down again, eyes fixed on Tige, water on his face like tears. Tige picks him up again and, holding him one-handed, swats him across the face. "You think somebody's going to carry you?"

Isaac's eyes flit like water bugs after Tige's every movement, all his concentration fixed on Tige that was before fixed on the rope, the gait, the ground under his feet, calculating. But now the danger is not rope nor gait nor ground underfoot, but whatever is stirring inside Tige as his face blackens. But though Tige yanks him up, he will not set his knees. Tige raises his arm again and swells against the woolen sky. "Don't you monkey with me!" And swats him again, the rest of us too miserable with wet to attend anyone else's misery, every man of us knowing it's on account of Isaac we're out here in this desolate bog, hating him for it.

Tige takes the rope off Isaac's neck and slips the loop over one of his feet instead. "Ay-God, you'll walk or be sorry! We ain't going to wait on you." And Loren, a smile playing over his face like light or water, jabs the Eagle and pulls him a foot or two over the wet marsh grass, Isaac's eyes big but his jaw set, you can see the muscle playing. When Loren stops, he rises up on his elbow and looks at the Eagle's crupper, but he don't get up. Tige takes and yanks him by the armpits from behind. But nosir, Isaac ain't setting his knees. Tige throws him forward. He falls on his wrist—I reckon like to broke it—and Loren gives his horse a heel and drags him maybe five yards. Emile is looking down at his pony's neck. Eustace is watching like his mind is elsewhere. Nobody says nothing till Mister Hite, looking in his rain-soaked misery like he's about to cry, brings out, "Now looka here, Loren." Don't nobody pay him any mind. Tige picks Isaac up. He still won't stand, ain't going to stand, we all know it. So Tige throws him down and falls on him and grinds his face in the mud while Mister Hite says again, "Now looka here!" Isaac comes up strangling, spitting muck. Tige would of picked him up to knock him down again, but just then Duncan yells.

We turn. A strange heavy wagon approaches along the wheel tracks. High sides, no tailgate, low to the ground—its little wheels nothing but rounds cut from logs—and the man in it standing up to drive his ox.

"Untie him," Eustace says. "Get that rope off him. No need to go into it with strangers."

But Tige looks at Loren. Loren says, "He ain't going no place. Ain't he been telling you that?" a taunt in his voice. Tige cusses, struggling with the wet knots.

The stranger looks like he might a gone right past like a man in a town, but hailed by Mister Hite he hauls back on his lines. He don't look friendly. A big dark fellow, he goes over us with a canny eye.

"Habitan?" Emile asks.

He nods. Emile puts something to him in a gibberish. He don't answer. He's looking at Isaac. He nods toward him. "Is sickness?"

Emile shakes his head. "Just tired and worn out with walking. He ain't got a horse."

He studies Isaac a moment longer. Then, *"Laba,"* he says, thumbing over his shoulder.

Emile motions to Tige and Tige says to Isaac, "Get in." Isaac don't move.

Cussing in a polite tone, Tige picks him up and carries him to the wagon and throws him down on the bed of straw.

"You know of a farrier hereabout?" Toliver asks.

"Ne comprend."

"A smith. My mare's thrown a shoe."

The man glances at Beth Pullen's hoofs and nods.

Then down the watercourse between the encroaching lily pads comes a boy in a pirogue so thin-shelled it'd float on a heavy dew. He looks shyly at us and drags his paddle, turning, jabbering at the man, who mutters back then clucks up his ox the way you call up chickens. The docile thing strains in its traces and we follow. The boy paddles rapidly away.

But when we come upon the cluster of buildings, he's there ahead of us, having come by some watery shortcut. It's one strange place. The house, roofed with piemetta fronds cured in the sun, stands on stilts like the egrets. Hanging underneath its floor are what first look to be cages of some kind but turn out to be nests for laying hens. The housewife could open a trap in the floor and gather eggs right into her kitchen.

The barn's on higher ground. The fenced barnlot is half land, half water. Some of the cows stand knee deep grazing on the tops of reed that should flavor their butter sweet and nutty.

So we spend the night in a barn of the *habitans,* who are said to have red bones. They do not feed us at their table, but their women in little unstarched bonnets bring us, where we sit in the wide barn hall, a thirty-pound sugar boiler full of steaming rice filled with prizes—mussels and crawdads and gobbets of chicken and pork—which we dip into with long-handled spoons. I never tasted nothing more choice.

The women watch, pleased at our appetites. One plump mother notes Isaac sitting his distance off where he's planted himself. She urges him, her hands making shoving motions toward the food. But Isaac won't attend.

She draws closer to him, stoops to peer into his eyes. He don't even focus on her. She makes her shoving motion with both hands again. He puts his face sidewards to her and won't take note. She nudges him. He moves like jelly, which finds its shape again.

We quit eating to watch while she dips her fingers full of rice and, crooning, holds it out to him. But he won't even look at the food in her hand. The women give up on him and return to us, watching us eat, commenting among themselves, laughing. One of them a girl so black-eyed, red-cheeked, fetching, Tige can't keep from touching. Soon as he does, their laughing stops. They turn and look, and we turn too. Tige curses. "I ain't done nothing! Oggle me I'll give you something to oggle at!" The women take fright and melt out the barn door into the dark and the rain, leaving us to ourselves.

Tuttle dips his fingers full of rice and holds it out to Isaac, who feasts his eyes on the hot food. He looks at Tuttle's hand, his lip trembles, his nostrils ruffle. But he turns his face away. The haughty look of him, refusing the rice, while we plainly hear his stomach, of another mind, railing at his stubborn mouth. I feel us all wanting him to eat. Eat because we have been so hungry and now, satisfied, don't want to have to know of hunger, because not one of us this day has used forbearance and don't want to be outdone by the likes of him, because something needs to be assuaged, righted, and nobody but him can give us that.

And won't.

But the minute Tuttle gives up and turns his back,

Isaac turns around again—like he's got to see is the rice still there. Tige laughs. Isaac, slow and haughty, gives us the side of his face again.

Tige grabs up a fistful of the rice and thrusts it under Isaac's nose and we see, again, the quiver, the ruffle, and also the forbearance, the will. And the look on him, scornful as a roman-nosed ass, would be comical if it wasn't for the hunger we hear fighting him all the way and losing to his will. Tige screws the rice into Isaac's face.

"Clean it off him," Eustace says.

Tige stares at Eustace a minute, then looks at Loren sitting there with his little smile. Loren just looks back. So Tige, silent and hateful and rough, shaves off the rice, using the heel of his hand like a razor. When he's finished, Isaac, eyes on Tige, has got the will and nerve to shove out of his mouth with his tongue what rice got forced in.

A person climbing the loft ladder and poking a head through the hole would see no one but Isaac off there in the corner where Loren's tethered him to the plate. We've all burrowed under the straw, where mice make their rustling transactions. Below in a stall a cow lies with milk sickness and a woman sits by her, keeping a clay firebowl full of burning knots that, out of the wind, gives off a steady rosy light. Ammonia rises to us off the fresh manure. And heats us too, the steam off the hot manure. It clears my head. I feel close with the cows and sheep and pigs and horses come in out of the rain. I remember one time as a child such a drowsy pleasure at going to sleep well fed and not alone, with a dim light burning.

Roused by a clatter the last instant before sleep, I rise up through the straw. An elegant gentleman with a silk goatee has climbed the ladder to visit us. I fancy he was out on business when we arrived and, coming in, was told by the old historian of a ewe that they was guests upstairs.

Another head pops up to see who's come: Isaac, thatched yellow with straw. The black-and-white billy goat spies him and edges toward his lonely corner, dropping his nose to investigate. Then, ducking his head, he nudges Isaac with the flat of his princely horns. Isaac reaches with his bound-again hands to close fingers around one of them. The goat sits down on its knees. Isaac touches the pieded gentleman's silky beard.

Full-bellied, warm, dry, feeling such a flood of pleasure, I lie back in the straw. The raindance on the shingles overhead lulls me toward sleep like music.

We are in Louisiana.

Duncan McElroy

It was getting Isaac ruint it. Before, it was all a lark. Look at him. You'd think it's an honor of some kind we're doing him. I reckon it was bound to happen. First time he's ever been the center of anything. Before, he was always on the edges, watching.

The way he stands waiting for the rope in the morning. The way he waits to see will he get a bite to eat or a drink of water. And accepts royally whichever way it turns out. He was always kind of pitiful. Now, worse off I reckon than he's ever been in his life, he don't seem pitiful. Stuck on himself—like some captured king. Give the devil his due, he's good at it. You'd swear he's older, taller, wiser in the face, like he has come over this unmapped way to a kind of knowledge.

Once I stole him from her and took him over to Big Rock swimming. I thought he ought to get on out and do something like other people, not just follow her to her garden, to her milking, on her hunts for the eggs her chickens scatter so. It bothered me the way he done nothing but trail around after her. Big boy like that.

I guess it was reckless, for of course he couldn't swim. The waterfall's dug a chasm. If you go to the edge, you'll just naturally fall down on all fours. And they say the pool below is bottomless. We were down there at the swimming hole. I'd no sooner got him in the water than here she come. Stood there with her arms crossed and never raised her voice but laid me low as a snake's belly. I reckon I got no more than I deserved. I could a drowned him. But I never meant mischief. It was just—big boy like that, it bothered me.

After that I let him alone. It wasn't my business to worry about him. I give up on him and left him alone like everybody else. Except Eily Jurdin.

Look at him. I wonder would a stranger looking at him now guess anything was wrong with him. King Solomon. And ain't nothing. No pa. Never had one. And his ma run off and left him when he was a toddler. Nobody but her— and he's lucky to have her, the women say. He'd no claim on her. How many women would do it? They all say it. Ma says she's won her place in heaven for feeding and clothing and taking care of him, her erring sister's child of sin.

I never would go inside her house. Ma says I ought to sometime, and see the cage—high as your chest—she made for some field mice out of that fine reed hogs are partial to. Inside are cunning furnishings for the field mice's pleasure. Ma says I ought to see it. But I never would go in.

She's got this fierce old one-eyed cat named Calico she trundled all the way from Carolina. It periodically breaks up the cage and plays the mischief with them mice. But she wouldn't be without her cat. The reed grows plentiful along the branch and the old Indian fields yield bumper crops of mice. Let the cat bust it up, she'll take and build her another like the first and outfit it with play pretties for the pets the two of them'll go out then and catch.

She'll sometimes call to me passing in the road and beckon me to her door for boiled goobers. I always have to go, polite, and take some. Ma'd switch me if I didn't. They're distant connections. You could make out a case for Isaac and me being cousins. I don't brag about it. Never says a word to me, just nods when I thank her. I've hoped to catch a glimpse of the cage and the mice, but I never. I like my goobers parched.

Myron Tuttle

Suddenly known he belonged to hisself and even in his present predicament can, like any man, pick as he pleases among the choices open to him. Like, he don't have to stand on his feet if he chooses not to, and nothing nobody can do to make him, don't have to eat, for it's him moves his jaws or don't, swallows or don't, nobody else. Don't have to set one foot before the other and walk.

Passed through a tunnel and at the end of it known he could refuse, and showed us all—refuse even food when he must a been starving.

I thought then he might refuse the whole of it—to move, to eat—and choose to starve hisself. What awe I felt.

But he didn't. Ate for me pretty as you please at breakfast. *I refuse* was the beginning of *I choose*. Eats what we give him, never a show of hunger, or even hurry. Chews every bite, calm, thorough, like mama's good boy's been taught, "because it's good for you." Good for your body which even now walks its cortege. And drinks his mouthfuls of water, no more. And walks.

We hit a low lawn ringed by a turpentine-scented pine woods, our way flooded by a sea of horned cattle, which we commence to part at a walk. They're feeding on wild oats, wild vetch, peavine. Unfenced, they're shepherded by graziers mounted on little Spanish tackies. Thick, ungainly, jug-headed—so unlike Emile's pretty pony, though they claim they're of a breed. One of the graziers falls in with Loren and I hear him tell that the cows belong to a French planter in the Teche and they themselves work for one-fifth the herd's yearly increase. Tige says, "How the hell would he know the year's increase? You could cut out half the calves and say the herd grazed onto something made the cows abort, and still take one-fifth of the half that's left and nobody the wiser. Hell, why don't I th'ow in with you, drop out of this pleasure jaunt and undertake something profitable?"

I woke that night we slept in the loft, amazed to see a goat with Isaac. All fours tucked under him, the goat sat still while straw by straw Isaac dropped a cover over him. I

100

watched for a time, but couldn't keep my head up. Later I woke again. The light under us still on, I could see Isaac sleeping. I took and crawled over and brushed straw off the mound beside him and sure enough seen a black-and-white patch of Billy. Then both the goat and Isaac, who they claim is deaf, woke up and the two of them glared at me. I had to chuckle. His face twisted comically, like a clown clowning anger, so I left them. But back in my own nest I watched while angrily he brushed away ever last straw of the coverlet I'd disturbed and commenced painstakingly to cover the goat afresh till no hair of him showed. Then, finished, he settled back against the beam. His eyes would close, then spring open to see had I moved, then close again. He'd done for Billy what a mother bird'll do where a hand has touched the nest. She'll labor away ever last speck of the contamination before she's satisfied.

Strange, such gentle care, such mothering, for a goat. I felt a sadness fall over me. Starved for sleep, I scarce could close my eyes for studying him.

Toliver Pullen

You wouldn't recognize him, firelight and shadow leaping against the night behind him as he rants, reeling like a prophet at a tenting, eyes like John the Baptist.

"I tell you I've looked in his face and seen a vision! All right. Don't listen to me. See for yourself. All you got to do is look! I tell you we're at the other end of that same rope!

Ain't we way out cheer because of him? If he hadn't a come out cheer would we be out cheer now? Well ain't that proof? What's that look in his face, *behind* his face, glowing out a his jack-o-lantern? Never had that in his face before, did he? What is it? Where's it from? *I tell you* it's from knowing who's general here. It's *us* tied to *him* by that rope! Ain't our pace set to his? Ain't thisere the place a his choosing? What did we have to do with it? Quit cher looking at me like I'm out a my head! Listen! I'm a-telling you we walk and eat and sleep and breathe and stop and go because of him. Without him, what would we be out cheer *for*? Answer that!

"Everything's got turned around, stood on its head. The first I knowed of it was when I seen *him* knowing it. Seen it in his face! It got thetere bald shine to it. I tell you he lifted his face like he'd seen the glory. Laughing at us! I ain't standing for it. Not Tige Fargus! Nosir.

"And let me tell you what's the worst of it. I would a run. When it come to me—and I never would a knowed if it hadn't just come to me—when I seen it, I would a run. Then, in that same way I knowed *it,* I knowed something else that's the worst of it. I knowed I would even been *running* on account of him!"

You wouldn't recognize what's coming from him as coming from *Tige.* If someone had tried to get him to understand the thing he's saying, they wouldn't been able to. He ain't theorizing, he's describing something he understood in one instant that has stretched his depth of field like a power glass.

Was it when Isaac on the stream bank wouldn't lock his knees and stand? Was it Tige learning he couldn't *make* him—could kill him maybe, but couldn't make him lock his knees? So if he couldn't make Isaac do, it had to be Isaac making him do?

I look around at Loren, who can manage him—because though Tige is hateful, Loren is more cruel, though nobody has seen all his cruelty, but that don't mean a thing to them, or means only that it's secret and therefore awful. The only sign of it is the mark it now and then leaves on his woman. In Carolina when I was a tad they tarred and feathered a wifebeater. But nobody interferes between those two. Like they're doomed to some private obscene beyond-ordinary pact. There's no ruckus. Maybe once a year the boy won't go near home for a day or two, so we know it's happened again. And somehow they know—did Hedy tell it to one of the women? I can't believe she did—but they know she put her foot down on one thing: he don't lay a hand on the boy. How can she stop him? How can she—frail, haunted, beaten—manage Loren?

When it happens, I'll find the boy in my barn. He'll dog my tracks, follow me with a cannibal eye, wanting. Wanting what?

Loren can manage Tige, but he's sitting there enjoying it. I'm waiting, wondering what it's going to be, when here it comes. With a reasonless leap, he stops before Tuck and slants over him shouting, "Are you laughing?"

Tuckahoe looks up. "I am not. It's something in the shape of my lip, I'd guess. I've been asked that before."

Tige hovers over him, silent for a minute, casting around. Then, "Howcome you don't ever take off that hat? Wears it while he sleeps," he says, turning to us like a barrister to a jury. And back to Tuck, "Wears it like his skin." And swipes the skin hat off Tuck's head. We stare. Tige's fingers nervelessly open. The skin hat drops to the sand.

"And so it is," Tuck says, his voice quiet but vibrant as the wing of an insect closed inside your hand, looking out of that fixed eye that can never completely close.

Emile asks, "Where did they take it?"

Tuck answers precisely: "In a village raided as reprisal for Nickojack."

Emile says, "That was seventeen ninety-four," for all the world as if there's not a scalped man sitting before us.

"I was a boy," Tuck says. "After the fighting I came to with only the dead for company, knowing they'd return, unable to run, an arrow through this thigh. In the silence the hoot of an owl that I know has no wing. Crickets, locusts, tree frogs all are quiet. My dear dead keeping their fixed watch. Then shadows move like ghosts from their bodies, strange ministering angels that hover a moment, then move on. And I have the choice of moving and winning the deliverance of a hatchet in my skull. Death seems homely, with all of these. And sweet, to blind them to here, now, and give that wonder look. Or I may lie for dead and endure the moment and live, if I can, out the other side. Someone bends over me. Long hair brushes my face. I smell the perfume my father brought last Christmastime from Charleston and all but start, thinking it's my mother. Then know it's my mother's scalp. The knife is very keen. It slits along what has always been my hair line. A sting to it, no more. And something like tears down my forehead, temples, neck. I think my scalp is crying. But more than the knife I feel the gentle fingers cradling my head for the operation. I want to weep to those fingers, kiss them for their gentleness. But I know I must not move. Fingers inserted beneath my helmet curl, take hold. In the moonlight I ape the faces of the dead who watch. The beginnings of cold. The fingers find a hold on my slick shock, rip it off. Lightning shoots through all my nerves. I never lose consciousness, feel horror and after the horror pain, and then again the cold on my queer new nakedness."

Tige still hangs there, peculiarly off-balance.

Emile asks, "You were pegged?"

"Found next morning and taken to a fort where an army surgeon pegged my skull." Then, as if we are schollars and he our pedagogue, he lectures precisely. "Pegged, you see, with an awl. A liquid emerges from the holes, like albumen from a pinhole in an egg, and spreads a scab over the entire skull, which, in turn, forms a scar, which is the specimen you see."

Tige bends sideways and picks up the skin cap. He holds it out to the Tuckahoe. "Put it on."

"Thank you," says Tuckahoe. He takes it but does not put it on.

Eustace asks, "Have you regretted the choice you made?"

Tuck says, "The boy who made that choice died as surely that night as if he'd made the other. He made the choice. The choice made me. So I can't answer. From the moment of his choice—the instant I was made as was, in another instant, Adam—I knew it's all the same, it's really all the same."

In the silence, we hear sobbing. Nobody moves. We sit like stones that can't hear sobbing. It's Loren's boy. He's fallen over on his face, sobbing aloud. I imagine I see his lip—his disembodied lip—full and pink and jerking. Moving that way, unaccompanied by the rest of him, it looks like a worm—that pinkness, those striations, that voluptuous movement. I find myself trembling at the sound of those grieving sobs off there in the shadows. For an instant I imagine it has been left to one child to grieve for the world.

Loren reaches blind for a handful of twigs and gravel and throws his trash at the sobs. A brief rain. The sobbing stops. Stillness. A retch. Another. And Loren's muttered curse.

Eustace Jurdin

Did I hope to be spared? One lost his scalp, the other his three wives, another his name, one this, the other that, another something else, and the open graves like turned-down beds for the coming night, and he, who has only his life to lose, will lose it at my hand. Did I hope to be spared? I thought no, but reserved *the one thing I cannot lose.* Take scalp, wife, name, take lands and all my plunder, every stick and shard, take my life, but don't take that, I bargained—but didn't know I bargained. And I'm answered: you can't live at all unless you can live with nothing.

I have buried her not to bury her. But she is alive, making her own way out of the tomb of my fashioning. Go back! If you don't you'll die. Like the mule.

But here she is. First so wise a being she's no need of words, knows what she wants—food, warmth. Add to that a smile sweet, knowing, self-contained. A babe, she grows younger to become a child.

Five years old, across the corner of the table from the colporteur who has called upon our patience as well as our hospitality for the night. Garrulous old bore. Confusing children with monkeys, he makes a monkey of himself, tipping his large head, rolling his eye, raising a coy finger to her. "Does my little lady practice virtue?"

She studies this specimen with interest.

"Answer the gentleman, Eily," her mother directs.

I answer for her. "As the bee practices geometry."

"Oh, very good! Well said! Ho-ho."

Twisting his head grotesquely on his puffed neck, he rolls his eye at her and would have spoken again, but Eily asks, "Howcome you do your head that way?"

Taken aback, "What way, little lady?" he asks.

Finding no other way to answer, she apes his monkey exactly with her unconscious-as-yet gift for mimicry.

"Eily!" her mother gasps.

I laugh.

"Eustace!"

"We have to punish her."

"I won't. What for? It was innocent. Served the old fool right."

"She mustn't be unkind. You favor her too much. It must be that she's the late child, and the girl—but you favor her too much. It's not good for her."

True. Favor her too much to get my work done. I find her and lift her onto my back and we're off for the barn where I keep my records in an office I made by enclosing and flooring the square corner stall—notes on veterinary doctoring, planting times, seeds (where got, when set), breeding dates, mare seasons, milk quantities, and the like. It gives me pleasure to put things down, to leave a history. And, too, the room's for cogitating. I give, to my shame, considerable time to cogitating. Eily takes after me. You'd think she's perpetual motion till she falls still for minutes at a time, cogitating.

I set the child atop a barrel and light a fire in Mister Franklin's stove.

"Pa."

"Eily?"

"I like it here. It's so nestly."

Shy away shy away.

Georgia Gem Hite

Ended one a his discourses yesterday with, "Try and see yourself by seeing what you lack," and I said, "Like trying to see the apple when ain't nothing there but the wormholes," and he never liked that none, so this morning—he notches a stick from one sabbath to the next, so he'll know when it's come around—we're all saddled up and ready and look to see who's missing and find him still setting there on a rock beside what's left of the fire. So Eustace seen it was Sunday and bowed his head and the others done likewise while Jay Dubya sucked his eyetooth and waited. Then looked up, sorrowful as the betrayed Jesus, and, hands in pockets sweeping his coattails back, begun so low we had to strain to hear him, a trick he's learned will drain ever last drop of your attention:

"In the beginning was the word." Silence. We waited. "In the beginning was the word and the word was God.

108

The word wasn't nothing else but to name Him. Yes. In paradise the word wasn't nothing but the instrument of praise—of prayer and song and poetry. Then come the fall. Man's degradation. And now the word is paper money. You put down words the way the pedagogue works numbers on a slate, hoping to find the answer. But I tell you the truth is not to be discovered thataway, out there on the slate or by that kind of figgering. I am speaking of what ought not be done. Words ought only be used for prayer or song or poetry or praise of God, ought not be used like numbers to come up with what they call the Truth. The Tower of Babel was made of words in just such degradation. Nosir. They ought only be used to describe it, to picture it forth so you can look at it and enjoy yourself. You cain't make Truth out of words no more than they could make a tower. They're to be used to describe the thought, not manufacture it. For that ain't knowing and that is not the Truth. Now let us pray." Here comes his favorite song. "Lord God be praised. The awful God be praised. Father bestow on me, in this plain of Moriah, nothing less than you give to Moses on the mount. Don't hold out your cup on me. I have strength to bear your finger. And will thank you to give the light to your humble Jay Dubya Hite."

Is he done? I reckon. Just stands there. Every minute you think he'll move. But he don't move till the minute you've resigned yourself to thinking he never will. Then puts on his hat and goes spryly toward the horse, leaving the mule for me, and climbs up to set facing ahead, waiting for the rest of us, as if *we've* been holding *him* up.

And that is one example of how I usually supply him with his text.

Emile

Extensive savannahs in early-autumn flowering. A cane meadow—the cane no less than thirty feet high, thick as a man's wrist. Cut any joint and get a quart of water. It forms a wall cutting off all air and passage, so we make a wandering gravel-bottomed stream our road. Then a small piemetta swamp. Intermingling gum and cypress. A close physical world. Intimate sounds of bird and insect. Beset by flies as intolerable in their bite as our burning flies, but exotic specimens. Green-bodied, heads of gold, these scarabs attach themselves to the horses and hang—pendant, splendid—among rich beads of blood.

They attack Isaac, too, while leaving us alone. The mule still faintly clings to him who clung to it. Vermilion-streaked face and throat and arm, chest skeletal, daubed as an Indian's from the fly bites, this half-naked brave advances with a strange lightfoot hop, as if his feet hurt. His lip reduced from its infant plumpness to an exaggerated signature across his face which, always mercurial in the changes flowing over it, has become a mask deceptively naked in its fixedness. A sunbaked terra-cotta ceremonial figurine.

What has this to do with a girl, a morning, a lip quivering between some unsettling hurt and that corner-down-drawn pout that makes three sides of a square as she says,

110

"And oh Isaac his name is Nyle!" as if the lip wants to speak, to say—what, Isaac?

What has this to do with that?

"We were left by ourselves a minute, standing in the yard, and I was so ashamed."

"Why shamed, Eily?"

"*I* don't know. Well, his hair's a kind of sorrel. And I wisht I'd a had my shoes on. His were boots. The softest leather. I couldn't help it, I said, 'Lord, your boots!' and had him balancing on one foot then another, turning them sole up across his knee. I had to explain: 'No, I mean I never seen leather like that there leather.' And he said, 'I thought I'd tracked something into your mother's kitchen house.' And my heart give a leap, for he was laughing in the eye. And he said, 'It's Spanish leather.'

"Spanish leather! Think a that! And he's big enough. We stand eye level to one another. I found a piece of my voice and said, 'Why me and not somebody else?' I know I'm pretty, I didn't mean that. But other girls are pretty. Oh quitcher—*I* know what I meant. And he said, 'Eily, I've studied it and studied it—is your name Eileen?'

" 'Eily,' I told him.

"And he said, 'Eily. I'll answer you, Eily, but it may take me all my life.'

"Then oh drat here comes his pa—he has this small jolly father, little side-whisker tufts like owl ears. They shook Eustace's hand and then they were gone on their big delta horses, nothing but a roll of dust down the curve a the hill to show they'd been there. I kept coming out to sweep the yard so I could look at that dust—just to be sure—till it was all gone. I wonder what was in his mind, what he meant to say, when he said that."

In spite of the mixture in me, I like the sound of Sidney's cornless cousin.

"Only—" She's making complicated patterns with her stick in the sand. "Eustace thinks I'm a goose." She looks off across my maize field toward the trees that mark the river. "Eustace and I, we had a good—feeling once. I never had to say, for him to know my mind." She complicates her pattern in the sand. "But for some time now, I can talk all I like, he mistakes everything. Mama clucks at his crankiness. There's one good thing—*we* get on better now. Don't you think she's pretty? I remember the faintest picture of her face leaning, and the least smile—pleased, y'know. Then for the longest, years and years, looked like she didn't care for the way I was turning out. But now we're friends again."

Duncan McElroy

We commence to see settlement. I think: food, company, sleep in a bed, at least under roof, and maybe some young'un to tell it to. Brag a little and feel better. It's something, ain't it—traveling so far, sleeping in the open, living off the land?

—You're looking at a murderer!

—Liar.

—Call me a liar?

—A deaf one to boot.

Then light right in.

Telling it I might come to see after all it *is* that way and just something the matter with *me*.

With them too. Moving off, skirting the least sign of a dwelling or community. We don't look good, they say. Dirty. Clothes in tatters. No call to go answering a lot of questions.

"You want me to see can I get some milk?" I ask Tuttle as we pass a ramshackle old place way off across a bog.

Shakes his head.

"Maybe they could spare some eggs."

Keeps on going.

Pa signals. I gallop back to him.

"I'm nearly out of lead. Go see can you get some. Here's my small knife. You ought to get right smart for it. Don't let yourself be cheated."

"Nosir!"

She picks her way through hummocks and muck, a humping ride, mud spattering up my thigh. I try and see if there's anybody out and around, till finally I lose sight of the house. But I follow a snaking trail, come out along a split-rail fence, and follow it till I see the shack again.

Nothing moves. A disheartening place, logs wide enough apart for marsh rats to get in without scratching their sides. No door, just an opening. I light and peer around. As I step up onto the rotting stoop, I hear a squeak followed by a squawk, squeak-squawk, squeak-squawk. I put my head in at the door. It's right dim so it takes a minute to see I'm looking at a face looking back at me.

"Traveling?"

"Yessum." She's wedged into a little rocker. That's what's squeaking. I don't blame it.

"Wanting directions," she sighs. "I'll tell you all I can.

Over that away, foller the rail fence till the corner you'll pick up a footpath if you look smart. Foller it till it cuts toward a dead cypress, you cain't miss it, and you'll come to a branch. Take the right fork and foller it till it passes th'oo a pond. You'll skirt that on its high bank. There'll be a clump a trees swallered in moss, and you don't go that away, you bar to the left till you come on a wagon track. Now. Bar to the right along that track a mile or two you'll come on a house. That'll be the Cleavers'. That who you want?"

"Nome."

"Then I don't know who you could be looking for."

"Nobody."

"Then howcome you astin for directions?"

"Wellum"—I clear my throat—"is your man nearby? I want to trade for some lead if I can."

"Only lead he's got's in his feet." She guffaws and sobers, never missing a stroke at the rocking. "Everbody wanting something. And everbody wanting something different. You might ast when you get to the Cleavers'. They might have them some lead."

"Mam, pardon, but how far is it to the next house east?"

"Your guess is good as mine. I don't get out much."

I take a step into the little low room. On a shelf beside the door, a large-based succulent that might have been transplanted in this marsh straight off the moon, its trunk thick as a man's knee, is wedged into a little pot, leaves shriveling, yellowing. Several lie on the shelf like dying bugs on their backs, curled up, making a cup of their poor bodies to hold their ebbing life.

She complains, "A woman in a wagon passing give me that for a bowl of honey. Come to me fit as a fiddle. Now look at it. Growed for her. Won't for me. No sooner come to me than it set about dying."

"Mam, in my opinion it wants repotting in a bigger vessel."

"Wail, another'll come along and have *his* opinion—*more* water, *less* water, *no* sun, *full* sun. How I'm to know I cain't make out."

A child enters from the other room, ragged, limbs like kindling. His eyes are dry, but his nostrils are wet and red and grieving. She eyes the forlorn creature and continues to rock. "I can't put flesh on his bones nor starch in his spine. One says tonic, one says purge. How am I to know?"

"Mungry," he mutters.

"Now he's come to pester me."

I make up my mind to venture on his part. "Some hold care's the physic, not the medication."

On she rocks. "One'll recommend this, another that. How am I to know?"

I turn to the child and ask, "What's your name?"

He dips his chin, thrusts out his bloated belly, and mutters, "Poke."

"Poke?" He's said all he's going to say. I turn to her. "Poke?"

Never breaks her rocking by a lick. "My old man he knows a man that swears Old Hickory prophesies a man name Poke will one day be president of these Unidet States. So we named thisun Poke on the off-chance. But don't look to me like it's agoen to be him. Don't look to me like he's got it in him. Childurn are a disappointment."

Spanking her through the marsh, I gallop after them

and overtake them entering a low prairie. As we pass through, the grass grows higher till it parts before our horses' breasts. We see a right smart herd of deer, fifteen-twenty head, and along a ridge of higher ground a litter of good-size wolf cubs black as bear. Mosquitoes big enough to harness. Earl says this land's so rich it would take a team of oxen to bring it under plow. Tuck says we're no doubt coming to a river.

And there it is, five hundred yards wide, a great pulled bow we can see for miles to the south, emptying out wider all the time, the color of pewter in this late light.

On its near bank—I hardly believe my eyes—the establishment of a ferry master. Then can hardly believe my ears that listen for objections and hear none. We're riding toward it, a four-sided building around a yard in the manner of the Creek. Actually, four buildings joined together at their corners by a roof: one house for travelers, one for the ferryman's family, one for his animals, the remaining one for storage. All built out of plain hewed logs and roofed with boards rived with a froe. The ferryman stands outside to meet us, not uncordial though eyeing Isaac on his rope, and tells us supper and breakfast together will be seventy-five cents apiece, ferriage twelve, feed and bedding for the horses two bits each. Eustace does the nodding.

Emile and Eustace and Mister Hite get down and hand their reins to someone else, and the rest of us water the horses at the river, then ride into the barn hall to dismount, unsaddle, and spread bedding from the loft. The ferryman, Mister Pepperdine, shows us plentiful fodder, a feast of change for our tired animals. Pa shoves Isaac down to set against a post and winds the rope around him and the post from his waist to his shoulders.

As the only other beasts in the barn are Mister Pepperdine's donkey, three cows, some frisky goats, and chickens already gone to roost in the loft and rafters and on the ladder, we assume we're the only tourists here this night. So we're surprised to enter the lodge and find the Indians. It's a big enough room, a fireplace at either end. Emile and Eustace and Mister Hite have already claimed one end of it. The other end houses a dozen red men playing at cards. Big strapping fellows, some with faces and breasts painted red, all with handsome feather plumes sticking in their hair, wearing calico shirts and buckskin breeches and moccasins. Some wear their blankets around their shoulders, others sit on them or use them for pillows as they lie on their sides, elbow-propped for the game, their bare posteriors exposed.

Their manner of transportation is now clear. Two bark canoes stretch the length of the room, suspended from the joists.

The kitchen door opens and a plump arm hands around it a bottle of porter. Mister Pepperdine, stern and anxious, hurries to claim the port and slam the door. He hands Pa the bottle. "Supper'll be along," he assures us. Then a knock, and he scurries. There's a giggle before the door closes again. This time he returns with candles strung on a twine through their necks. He stretches this contraption between nails across a corner of the room. He lights a taper at the fire and sets the candles blazing.

The knock, giggle, doorslam are repeated till every corner's lit. Emile calls out to the red fellows a spate of Indian words. They look up. One calls something back. They go on with their card game.

"They're Flatheads," Emile says. "Choctaws."

Our porter almost gone, the door opens and there stands a gal I'd reckon right at six foot, holding a large pan her father rushes to take, shooing her back. He slams the door on her, then brings us the food and some wooden spoons. The fish stew is good, with hot biscuits and a platter of shoat ribs. The Indians get another bottle of port.

By the time we're done, it's dark. I stuff a biscuit in my pocket and make for the door, fumbling at myself so they'll think I'm gone to pee. Once in the dark, I head for the barn. I've already got the biscuit in hand, glad to see there's a lantern and he ain't in the dark like just another animal. Then I see Earl standing there. I hadn't even missed him inside. So I take a bite of the biscuit and don't even glance at Isaac.

Earl says, "Reckon they're happy to be indoors tonight and fed and bedded."

"Eyuh," I say. "I wanted to see if they was quiet."

"They're quiet," he says. We stand looking at a horse, nothing more to say. Neither of us looks at Isaac before we go back in.

Tuckahoe has crossed the room to stand overlooking the Indians' game. Soon he's squatting, pointing, grunting questions. Little by little, he's talking their language. He joins their gambling.

After a while, they's a ruckus. Tuck springs up, and a big bare-ass fellow rises, dropping his blanket to reveal the two arms of Samson, each bound with a copper bracelet above the elbow. Tuck steps back in awe and laughing sweeps off his hat. I catch my breath. The Indians look up.

The tall fellow reaches out a finger, touches Tuck's crown, and laughs. They're all laughing, pointing to Tuck's head as though it were a pleasant joke. Tuck talks, describing with his hands, and gives the big one's braid a jerk. I would no more a bothered that braid than I'd bother a bear's ear. The fellow doubles up and hollers. I always heard Indians was morose, but they're a wild giggling company.

Another giant girl appears. Mister Pepperdine shoos her back into the kitchen and brings the Indians their pot of gumbo and platter of shoat, which they dive in to their elbows, after tossing their spoons at Tuck, who is having his second supper.

Tuck and the Indians are still gambling when I fall asleep. I dream all night and wake in the morning to find the Indians and their bark canoes vanished downriver and gone forever, like my dreams. The men sit quiet at a trestle table let down off the wall, eating white meat and eggs and pone and passing a large tureen with a tin top. I reach for it, thinking it's hot tea or coffee. But whiskey scalds me, lip to belly. I come up gasping, coughing, the top of my head flapping as easily as the tureen's tin lid. The men whoop and holler at my expense, pointing, aping me with faces.

The door opens and I see the daughters giggling at me, demure but knowing. One of them holds out her arms to me, and I'm faint with the need to run away, everybody laughing but Mister Pepperdine who, blanched as white bread, rushes at the door, shoos them back like a bevy of hens, slams it, then lays back against it panting from the exertion. And some of them girls greying in the hair.

We think we might almost ford the river, and what we can't ford will swim our horses. But this agitates Mister Pepperdine. He shakes his head, closes his eyes, and waggles his hand at us no-no-no. He says the waters are treacherous, the undercurrents can drag a horse and roll him and wash him away. Eustace asks how, then, are we to cross, and he eagerly explains a contraption he's invented, which we find to be a raft with an open slot in the center. Into it you walk the horses in the shallows—a brace to a raft. Fixed in a loose rope harness that allows the raft to rise and fall with the water level, the horses can wade inside it, then swim with ease, the wooden raft keeping them buoyantly afloat.

These rafts appended behind the pirogues carrying ourselves and our equipage and such small stores as we've got from the Pepperdines, like Noah we set out. Who maneuvers the pirogues? The daughters, all fine sailors. We anxiously watch the horses, who stretch their necks, keeping desperate eyes upon us in the boats. We shout encouragement the whole way across. And no mishap.

On the opposite shore—the square establishment upriver and across now hardly more than several neat-stacked cords of wood—the horses shower us, shaking themselves dry. We're so relieved to put the river behind us we shout with laughter as we're drenched.

The daughters produce biscuits and honey, which we eat while the horses rest after their swim and graze on the buffalo clover. Mister Pepperdine waves the big girls with their baskets back into the boats, where they sit waiting while we chatter with their pa. Then, waving, they ship off and begin their haul upstream, keeping for the time close to shore.

We've seen them in midchannel before we pick up and saddle. Some time later we stand on a hill and look back at where they've disappeared. And the river like a great worm that's thrived on every speck of life for miles, rendering itself fat but lonesome.

Part Four

Toliver Pullen

Passed this morning through a grove of illicium, callicanthus, magnolia auriculata, then crossed a broad meadow of high grass to come on the capes of another river. We followed the shore of a lake with surface acreage to make a small plantation, and totally cultivated—a field of floating paddy leaves, pale butter-colored blooms on lithe stems three to four feet tall, each flower broader than my hand across. Then into a meadow tufted with groves and by and by a lush savannah. We nose our horses northward. The morning passes.

KEEP OUT
OF THIS SWOMP
LESSEN YOU WANT
YER HED BROKE

Tacked with a rusty horseshoe nail to a cypress at the margin of a swamp, lettered—as I climb down off Beth and discover—on the reverse of an advertisement offering a reward for a runaway named Hemp, "a medium size thutty odd year old dark brown boy with one light eye and a notched left ear, the othern bit clean off in a quarl, slight but that deceptive so watch out."

123

The trace we've followed for two days falls here into disuse and peters out. Another barrier. The pull of all this thwarting sings like a strummed wire in my head. Is something bent on balking me? I lift the limp umbilical joining our pedestrian to Loren McElroy and, ducking under it back to Beth, get an upward view of him staring straight ahead with eyes as sightless as the woodgrained eyes of a carving. Every other man of us sags inside his skin with a dull days-long exhaustion that now feels only natural, but Isaac, who has walked every step of this long way, stands asking silently, "Why ain't we getting on?"

I stretch to my full height for the sake of looking down on him, of getting him shrunk to more reasonable proportions. Nothing. Not the flick of an eye. He will not look at me. I test the binding on his wrists—for some reason I have to touch him. Learn patience, I tell myself. Learn tedium, thwarting, boredom, exhaustion, pain, to bear them this way. For whatever reasons. But what are his?

Georgia Gem—in that getup she might of borrowed off a scarecrow, taller on Rufus Mule than any one of us—sets watching me with that look, constant for her, of patient mockery. So I set the ball of my foot in the stirrup and swing heavily up. This swamp facing us stretches north and south clear out of sight. As it lies in our way, we must go through it—and for the same good reason the chicken crossed the pike.

Georgia Gem Hite

Stands to reason if someone gone to the trouble to fell a tree that size, they wouldn't just leave it lie. All of them looking at it, saying nothing, it lying directly across our path, roots thrust chest high to the horses on the pedestal of old dead branches. Clearly it was axed and felled precisely that away, across the path, and I mistrust it. They don't though. Loren steps around the buttcut, leading Isaac on his string, and the rest of them fall right in and follow. The horses have better sense. They're uneasy. Every ear of them tuned, little riffles across a flank, a shoulder.

Stepping into this place, we might have stepped into a later hour or might, as we penetrate deeper, be walking the floor of some green sunless sea. Away off up there over our heads, that dense canopy makes another landscape that, seen from a hill afar, must look like the rising, falling, wavery surface of the deep, and no sign of this second-layer seafloor landscape we walk down here. Between the low piemetta growth and that high plumage, the middle distance stretches open, parklike as the preserve of a suzerain. But in all this openness, such a sense of concealment. A yard to either side of me, I can't make out the earth for them beckoning slim-fingered piemetta hands that cover the swamp floor far as eye can see, brushing aside as we pass with the papery whisper of wind in hides hung up and dried for curing.

The faint trace entering the swamp followed the run, parted company with it, now joins it again. In what could be giant footprints sunk below run level, midget cypress knees pop orange heads out of the muck. Whole deformed colonies. The fetid smell is overpowering, strange, heavy with decay but swollen with a hot breath-sweetness like the breath-sweetness of wild hogs, which I take arises from the continual germination.

The road commences to writhe like the serpent and us with it till the foremost—Duncan, Toliver, and me—are brought up short where it noses into the run, loses itself awhile, then climbs back out on the opposite shore upstream a way. Between the severed ends, clear water runs noiselessly over bleached white sand which depth here and there turns blue.

Here, too, on the downstream side where the run looks shallower, the way is blocked by another of them purposefully felled trees, a rotting loggerhead nosing its upstream side.

Toliver, too, seems caught by something in the stillness, in the air, in the sound—wrong on the ear—of them signaling birds, so high, so distant, that don't sing but cry long same-note killdee cries that float away and echo. But Duncan clucks Maudie on into the run, commencing to whistle as he steps into the water. We set watching him, watching his back as if, just this side of knowing, we wait for something. Then all of a sudden in midstream the horse looks like she's laboring without making headway, like she is using all her strength—and she's a big mare—to move but can't, the way it'll sometimes happen in a dream. Duncan leaves off whistling to coax her on. That failing he gives her a cuss, then raises the ends of his reins to wallop her plump white fleabit rump. And us watching him whip her, knowing before we can bring ourselves to think it what's happening out there. They're sinking, boy and horse. And us not saying nothing, holding our breath like really we are in some sea and our life depends on holding it.

Then Toliver steps his mare up to the stream edge and, clearing his voice, keeps it an an ordinary pitch to say, "Duncan." Duncan twists around in his saddle, face breaking up in patches of pink, patches of white, mouth lax with some still unnamed fear. Toliver says, "Quitcher hitting her and listen now. She's in quicksand."

Duncan turns back like he ain't heard, cussing her in a reedy voice, and her struggling, snorting, tossing, going down, and him hitting her again. When first she stopped on that spot, his boots was hardly wet by the stream. In just this little time his pantsleg's soaked halfway to the knee. Maud tosses her chin and whinnies.

"Duncan," Toliver says. He might be gentling a colt, but Duncan twists around and shouts, "I ain't a letting go a her. I ain't a letting her go. Goddammit!" And beating on her, cussing her, kicking her, legs like flails.

"Duncan."

He twists, sullenly silent.

"Now listen. See can you undo the girth." Duncan stands up in his stirrups and starts to dismount. Toliver yells, "Stay there!" Duncan stops and stands in his stirrups, listening the way an animal listens, his sideface toward the sound of Toliver's voice. And us measuring with our eye how high the water's climbed. The others come up and set dumbstruck, watching, keeping out of it. Toliver says, "Now bend down, see can you reach and undo it."

He bends. "I can't. It's wet and she's all swole up." Water licking his kneecaps now.

Toliver says to Loren. "Get that rope off Isaac and hand it here." And Loren don't say nothing, do nothing, just with that little smile of his gestures Tige to get it. And him the boy's pa. You'd never know it. Tige throws the rope to Toliver and snakes off his belt and binds Isaac with it to a sapling thick as your arm.

Out there the mare already holds her nose high, whinnying, outraged. Toliver yells, "I'm throwing you this rope. Catch it now, hear me! Stick to that saddle!"

"Th'ow it."

"Ready?"

"Th'ow it!"

Toliver takes and swings it underhanded like a hoop, and it snakes out slow, uncoiling as it goes. Duncan catches it. "Now knot it around yourself and ease down on the water," Toliver says. "Paddle easy. Don't thrash. Take your time. I've got you."

But Duncan ain't doing a thing he's told. He's leaning, pretty near standing on his head, to draw the rope under her barrel and snag it in the girth. Then leans down the other side to pull it up and knot it around her. "Now," he screams, "pull, durn you! I ain't a-leaving her!"

Toliver curses. Tuttle cajoles. Tige yells, "Come outa there. Your pa'll skin you alive, mess with him." Loren ain't said a word. Emile steps down off his pony and moves up alongside Toliver.

"Pull!" Duncan yells while Toliver motions and I bring up Rufus Pachydermus. Toliver hands me up the rope and I fasten it through the eye of the saddle tree and commence to saw the bit sidewards, backing him.

"Pull!" Duncan screams.

I'm pulling. Rufus Mule, who can snake a mess of logs off any ridge, can't do better than he's doing against the quicksand. But I keep sawing, backing him, till the saddle gives under me and I have to cut the rope to keep from going. Toliver grabs the end as it whips past him. At once, without the small holding power of the rope, Maud noticeably sinks, all of her covered now but her withers, neck, head.

"Duncan!" Toliver yells, "Cut that rope off her. Tie it around yourself! Do as you're told, you hear me!"

But Duncan slides off the saddle and paddles around to his mare's head. He's holding her head up by her cheek straps, struggling to tread water without the depth for it. "Get up, gal! Durn your time, get outa here!" And lays his face on her dark muzzle, crying, cussing, "Hod damn you, Maudie, get on up! Get—" Words swallowed in water or sobs. Then his whole face opens up in terror. He's tried to move his feet.

Pa begins to chastise God. Toliver shucks his boots, lies down, and rolls himself into the run the way you'd pole a log. That way, he's able to dog paddle till he can get him some depth. He's swimming. Out there in the middle just Maud's face is still above water and now Duncan himself wildeyed. Eustace walks to the water's edge and stands with Emile, one arm lying on a diagonal behind him in its usual way—palm, soft underside of his arm outward, thumb lying across the palm. "Earl," he says, and Earl's beside him. He mutters, pointing, lining something out with his hand on the air, and Earl nods and springs up the exposed roots to inch out onto that raccoon bridge. He reaches midstream on the log as Toliver reaches Duncan and sets to prying his fingers loose from Maud's cheekstraps, trying to keep his own feet out of that buried treachery. But without foothold how can he haul Duncan out? Now Tuckahoe's inching out toward Earl.

Toliver himself is gasping, and him a strong swimmer. Gasping, prying, no sooner getting one finger loose to go to another before the first one's latched on again. Duncan has lost his wits, fighting him all the way. "Durn you! Get off me! Pull, Maud!" And the mare's rolling desperate glass eye fixed on Duncan's face, which looks like a mask floating face up on the water.

So Toliver takes and climbs up on the back of the doomed horse. He grips her sunken shoulders with his knees, reaching out for Duncan. All of Duncan under but still visible, distorted in the water which, for all that activity, seems too still, like some thicker element. Toliver takes hold of Duncan's head in both hands like a bowl he aims to drink from, then, leaning off-balance, manages to get him by the armpits and tries to raise him up over Maud's head. And Duncan limp but for them hands still fast to the cheekstraps, a surprised look on his wave-washed face.

Maud's head sinks, her flattened ears, her wild, mismatched eyes. And Duncan can't let go. He's forgotten he clutches her. Toliver on the living platform of the drowning horse—ignored, used, not even left in peace to die—Toliver strains till I can see from here the ruptured vein crawling down his forehead, down his neck.

Earl strokes toward them, lips puckered over the hunting knife between his teeth. I yell to Tige to pick up the end of the rope still lying on the bank and hand it here. Earl takes knife in hand, swallows a lungful of air, and goes under. I fix the rope again to my saddle tree, so when Earl surfaces, yells "Pull!" I'm ready. This time, with Earl and Toliver both out there prying him upward, and the rope Earl's cut free of the horse fixed now around Duncan, Rufus and me we take effect. A peculiar soughing, like water swallowing itself, and here he comes, floating free on a rising gorge of sand. Toliver eases himself off the sunken horse to float on his back and, taking Duncan's shoulders over his fork, gasps, "Now!" I saw on the bit, backing Rufus, and that way, like a clumsy, swamped, wallowing vessel, they get hauled in.

Tuck pulls Earl back onto the raccoon bridge and he sets there panting. Then they creep along it to dry land. Tuttle struggles over Duncan, pumping, till here it comes belching out of him, an impure stream. His chest swells, waits, collapses with voluptuous satisfaction. Beside him, Eustace rises from his knee and turns. We all turn and watch the water out there clear ever so quickly after so much churning, till right soon again we see the expanse of bleached white sand in the bed of the run, clean, swept, not a trace of her or of what went on.

Earl

Heard it the minute they left off calling. Them unconvincing birds. Heard the sudden silence the minute we turned with the path down that little dip to the run's edge. And when I heard that sudden silence of the birds, at that same minute I saw the original road had not dipped where we dipped toward the stream but had gone on maybe twenty yards farther and *then* turned in to a ford. And as I seen all this, seen too that second felled tree lying across our path, funneling us into this new ford. Then known I'd seen too late—there was Duncan already sinking. Whoever they are, they certainly gone out of their way to lure us to this treachery.

When it's over and he's safe, while we stand looking at that already-cleared-again streambed, gasping for breath Duncan says something to Toliver and Toliver turns on him, dresses him down angry as I've never seen him, pure trembling with rage. But just then Tige lets out a whoop and we all turn. Isaac has disappeared.

As soon as I see it—the belt Tige fixed him with to the sapling knifecut clear through—still gripping my own knife I feel them looking at me. My face swells from a sudden pressure behind it. Think I done it! Why would I haul off and do such a thing? Why put it off on me? I blame Duncan. At Pepperdines when I went out to the barn and shoved some biscuit in his mouth and held a handful of water from the trough for him to drink and here come Duncan, I thought he seen me. Damn him, never let on to me but went and blabbed to them! But I never cut him loose!

I turn to face them down and find ain't nobody looking at me. Ain't nobody *been* looking at me. They're all looking at that knifecut belt. Tige keeps having to touch it. Howcome such a strange thing to come over me?

Then we're startled by a shriek—loud but distant, echoing. We spin toward the sound and glimpse someone— dark, far off, indistinct—who stands up and runs and disappears in the gloom. Tige jabs his nag so hard it stands straight up and comes down running. We yell to stop him, but he's running right where he's been goaded into running. Then, screaming, his nag stands up again, Tige hanging on up alongside his neck. In that minute the horse stands poised, we see the shaft hanging heavily from its breast. The shaft is raised like a flagpole as the horse goes over backwards, Tige leaping wide to keep from falling under him. I duck at the concussion of all that weight and all that wind busting out of him.

Leaving our own animals, we approach gingerly, half expecting something to spring at us from the very ground itself. Loren grunts, parting the piemetta where the horse hit the spike. "A whole phalanx of the things," says Toliver. Their mean points slant up from the hard black earth where like a slanted paling fence they been planted in hopes of a cruel flowering.

Tige picks himself up and crawls to his thrashing nag. Tuttle says, "Get aholt of the legs so he can't catch somebody with them shod hoofs." Tige and I fall on the waving legs. The horse's neck twists like a dragon's, lips raised off his long teeth. Tuttle takes firm hold of the shaft with both hands and brings a steady pull to it and it eases out, bloody for half a foot. He leaps back out of reach of them teeth as the crazed horse tries to lunge. Eustace grabs its head and sinks down with it muzzled in his lap. We watch Tige run a finger along the bloody spearhead, axed to a fine point. It comes away with an unnatural thickness to the gore. He brings finger to nose, sniffs, flings the stuff off his finger with a spasm of disgust. "Shit! Hod damn em!" He's turning in a circle, fist raised, about to holler at them silent woods, but Tuttle, with his long reach, laps a hand over Tige's mouth. "You be quiet," he says. "Now give me your shirttail."

Muttering, Tige pulls out his shirt and rips it. Tuttle mops at the big wound in the cleft of the gelding's breast. Looks like the blood won't stop. Don't pulse though, just runs. That's good. The horse quiets some. I rip off what's left of my own shirttail and run soak it in the water, nearly stumbling over Duncan sitting in the path, his forehead on his knee, absolutely still.

"Build me up a fire," Tuttle throws at us over his shoulder. And when we've got a blaze, he takes and lays my knife in the blue of the flame. We set on the horse while he cauterizes the generous wound. The smell of cooked flesh and scorched hair makes me hungry and that makes me sick. I stagger off and vomit. Somebody laughs. The horse goes limp long before the end of it. "We'll see now," Tuttle says.

We're all huddled over the horse when we hear another sound and turn in time to see our animals scattering into the swamp. We start after them but Loren yells, "Hold on!" We stop. "Ain't you been led like lambs to enough slaughters?" Clearly someone ain't committed to our prosperity. But how'd they scatter them horses?

Loren straightens and shows us his fistful of pebbles, and then we see it's showered pebbles. As a man can hurl a rock only so far, we stand feeling close-surrounded in the open empty woods. Loren says if we want them horses we'll have to go after them before good dark. We can see them wandering off there among the trees in the uncanny light. He tags Tige and Tuck to go with him, and takes Toliver instead of me, though he always makes light of Toliver. Which does he want the best man for, to go or stay behind and look after things? Turning, he stumbles over Duncan in the path, and righting himself rounds on Tige and Toliver: "Are you coming with me or not?"

I stand looking after them, then go collect them pikes. We might can use them, for away out here where we can't reasonably have an enemy, we have nevertheless unreasonably got us one.

Myron Tuttle

Like to never got him out of the path, onto his feet, up to the fire. Like to never wheedled him out of them wet clothes and into the india rubber coat. Now just lies there dead but for jerks that catch him up. Never saw such dark. Pesky fire! Wood damp clear through and rotting. But the coffee's still some of the Cajun stuff. And boiled till it'd float a wedge. The yams are done.

Who can it be deviling us? Damp comes through your clothes. Mosquitoes part of the element. I'd sooner be caught in a fowler's net.

He opens his eyes and frowns at me, so I lift him and bring some coffee to them blue lips. He takes a little, and tastes a bite of a banana yam. Anything hot inside him will help. And says to me, "Of course she drownded first."

I nod.

"They say just takes a minute."

"Not that." He's a sweet-faced boy, like Toliver at that age in the coloring.

"I done all I could do. Could she a knowed it?"

"You know it."

Eyes all over my face, then closes them.

No sign of Toliver and them. Wet to the skin and out hunting horses! No use to think about it. You do what you can do. And this child—nearly drowned, belching water—

looked up at him, worshipful as usual, tried to speak his thanks and Toliver flew at him. Never saw him that way. Wild. Something wrong with him. It's this obsession, so bound and determined to stop for nothing, to get back home, driving hisself and herding us beyond endurance. The least flinch in Duncan's eye, and that look of love slid into something just this side of hate. Ay-God, I known then Toliver never done it for love of the boy but just to retrieve him so we could keep moving. I don't doubt Duncan known it too. *I could tell you this: you are better off away from her. You're a man apt to lose hisself.*

Craves her too much. She fears *she'll* lose *her*self. Howcome her not to know we've all got to lose ourself? Where'll it end?

Where'd it begin? Talking, talking, following her around the place, talking. Talked till he give out, till he couldn't talk no more. But some dam in him had give, washing up a shoal of pebble words. He had to do something with them. They ground to sand sharp-edged as glass inside him, killing him, tearing him up inside. But he lived through that. Then I seen the sand remains of all them pebbled words was ground off rounded, smooth as marbles. Drop a weight in them, they'd turn together till they'd buried it. That's all this quicksand is—sand tumbled so by water it's lost its edges. With nothing to catch and bind, it just keeps turning while the weight of a body—or a mind —is lost in depths too deep to be retrieved. And, last, I seen him fight the quicksand by talking to hisself. His lips move. He'll gesture with his hand. Feared he's unclear, he struggles, illustrates, goes back, working too hard at it. And sinking anyways. No one attending. Buried already to his armpits in his deadly predicament, says to her with his eyes: *You could save me if you would.* Could she?

136

Then of course there's her side of it.

I hear something—a sound like a hand shoving water. Toliver and them returning up the runbed? If they was to get lost out yonder, it would make clever sense to return to us that way. But there's the sink. They'd know better. So what's that sound?

Eustace lifts his head. Earl sits up, pokes Emile. Georgia reaches for a spear. I ease Duncan's head off my lap onto the ground and take up the one Earl's laid by me.

Duncan McElroy

A blow at the back of my head and I'm a barked-off squirrel getting my killing by concussion. In the sunburst's center Toliver's face curses me chapter and verse. Then know my head's on hard ground that was on something softer.

I roll a little, groan and hear it, open my eyes and know I'm daft. I'm looking through a row of trousered legs braced between the horrid thing and me. But no matter, it's on my low level, so I'm alone with it in spite of them trousered legs and their hands clutching the spears. My eye's a bubble froze in glass.

The line of legs moves toward it away from me. The apparition stops but don't retreat, then lifts its head and trumpets thunder. Then I see they's more than one. A line of them's come up out of the run, the color of certain roaches' shells, no fear in them, just a canny eye, a pulse

137

in the bloated throats lying along the ground. From the look of them, they'd feel like mud shale to the touch. Them wooden spears ain't weapons against this armored visitation.

They pause and eye us, then the head one turns—first his head, then he moves in that direction. The short little legs don't even raise his belly off the ground. Where he goes, he leaves a smear. His friends pick up and follow and I know they're headed for Tige's horse lying out there beyond the fire. So I leap up. It all goes black, pinwheels of colored light in it. The round world spins and me upon it, a large sensation. I try to hold onto it. *Nothing's like I thought* echoes, repeats, vibrates, astonishes me.

But can't hold onto it. My eye clears. A brand from the fire has come to hand. I yell, "No more!" and launch myself toward Tige's horse. But Earl catches me from behind and holds me. The world spins again in its socket of universe, us holding on for dear life. And close enough to hear the jaws work, the flesh tear. The horse ain't made a sound.

"It must a been gone," Earl says, letting go of me.

I lunge, yell, and at my own yell the scalp crawls round my skull like clouds round a spinning world, but I rush at the crocodiles with my fire. They take note, so Earl and them pick up firebrands too, and that way we fall on them. But it's our torches they respect, not us. They ain't afraid of us. And in the torchlight see the horse, its flesh all ripped, smell the stench of its opened stomach sack, with a dark miscellaneous lava falling out of it.

Strange silent scene. Rush at them with our torches, they fall back—but not no farther than just the outer rim of light. No driving them clear off. They half ring us, mean little eyes under brows that set up off their heads like stobs—you could knock them off with a stick—picking up our torchlight, throwing it back at us, gleaming like cateyes. Evil old armor-plated worms. Slither on your bellies. Tails like broadswords. I run at them, knowing this time I ain't going to stop, and they fall back, stop, fall back, stop. Now some are turning, slithering toward the run, me worrying at their heads with my brand, the swamp alive now with sound and Earl and them yelling their heads off at me to watch out! come back! come to my senses! listen! and finally them things driven before me into the run. You can hear the little whirl they make when they drop off in the water. So I turn around, panting, thinking I'm done, and see, between me and them, turning in his pondersome way to get his jaws at me, his lordship himself, twenty foot long and big around as a cow. And then I see him wait.

So yodeling, I fly at him and in the rush of air my brand that's been a coal flames up. He rears his head, opens his three-foot maw, and roars like a bull, shaking the ground till it's more than me that trembles, and I thrust my fire in at his cruel mouth, into the long cave of his throat, and first thing he tries is closing on it, but the burn sears him open again and my arm explores to the elbow as his slow head twists with the savaging pain and I'm enveloped in a powerful stink off him that might be his breath or might be his pain-freed fart and this time it's Georgia flings herself at me. I knock her off. The ugly, monstrous thing all but rears up on them little legs, flailing his head, tail apt to make a trivet with them stunted hind legs as he rears and yawns, trying to vomit fire, and then falls down. I shudder to know such pain by me inflicted. He waves his ponderous head like a baying hound, with that outrageous muzzle. Farther in I thrust, and feel the soft parts tear at the back of his throat. I don't let go, I work it deeper, wait for him to open, work it in some more, yell, "*No more killing!*" and plow it home. His enormous weight wrenches my torch. I feel the awesome weight go dead, then stand there pumping, lungs like a bellows, and looking down see who done the killing this time. The bellows forces out a laugh that could a been a cry. The joke's on me and it's so funny I can't stop laughing. I see that everything is its opposite too. Try and change it, you turn it like a pocket inside out. All you've done is make another pocket. No cheating around it for that's what's true and it's up to you to find some way to think it.

The others bring up their light. Panting over him, I look. He ain't nothing. Just a crocodile out hunting his supper. And the horse might a been dead already. Then tremors again in me, my whole person caught up in them. Tremors and jerks, like I'm about to have me a conversion. Tuttle and Georgia drag me to the fire. I set with my arms hanging off my knees, in a curious lax state of wanting, wanting. When I hear the sound, at first I'm annoyed to be distracted from this curious pleasureful wanting. Then the sound repeats and registers, and I know it's the killed lizard rising up alive. And I leap up, grabbing my torch, ready to kill as many lives as he's got at his disposal, and find him still soundly dead. It's his brothers come up out of the water, devouring him, not even looking at the horse but tearing my kill apart, the hungry cannibals. I drop my stick and walk back to the fire, leaving them to their feast, knowing that's all it is—a wrung-neck chicken, gutted deer, felled tree, head-smashed squirrel, or murdered girl—it's all the same. And riding the tail of this new knowing, an emptied feeling that leaves room in me for anything.

Toliver Pullen

If the learned gentleman's spectacled eye can penetrate this gloom, it will discover a wet-through, hungry, hot but shivering, angry, unphilosophical philosopher squatting in still deeper gloom, in total discomfort, on his raised heels, staring into the dark in the calm of utter defiance, moving his bowel. Thinking: *It was a gift!*

Dismayed him he hadn't known to have it ready and waiting before bringing her home from her pa's rich tideland place, but he'd never had call to think of such a thing before. None of the other women required it, or anyway didn't *have* it. Always too many other things needing to be built—barn, shed, corncrib, smokehouse, cold cellar, forge. *Who'd think privy?*

It wasn't nothing any of us required, he explains doggedly to the gentleman. Not Eustace's Kate, not Min Hite nor Loren's Hedy.

But saw them in the tidelands, so soon as I got her back home I left everything to Tuttle one whole day while out back of the vined garden fence I built her a right good piece of architecture, with leather-hinged door and dug pit.

I thought she'd be pleased. How was I to know they'd step over from every direction for the next several days, to squat or stand silently marveling, women with arms crossed under shawls, some righteous, some wistful, children requiring explanations, then sniggering behind their hands, pointing, nudging one another, the men chewing grass stems, eyeing it. And Sidney won't go out of the house, won't talk to me, won't meet my eye, so angry she's turned to stone. And I can't face her *or* my thoughtlessness, bringing her such chagrin. She could have killed me, I saw it in her eye. You'd have thought I'd done it on purpose. I hear it going the rounds again how one moonlit night Tige and Earl arranged for me, returning late from calling on her, to meet the apparition of a hanged man. As the lane brought me up a gentle rise between dark treelines, I saw him swaying against the sky, stilling my heart. But Beth and I ambled on and, passing, lifted one of the matches her pa'd given me at Christmas from their tooled leather case and set fire to the poor devil. He blazed and was gone—being nothing more than Tige's underwear stuffed with pine straw. I hear them teasing Tige again, asking has he got on his underwear.

Gentlemen, observe: our angry friend is laughing. "A man ought to be able to build his own wife a privy!"

"What?" whispers Tuckahoe, some way off in company with the others and the recovered horses, all of us caught together under the net of dark.

"Hushup," Loren whispers.

But our philosopher has doubled over, clutching himself as he is clutched, sweat running off him freely in the stifling air. "Dear God," he prays, "don't let me be sick," then starts at the thought *If I die out here I'll never get back home.*

"Look!" Tuck's voice.

Tige says, "I'll be!"

Groping back to them in the clearing where we're waiting on morning I see, some way off, what they've seen. Lights. As we look, they commence to flare and brighten, animating the tree shafts, making them a paling wall which then falls, like a trick of vision, into deep perspective, becoming a wall you could walk into. At this distance, the light comes from fissures in the forest wall the way fireplace light will come through chinks in a loghouse. But the log wall of forest is perpendicular. The lights are up high, appear to be on a hill. Whoever heard of a hill in a swamp?

They discuss in whispers what to do about these lights while, racked by a right smart fever, I find another tree. Nothing outside me is real—not this night, this place, these people, those eerie lights—but only the rack, the sweat, the waves, my heavy entrails reeling on a spit, and the need for tears I'm stifling in the dark, swallowing warm saliva.

So how do I come to be crawling with Tuck and Loren —Tige left behind with the horses—on my cramp-strung belly toward the leaping flares, collapsing beside them, lying still, trying to focus my eyes and see? What are they? Tree houses set on a log platform high off the ground, their corner posts trunks of living trees to which are fixed their sapling walls, roofed with palmetto. Closer to the ground than to the ceiling of the swamp, reached by one sleyed log ramp leaned at a stiff angle from the ground like a chicken run. In the leaping light, leaping shadow, in the uncertainty of my sight, the scene moves and fractures in my eye.

The platform on which the houses set, roughly a square, has been piled a foot deep with dirt. It is the floor, too, of the breezeways, dogtrots, and alleys around the houses, joining them. This dirt floor also supports the bonfire which lights up the village and the surrounding swamp. Roaring in the middle of the main plaza, it is also their cooking fire.

A whole tree village. Never saw such a curious neighborhood. In the firelight, a black man moves against the black wall of night to disclose Isaac, sitting tuck-legged on a chest, gnawing a bone clean and casting it with a lordly gesture off into the palmettos below, his brows dipped into that bold black unbroken keel that lifts its prows above his temples, that pea at the center of his upper lip catching the bonfire light. No ropes bind him, he holds food in his free hand, with the help of his new friends he has eluded us. But his worried eye sprints after each move the cook makes as he stirs the pot or dips clustered fingers into the stew and tastes, then absently adds a dash of something. Whoever they are, what do they want with Isaac?

Isaac and the cook seem alone except for the skull wedged onto a stub of limb, watching with fathomless eyes. We edge closer—Loren, Tuck, and me—the bonfire close enough now to light the pale eye of Loren's near profile.

"Stay here," he whispers, putting a hand on me. "I'm going to get him back."

With a curse, Tuck grabs at him. But Loren is gone. An instant later, live lathes snake round us from behind and pin us. I try to turn. A large hand takes the crown of my head in its easy grip and screws my face forward. A voice complains, "Ain't but two ob'm."

We're thrust and kicked toward the tree village, finally given the freedom of our hands long enough to scurry up the steep chicken run. As I look over the elevated floor, I find myself eye to eye with a socket. The skull is the dwelling of a hirsute citizen who sits in his window watching.

144

Isaac sees us. His whole expression shatters into light. Again I see his face dart out of the carrion mule and burst into joy at sight of us.

Then a swarming up the log ramp and we're surrounded by the whole black company returned from ringing the village in hopes of luring all of us like deer to their light, grumbling, blaming each other that they've caught so few. Thank God they haven't caught Loren. Then a vine net cranks up on a pulley. They reach out, swing it with its huddled freight onto the platform, let it collapse. And there he lies, sprawled on his belly, his face plowed into the dirt, eyes closed, cheek barked clean, a grated iridescent injury over the visible side of his head, as if a big flatrock's been lammed there not quite neatly, scraping, perhaps flattening his skull, though with his head half buried that way in the loose platform sand, it's hard to tell. And can't tell either if he's alive or dead.

Tuck and I get our arms girded to our sides with swamp creeper. I'm yanked backward, slammed down onto the dirt, hauled up and bound to the very tree serves grinning Jack as his trunk and limbs. Dear God, don't let it be an augur. Tuck, across the fire, is similarly bound. Stunned by the spine-shattering, I'm overwhelmed by nausea as, with so many steps in conflicted rhythms, the platform moves like a hanging bridge till the movement is continuous, a complicated sensuous rhythm to which these fellows move like riverboatmen.

A black man bends in front of me to the pot, his naked back a tracery of scars—delicate, or cruel, or puckered in relief.

"Wiley!" I cry, but deaf to my own sound.

He turns and looks at me. Is it Wiley? Here? Why can't

I be sure? The fever's fit, on me again, coats sight with a membrane. When it slides, I see the whole half-naked host of them, silent, hogging down their stew, not sitting, milling, wood bowls held up to their mouths, served by knives or by their elegant oiled fingers. Every back is similarly laced—each one the map of a private pilgrimage. I bear my feverish eye on one, then another, but can no longer be sure of the one I took for Wiley.

The air like mucus thickens, swims, clears like fog from a small space in which Isaac kneels before me, peering into my face. That blinded grin, lip caught under teeth as even as a row of kernels, sitting on his heels he bends toward me a raw breath you'd expect from some innocent flesh-eater. I reel. Close to my ear, the breath of a voiceless laugh. Fever flushes my guttery. I spin on a dizzy axis, shoot out arms that telescope into the living leaf-fingered limbs of Mister Death himself. A variable moving map turns in my eye, its traceries in black on black, a kaleidoscope falling into new and newer figures. Stop! Hold still! Do I veer off? Turn? Bear left? Bear right? Oh which road rides me home?

The Tuckahoe

I never saw such a carved-up company. These scarifications, slits and notchings, elegant scrollwork brands of an altogether different origin, ironically remind me of the African's self-inflicted beauty. Hateful mutilations, yet apparently required for membership in this fierce brotherhood.

Above the heads of my captors, our Chief of State grins mindlessly, swaying in rhythm to the rising wind as if absently keeping time to some bright air. Below, Isaac perches like a grasshopper, a second grin framed by the stiff angles of his jutting knees, upon a mummy-shaped chest—no, it's a coffin.

A fit of nerves sets my tongue rattling. "I'm told," I say, "on authority—by a dean named Phillips, as I recall—that each plantation quarter billets one man who cannot be slaved. Now this dean told me that this solitary man who lacks the talent and hence simply cannot, even for his life, be slaved, is called *a bad niggah,* for, rendered strange by his peculiar lack, he is always feared. As of course you will agree this lack of the talent for slavery renders any man fearsome, whatever his complexion."

An insolent rogue passing in front of me stoppers me with a hot pone he happens to have in his hand. I sputter, gag, spit, and swallowing some of it burn myself clear to the stomach, while they laugh uproariously. Their newest member joins the merriment, quaking silently atop the coffin. The jollity echoes far enough to reach even Toliver, off in his distances. He lifts his head. It rolls. Between drooping lids, the whites of his eyes are bronze. His bright wet face reflects the rosy light.

I swallow the last of the dumpling and continue: "I assume from the decorations lavished upon your persons that you all might represent a convention of these—"

"Bad niggahs!" one pronounces, throwing back his head to holler a laugh. "Watch what you say, boss!"— a thick-muscled fellow with a bush of hair I envy, holding a rib bone in his hand, using it emphatically as he talks. "Dey feahed of us awright. You hit it. Feahed a disere swomp and us in it! Cause dat pure-dee too much dahkness all at once to suit de likes a dem."

"It's a big swamp," I say.

"Hit a grebbig swomp!" Bush, wagging his head, agrees.

"You ain de patrol, is you," states a small-eyed, narrow-faced, light-skinned man.

"We are not," I say.

"We thought you's de patrol," Bush says.

"No."

"Thas bad," he sighs.

"Bad according to what?"

"Bad according to he say so," says Snake-eyes.

"What do you want with us?"

"We ain got no use for you," says Bush. "We thought you's de patrol."

"Well, now you're satisfied we're not, you might untie us and let us go."

Snake-eyes, smiling, touches the protuberant pad of his forefinger to the tip of his knifeblade, then delicately applies the razoredge to my throat just under my chin and tilts my face. He shakes his head. "Das aginst de rule," he says.

Never saw a rule I liked, now here's another one. He tilts my face at a steeper angle. I feel the shallow slice, the sudden thickening of the sweat running down my neck. And chuckling he turns wordlessly to point out to me His Grace, grinning absently down upon my predicament as he rocks to the accelerating rhythm of his reel.

Toliver Pullen

"It's not good dark yet, don't go in!"

Chasing lightning bugs in the duskdark churchyard, catching them in lamps of loosefinger fists where they flare and die and flare and die. A goalie guards the graveyard gate we've designated Home.

Voices in the twilight off the near ridge call the bairns to come in, but no such womanly voice for me. I lie in terror behind the trunk of a fallen tree, for it's dark and the wind is rising and It sees everything. The others one by one fly past, crying at the gate *Homefree!* But fixed on me It stalks the dark. I see his fleshless face. Voices call the children to come home, but no such motherly voice for me, and every night dashed at being left behind, the last, alone while dark falls, as one by one they grumble and obey.

Homefree! Homefree! flies past me in the dark. I take Its place and guard the goal. "Let no one pass!" *Or I'll be alone, sick and abandoned, despised.* But here on my limb I've such a vantage of this hidden land of outcasts.

Whisper of rushes, of danger, of the night. A dragon roars.

"It's the gators playing."

"Ain no gators."

"It's blowing up a storm."

"Hushup, Tucker."

"Listen at dem gators! Tawkin back to thunder!"

But I cannot move, bound to this tree while they fly to and fro. Children, your goal is always home! *And to and fro.*

Dark which hovered now descends. The lamps of the valley all go out. Even the fireflies douse their wicks. Now only the stars. And only cicadas call my name.

"What's dat one's moniker?"

"Toliver?"

No motherly voice for me.

"Toliver Pullen."

It's only Tuttle.

"You have some interest in him?"

"Don't mix yourself up, Tucker. I the one ast the questions here."

The game has changed. We play at riddles, bob for secrets. The wind whips a shower of sparks into my hair.

"Well, you ain de patrol, but you is white. You take, they's a grebbig ol live oak tree rat on the marge out chonder. Some little while back, patrol it flush thisere whole swomp and hung ever mother-humpin son of a bitch at one an the same time on one and the same limb a thetere selfsame live oak tree. Like blackbirds, it was said at the time, as I recall. But what I recollect bes bout dat whole episode—one a them niggahs wan't a slave. He a slave owner. No Mistah White had papers on him. He had em on hisself, he was his own slave, I know it for a fack. He was a wheelwright rented out his time from the mastah till he saved enough to buy hisself. Then one by one he bought him some other slaves—his wife, his mam, his brother, an his baby boy. That was a rich free niggah they pick up jus by accident. Now does you git the point a thetere yarn?"

"Wait, give me time, let me think!"

"What he jabberin about?"

"Toliver?"

"The moral a that story is—that man wan't hung for a runaway. His crime wan't nothing else but bein black. Now sho'ly you see the point a dat."

"Surely you see the point of that!"

"What he sayin?"

"What were you saying, Toliver?"

"What learnin I has come by, I picked up from the Book a Mistah White. And I count thisere what I moan tell you one good lesson I learnt from thetere book a revelations. See, the moral a that story is—if that man kin git his killin jes for bein black, then you all kin git yoan jes for bein white. Ain dat rat."

"Wrong!"

"What he sayin?"

"Gentlemen, I give *you* a story. A rattler swallowed a fox, and a woodsman, outraged at such wanton murder, hacked the rattler in two, The hungry fox, released from his warm prison, fed on the rattler, but having a rising on his gum, when he tasted the rattler's poison, died."

"What de moral a dat?"

"Pshaw, means Whitey got medicine ginst his own poison but black man if he touch it die. Don't insult us widdit, Tucker."

"Playin on niggah feah of haints. Means kill him and his white cawpse will deal out retribution. We ain feahed a no white cawpse, Tucker. Raise yo eye and see the evidence up yonder where we pegged im on dat tree. He smilin at cho ignernce. He was white once, Tucker. Cut to the bone, we all the same tint."

"Hushup. You tawk too much. Means white man immune to evil, but black man ain't. Like Injuns ain immune to de *malare.*"

"Where de justice in dat?"

"Means killers git kilt."

"Mean White a snake and Black a wiley fox. If fox change his nature and come to be snake, he the same as kill hisself."

"A diffrunt country heard from! We call thisun Fox, Tucker."

"Means when the tables turn, don't give back what you got."

"Which ob'm rat, Tucker?"

"Nobody's right. Everybody's right. When I'd peeled that skin I'd et the onion."

"You'll lose this game for us!"

"You know what we gone do with you, Tucker?"

"My turn! Give me a chance! What game is this? Why don't you listen? I'm never understood! Put out that fire! Hold still! This rocking makes me sick!"

"We gone make bait outa you. We gone bash in yo haids and spill out a little brain, then we gone rip open yo stomachs and stake yo carcass out to lure us some razorbacks."

"All but dat little small one yondah."

"What do you want with Isaac?"

My turn! Mine!

"He a likable little feller. He don't tawk lak some we might could mention."

"I don't think it'll serve any purpose to do away with us."

"Das white-man thinking. We ain burdened widdit."

"I'll tell you a story, Tucker."

152

"Thas rat, Fox. Yo turn."

I'd know you anywhere! I read those lines on your back!

"Listen to thisun, Tucker."

"I'm not a slave. And every man here would say the same if he had the metaphysics."

"Ain I tole you? Listen at im! He a match fo you, Tucker."

"We all knows who we belongs to. If we ain slaves, howcome we in thisere pestilent place?"

"You cain tell nobody nothing they don't awready know, Tucker. And if they awready know it, what the use tawkin? When kingdom come, the world be silent."

"That's not a rule! The rules keep changing! That's cannon in the distance!"

"Po Fox he tetched in the gallery."

"No, he's not, you're sane, Fox. You're in this swamp because you think you're free, they're here because they think they're slaves. They act in spite of their belief, you don't. Oh yes, sane, for sanity's only this—the eye of reason and the eye of sense—I mean feeling—in focus and not walleyed, one scanning one horizon, the other searching out another, each autonomous, no communication between them, like two vessels under sail to any wind and quite at sea. One man in ten thousand enjoys such true vision. Can it be? Here? In such a wilderness? In such a skin? Or are you a figment?"

"Whoo-ee, cain he tawk! Keep it up, Tucker. When you gives out, when we gets bored—"

"Will you survive this shipwreck or die in this bog of your own weight, like the dinosaur? Will your seed give its stamp to generation, or will it be that other, of a different stamp, that blows on any wind to its survival, can live

like the air plant on nothing, or on indigestible leavings—
I mean shit—can adapt to anything but death and therefore
is immortal?"

"Whoo-ee! Slit im some mo! See kin he do it agin!"

"One a these days, Tucker, when our lot's improved,
you'll see."

"Beware your Improver—he's a man will sacrifice any
lamb to an idea."

"Tucker, I'm innerstid in the question is change possible. Follow?"

"I'm coming! Wait!"

"I'll bargain wid you, Tucker. To Mister White all
niggers look alike. Now take this Tulliver. He once swap
his mare for me, and that the bes value I ever had laid
on me too. So I recognize him. If he can recognize me, I'll
do you a good turn. If not, the turn be bad as it can be.
Tulliver, lookie here, you know me?"

May I?

"You and me in a different wood tonight. Can you call
me by name?"

Still as stone, cold as death. I'm asleep, Wiley. Run
while you can!

"Tucker, I haves this awful innerest in change, a scien-
tific innerest in this question is change possible. Know me,
Snowman! Satisfy me one man can change! What's my
name?"

"Fox, you're a slave after all. Toliver's slave."

"Watch yo mouth, Tucker."

"If you're not, why must he prove to you what you
might prove to yourself? *I* know change is possible because
I once changed myself and left off hate."

"You full a tricks."

"I'm tired!" I want to go home. It's starting to rain. Too

much lies hidden in these games. And behind your eyes. "Oh why won't you open your heart to me?"

"Whad he say?"

"I'm not talking to you. There's some confusion."

"Fox, you're our hope or likely our despair, because of the hate in you. Oh yes, hate. I've a peculiar sense that can smell hate no matter how soft the fart. Bush or Rattler here might kill us or let us go for sport. But you're not arbitrary."

"Hushup, Tucker. I had enough a you. Tulliver! Do you know me? It's your life!"

Only the name I gave you. Not enough. "Who are you?"

"There. You lose."

And must go back, go back, go all the way back. Run home, Toliver, or you're out. And never will be homefree.

The Tuckahoe

The wind stirs the huge old forest trees and shakes our platform, whips up the fire till sparks threaten the thatch roofs of the lean-tos. Cookie tips a rainbarrel, dousing us in dark. The tempest takes a lash to the forest top. Through rags and tatters we glimpse the sky where lightning blooms like branched candelabra, and I quake like the platform we ride. "I'm sick!" cries Toliver. "Hold still!" A mess of moss flies at him, beards him, muffles his cries. Like a ship in a heavy sea, the platform rolls and snaps at some indeterminable point with the crack of a mainmast going, then shudders to a list. "Catch dat ramp!" There go our captors, scrambling down.

"Untie us!" I yell. But they rush past. Now helpless—Loren, Toliver, and me. Big limbs fly by like twigs or leaves. And with the canopy torn, floods drive down on us. We lie in throbbing dark and bright. The crippled platform groans and thrashes, a wounded beast. Bound to collapse. The tree I'm tied to moves counter to the platform, rubbing my chest, arms, shoulders raw, and rain like quills—I bow my head to protect my face. Something lands in my lap. In the lightning, I stare into the empty grin. Then the storm flings him off into chaos where he belongs. Toliver cries out. In the furious dark, hands grope over me.

"Loren!"

"Hushup, Tucker. Be still." Fox! Wielding his knife! I scream, but the wind tears the sound away. "There," he says. "You're loose. Hurry! Pick up that'n. I'll take Tulliver."

I try to stand, but the ropes have cut my circulation, I crawl and, after a stormy voyage, reach Loren where he lies, but someone's there before me. In the lightning, Isaac —I had forgotten Isaac—bending over Loren, nudging him, frowning.

I roll Loren toward the listing ramp then scramble down. Fox lifts Toliver and Loren into the vine cradle and lowers them to me. Saddling Isaac on his shoulders, he shinnies down. Somewhere I find strength to hoist Loren. Fox lifts Toliver. With Isaac tailing after us, we stagger through mud a howling quarter mile to where Tige, hunched and muttering, holds for dear life onto the frightened animals. "Hod damn, you never said you'd be all night." Then he sees Loren.

Fox throws Toliver across a mule, I lay Loren over his own horse. "You and him ride double with these two."

Tige and I mount obediently. Fox settles Isaac on Emile's calm pony and hands me the reins. I look down at him—wiry, about my height, very black, eyes like an Egyptian, I'd guess Senegalese—standing there in the lessening rain as dawn shows its dirty face. I put out my hand. He eyes it a moment, looks up and laughs, then turns and shortly disappears into the dull light and the broken palmettos.

Part Five

Georgia Gem Hite

Here they come, soaked, scarce alive, drowned by the storm but fearing the devils are on their tails and no time to lose. In the dim daybreak we mount up and, wild-eyed tatterdemalions, bewildered of direction, haunted by fear of hidden dangers from unlikely foes, we flee the swamp, three riding makeshift—Toliver bound rollicking astride his mare, clutched by Tuttle, mounted up behind; Duncan, after standing ready to fight Tige for the still carcass of Loren with his poor barked face, up on the Eagle's round rump, the limp package of his pa across the saddle in front of him; Tige, the loser, on Tuttle's mule, and Isaac, light enough, riding Emile's shirttails.

Giddied by flight, we might blindly have taken the same path out we taken in, but free of that distempered place, we find ourselves on a king's highway atop a levee which furnishes this landscape its only rise. Off in the distance slaves harvest a white sea of the vegetable wool, dragging long cloth sacks in the sand behind them, chanting to their work. If they was to spy us across the distance we'd likely appear as the topmasts of a vessel on the horizon of a sunny ice-locked sea. Sound of their singing comes to us fitful on the wind, a mournful tune and pretty. All the cultivated land lies below the level of this high road we have to travel single file.

Never seen earth so black and evil looking. Tuttle, he says it's rich as the delta of the Nile, but Tuck he says there's no comparison, this would put that to shame. "There the soil's nothing, but it's renewed each year with silt brought down by the river. This soil's so deep and rich a plow'd require a team to lug it."

I'd hate to set bare foot in the manurish stuff. Our land at home ain't of the richest, but it's a bonny sandy loam, easy to plow and plant and cultivate, early to lay by.

We make for a little tufted wood at the far end of the levee, like an island in the boundless cotton. No telling what devilment this ride's done to Loren and Toliver.

In the shade of the trees, cooled by a breeze, we come on a family plot, shamefully neglected, surrounded by a black iron fence festooned with black iron grapes, the sagging gate entwined with black iron roses from the selfsame black grapevine. The markers lean ever which way in a drunken fellowship. The principal grave, instead of the usual mound raised like a cover by a sleeping form, is sunk several foot below earth level so that the reeling marker seems to mark a grave long since rifled of its holdings.

We slide off the horses. They won't forsake the shade and the grass, so we let them go. Leaving Toliver and Loren with Duncan and Tuttle, the rest of us stagger to the wood's edge to fall down and lie letting the sun dry our clothes and bake some sizing into us. In no time Emile and Pa are snoring in sacred harp.

After a little here come two young black gals at an easy trot with a wood yoke on their shoulders, an oak water bucket swinging from the shaft between them. Parched and thirsty, we draw bead on that water bucket—meant, no doubt, for the field hands yonder—as here they trot bare-footed. Hardly any ways off from our island, one of them looks up and sees us. She stops so quick the yoke comes off her sister's shoulder and their bucket sets down, splashing out half the water.

Wildeyed, they grab it up and turn to run, but Tige and Earl fly at them and grab at the bucket, spilling what's left. The water carriers drop it and show us the pink of their soles.

Tige and Earl stand humpbacked looking at the empty bucket. Then a rumble and a high-sided wagon comes to a halt at the end of a distant row. The field hands leave off singing and pick to it and empty their cotton sacks. The wagon pulls away. Then the slaves shuffle toward us across that flat expanse where the cotton fades and reappears on waves of heat. As we stare, the field divides in two and a top thin layer of it, slaves and all, reappears in the air above what was the horizon. Above *them*, setting on a cloudland of cotton, a big house trembles and blurs. Tige yelps, pointing, falling back. But Tuck says "Mirage" so calm we guess it's nothing to be scared of. I'm minded of Ezekiel as the house fades from white to blue and vanishes. The two layers of slaves draw closer till the bottom layer walks out of the vision, becoming its original number, which is aplenty. They're heading for our little woods, no doubt to claim their morning drink and rest in the shade. They's more of them than of us, though a number are merely women, but what with their water bucket lying empty and what with yesterday's encounter with others of their breed, we nudge Pa and Emile awake and crawl back into the wood where myself and Earl stop and lie in a hummock of weeds, parting them to watch. They all but stumble on the bucket before they see it. For the longest, they're too undone to have anything to say. They just stand eyeing it. We can commiserate. Then they all take the notion to talk at once and set up a gabble.

Now here's another actor in this entertainment—a stout man in a broad-brimmed hat, boots laced up his calves, riding a tall sun-rusted black horse along the row the water carriers traveled, a gun in a holder on his belt.

The slaves squabble with outrage, pointing to their bucket. The man passes a hand over his mouth and stubbled jawls and wades into a litany of swearing the slaves quiet down to admire. Not till he's got through the text does he ask howcome the bucket to be spilled.

One of the women—fine, muscular, shiny, tall as me, every feature of her face outsized, like a child's picture of a person—points back toward the swamp. "Them renegades."

The overseer goes into his profane song before he answers. "You're lying, Het. What they want with a bucket of water? Water enough in there to float an army."

The woman says, "They was after the gals, not the water."

Then along the levee comes a black buggy pulled by a true black horse and driven by a white-haired black man. Behind him, a veiled old lady so shrunk by age she's all but vaporized, all dressed up in funeral black. The driver pulls up beside the congregation.

"What's this? Howcome you to stop? Are we there? Who is it? Speak up!" says the old dame, rapping the driver's shoulder with her black umbrella.

"Mornin, Mizriz Lumpkin," says the rider.

"Is that my overseer?"

"Yessum," he confesses.

164

"Setting in the shade, Mister Roark? Tippling, I expect!"

His steam gone out of him, he flushes to match his nose, looking guilty as charged though we ain't seen him tipple and surely he sits in the blazing sun.

"Are you alone? Who's with you?"

The slaves press around her buggy and stare down at her as if pleased for the chance to inspect her at close quarters.

"Some of the hands, mam," says Roark.

"Why ain't they picking my cotton? Answer me!"

Thrown into confusion by her rough tones, Roark stammers, "Wellum, wellum," casting around for an answer, lighting on, "It was them renegades in the swamp—trying to make off with the water gals."

"Liars!" she shrieks. "Every shoat that strays, ever kidnapped calf, ever pie stole off the windowsill, you lay it to them runaways. Never saw such a pack a liars! You'll steal me into the poorhouse! Then who'll care for you?" The ferule of her parasol jabs the driver between the shoulder wings. "Move!" He clucks up the horse. "Cain't turn my back a minute!" They round the tip of our isthmus and put in at the gate. "They'll do me out a house and home! Parrots in the corn! What's this world acoming to?"

"Rack and ruin," chimes her coachman alighting sprightly as the cricket he favors with his spindle limbs and frocktail coat. He hoists a wheelchair out of the buggy, flips the step in place, and helps the old lady make her way to the ground. She stands while he shoves the chair up against her knees behind her, then sits hard. He bustles her over hummocks, rocking and tilting her like a plaster doll till he halts the chair in front of the sunken grave. Though this little wood is full of us and our horses, it ain't yet full to saturation. The field hands seep through the trees till the whole host is gathered except for Roark, who has stepped off his horse at the margin of the shade to mop his face and fan hisself with his hat.

The field hands and the buggy driver gaze at us. The old woman stares at us with her blackberry eyes.

"Is the plot in order, Rafe?"

We set still, wondering have we lost our substance.

"Yessum." He glances over the weedgrown place. "Ever thing the way you likes it."

"Grass cut? Hedge trimmed? Fresh flowers in the pots?"

"Some ob'm beginning to show the least little sign a wilt."

"Have them replaced at once."

"I'll do dat," says Rafe.

Toliver lying in the grass opens his eyes and cries, "Why don't you let me rest?"

The slaves gaze at Toliver. The old lady's hand clutches the cloth violets on her breast. She gasps and cries out, "Rush!"

I expect them to fall on us, but nobody stirs except to turn from staring at Toliver to stare at her. Looking skyward with her bright eyes, she puts a finger behind her ear and tips it forward. "Hear that?" she whispers. "As I live and breathe!" Then, speaking up trembly, "Rush Lumpkin, I'd know that voice anywhere! What's ailing your rest? Tell me and bless if I don't remedy it."

"Why won't you open your heart to me?" cries Toliver.

The black folks look at him, watch Tuttle struggle to hold him down, turn back to the widow to see what she'll say to that.

166

She gasps, her hand flutters to her breast. "How can you ast me a thing like that?"

Duncan grunts urgently. We turn and see Loren move, open an eye, and lie staring up at the trees. His mouth works. Looklike we're due for a debate.

Toliver cries, "I've given you many a gift to win you away from yourself!"

"He's talking riddles," she gasps. "What can it mean?"

"Never a proper wife to me!"

The widow bristles. "Rush Lumpkin, you're one to talk with your mollies and maggies!" Then changes her tune. "Oh I know I ain't been out here often as I'd like, but you wouldn't th'ow it up to me if you knew what I have to contend with—the house and land and cotton and timber and livestock and orn'ry slaves and"—she brightens— "them blessit runaways in the swamp! Just this morning swooped down on my water gals!"

Toliver, bewildered, frowns, casts around, stares at Tuttle, blinks.

The widow waits, then satisfied she's put a cap on the conversation, bustles around in her chair. "Take me home," pulling on her gloves. As the old man hauls her back to her buggy, she mutters a pleased complaint: "He ain't changed one bit."

A dozen hands reach out and raise her gently from the chair and settle her in the buggy. Another dozen press her robe about her knees and settle her pillows in place while she runs on: "I've got the responsibility of ever thing. Childurn, helpless childurn, the whole pack. Where would you be without me, answer that!"

"No place. Nosir," old Rafe mutters, driving off. We glimpse the buggy here and there between the trees till it stops in front of Mister Roark. "Have more water sent out to them good-for-nothings and herd them back to the field sometime before sunset, please." With a groan, the overseer gets up and, cursing his horse, mounts and, cursing the heat, follows the buggy at a little distance. Now here we set in a ring of silent faces.

Earl

Looklike them runaways get a heap more credit than they're due. Looklike we're in that land where the least shall be first—them strapping slaves at the base, that flabby overseer on top of them, and resting on him a ridiculous helpless widow, and finally over her a ghost.

Eustace asks sternly, "What's been at that grave?"

A nervy light-skinned oldster says, "Well, I tell you what we think might could a happened."

Tige snorts, "Them runaways stolen the remains."

The spokesman waits while we have our laugh. "Marse Rush he always a man like to get away from home and find hisself a livelier company. Well, so not long after he pass away, Mizriz she put up her own headstone rat by hisn. Dare. Wan't long after that his grave commence to sink. He must just been disturb by the prospeck of such a spell of the Mizriz' company. So the grave it commence to sink and he slip away quickes he can. Roke, he had some of us dig to see what went with him and we dig and dig till we struck water. They a little underground river run rat

168

under the grave, and Marse—we ain't seen naire sign a him—he must just set down on that stream and sail away. Somewheres that river meet the light a day. That where you'll find him."

Tuck says, "That river surfaces yonder in the swamp. I've seen old marse just this past evening. I had the pleasure of supping in his company, rode out the storm with his head lolling on my knee."

"Well I declare. How he holding up? He looking well these days?"

"He's just one better than skin and bone. There's not as much to him as they used to be. But he's kept his spirit, always has a grin."

"Das him," they chorus. And the old man nods. "He was always a man to have his little joke. You nail him down rat pat in dat."

Loren McElroy

My only weapon this smooth stone in my hand, a smooth wet stone—a whetstone in my hand—drawn by light, prowled the dark like a painter till the side of my head shaped to a flat rock and my dark lost in a dry flood of light, lids parched and cracked, obliterated. Curse what cock crowed in this day. The roebuck whistles. Bleat like the fawn and bring the doe.

She was my first deer. After the kill, took and split the doe to gut her and found a fawn in the nest of her womb and knew split the fawn I'd find its twin, open the twin, disclose another, split that one and on and on, another and another. No end to this mystery. Whet by the blood of my first deer: here, inside her, something I must know. Knife flaying, hacking muscle, tendon, bone, dividing every part, then parting again, till diminishing diminishing, each part again a whole, so my ax in a frenzy pulped the multitude she's spawned till, a jelly of herself, no recognizing her but for the dainty cloven hoof—not that, she could a been the Devil. Never give up her secret. Then my brother smashed the side of my head with the stock of my gun and knocked me winding. Drove me, booting me, to get a shovel and dig her a grave and bury her. And I dug and while I dug swore to repay him and shoveling in the multitude she had thwarting me become, puked to bury some of myself in her. I taste it yet.

"Pa."

Died last spring aplowing. The least a the hateful bairns spawned year by year clings to her, still asks for him, won't believe he can't come back no more.

"Pa."

But I know better. He's dead and in his grave. And now my brother too, shot in the woods, leaves me alone.

"Pa."

How could it know the difference when I am, beardless, the hunter who provides? But smile at her, get a vacant look. She loved my brother best, the sweetness in him. I am what I am.

"Pa."

Retch and strangle and open my eyes to clean mossy ground.

"Pa! Are you all right, Pa?"

Turning, stare at my youngster self. Bewildered, see a

wood, but not that wood; faces, but different faces; a day, but never again that day. *Lost* ricochets through chambers of a broken skull. Lost place. Lost face. Lost time.

"We ain't lost much, Pa."

I look at my younger face. *I don't care for you.* A child is a pity and a disgust. My breath like a roebuck's whistle. "Give me my gun." The effort splits my headbone. Retch again. I taste it yet.

Duncan McElroy

Not hardly breathing, waiting for Tige's shadow to part from the moon-cast shadow of a sweet gum clear the other side of the pasture, then vault the split-wood fence, land running and drop again across the branch from the horses, a dozen and more, bunched together, cropping grass. The belled cows drift past toward the barn. It's nearly dawn when their bags commence to ache. But we got time. Enough, I allow. They're dawdling on their way, still grazing.

They get clear past and there, the other side of the branch, the herd. I'm up and moving, low to the ground, almost running on all fours. A big mare with a colt lifts her head toward me, quivers her nostrils, swivels her ears, trying to pick up something. I drop. But uneasy she swings off at a lanky jog and the others follow. I'm breathing out loud and can't help it. My heart's doing something fancy. There's Tige again, a dark thing streaking the moonlit grass. Downwind, he's nearly on them before they know it. Here they come thundering, churning the branch, rumbling the ground, but I wait and take my pick. It's got to be big. Tige asked Pa what me and him would do for horses, and Pa said, "You asting me to go get some for you?" So Tige give a funny unsure laugh and turned to me. That's howcome us to be here, now, in this dark, me waiting till they're all but on top of me and I'm splashed good and wet before I take my pick and fling myself at a rawbone customer. Swing on his neck, hang on for dear life, shirt so belled by the wind I feel naked. My weight on his neck slows him. Tries to toss his head, but I'm too heavy. So he ducks so deep with his neck straight down, and gives a buck and I almost go down the slide of his neck, off at his muzzle. But there's his mistake, for he had almost to stop to perform this acrobatic. That's my chance to bound off my toe and spring. By the time I'm up and over, he's stretched out at a run. Unsure of my directions, just clamping my legs and holding onto a hank of mane and doubting I'll stay with him when dead ahead, the barnlot fence, but I see we ain't going to let that stop us. Oh Lord I'm in the air, surely we've parted company, then land and what a shock his sudden presence! He humps a sunfish and tears across the lot, into the barn, down the hall till we're brought up so sudden I'm throwed onto his neck. The stall gate's closed. That's luck. He'd a rubbed me off in there. It ain't but minutes till dawn, so—eyes watering from the shock in my fork—I circle his neck, lock fingers, and slide on down. He throws up his head and steps back, rolling a wild eye, neighing. That sets off a dog somewheres. I got to hurry. Too dark to tell his color, but not too dark to see he's wearing his ears flat, a dangerous fashion. He ain't above taking a bite of me.

172

With one hand I undo my belt and snake off it the hemp hackamore I strung together. I manage somehow to get it on him, him fighting me all the way. Then bounce off a stall gate onto his back, wheel on a dime, and dig in my heels. We clear the barn, picking up speed. I set forward and pluck him over the barnlot fence. We land running and cross the pasture like it might a been a vestibule, sail over the snake-rail fence, tear down an aisle between tall rows of corn till the field plays out and we bust into the open, his head flat out on the wind, and I see he's got him a handsome dished face with outstanding eyes and nostrils at a flare. Daylight soaking up the dark when I find the wagon road and let him have his head. I know I'll make it now, and know I've got me some horse. Let's see can I keep him.

Myron Tuttle

Looklike ever conceivable obstacle's been thrust in their way, like some power's bent on keeping them from their destination. Destination. When I think what waits on them in Culloden, I don't wonder that power lies somehow inside their selves. But malaria don't. Runaways don't. Quicksand, hurricane, river-to-cross don't. Yet all the same here we lie, so destitute we've begged help off of slaves.

Eustace has walked yonder to the edge of the bluff and stands looking down the delta we've left behind, one arm lying on a diagonal behind his back in that way he has—palm of hand, soft underside of arm outward, thumb across palm like arm across back. Then turns and walks over to me where I squat beneath the sickroom window and squats with me. Eustace loves him like a son. I give him that. Veined eyelids lowered, big hands hanging off his flat-boned wrists, he watches some ants in a caravan cross the sand yard, their Sahara. It's worst on Eustace. She was his love and his loss. And the killing will be his, as the victim's next-of-kin. It falls to his hand, not for revenge—though if his heart craves that, it'll serve—but because of what's called justice. Well, it's just that you can't ask another man to do for you what you might be loath to do yourself. Guilt ain't transferable or divisible. If your hand kills, though you're a hooded executioner, it's your soul marked and don't forget it. Can't nobody do it for him. It's his right, if any right there be. If he forswears it, Isaac will live. So it's worst on Eustace.

"We can't stop here," he says.

"Move him, it'll be his life."

But both of us know it might be that for Toliver whether he moves or not.

"We got to leave him," he says. My eyes leap before I can stop them. His lids slide up. He looks at me with them greys of his. You think he's dying, but you go. Where's Eustace? You're not Eustace. Imposter! You look out of his eyes, you've taken his hide. You've done away with him. Eustace is dead.

I say, "Reckon I'll be staying too."

After a minute, he asks, "You can find your way alone?"

I can't let it pass. "Toliver can," I tell him. "You can't fault Toliver on directions."

Closes his lips and nods.

When they're ready I walk with them to the brow of the hill where the path noses down. He puts out his hand. They're looking so I shake it. And watch them go till they're lost in trees. Then set on a rock and whittle till they bob back in sight far out in the valley. I watch them awhile, but they'll be visible some time yet from this rock. So I shove my knees straight and hump it back to the house, not thinking no more of them, but of Toliver lying so still who been in such a hurry.

Duncan McElroy

Pa waiting, cussing soon as he sees me ride up. But never tells me, tells Tige, there already with a little brown hackney. "I reckon he showed some sense. They'll hang a horse thief outright, reserving more delicate treatment for anybody steals a brute. They'll geld him and let him go." I spin to look at the big horse's crupper. His tail's just then swishing a fly. They laugh at the look on my face. In the dark that away, how could I know? Tige prescribes the way to geld him, if I want to keep him from bleeding to death, is to bite them off. They discuss the one-sided contest they say it's bound to be and both bet on the horse.

Short-coupled, well-legged with upstanding pasterns, wide-loined, long-necked, deep-chested, a swath blazing

175

the dished bright sorrel face, nostrils always at a flare, and seventeen hands if he's an inch—I've got me a Mister Fancy.

The hackamore has to do me for bridle, and to keep his flung head out of my face, I fashion a rope martingale I can fasten to a leather band I swapped off Tuckahoe for my folding knife and made into a girth, string stirrups, and crupper, Indian style. All the saddle I've got. And just as well. Without a bit, I've precious little say about what comes next.

So nothing all day but the buck and wing, me his unwilling partner. Not once after that with the others—though I see Eustace and them are back now from taking Toliver to be doctored in the night. Back, but way behind Pa and Tige. So all day prancing wide off to the side, dancing way out front, rearing, pawing, flinging his head so high he like to knocked me winding even with the martingale, we make a regular circus, Tige yelling, urging me on, betting on him to sunfish, buck me, throw me, paw me, run away with me back home so I can collect my comeuppance, which sets me on the suicide course of sticking like a louse. Do what he will, I'm bound he'll shake the brain in my head before he'll be shed of me.

And finally let him have his head and run him for miles over broken country—up hill, down dell, over branches and now and then a fence, rubbing his tail off hunkering at a skid down the face of a bluff, then through a stream and up a hillside over loose gravel where I don't know how he can keep his footing, till late in the day, the last of the steam run out of him, he stops, to stand, sides flaring and falling, snoring with exhaustion. Prod him with a heel, he'll take a few steps. Kick him, he'll budge for a foot or two. I've pure run him till he's pleading for mercy. Then swing a leg over his head and slide off and show him my scorn by dropping the reins, then lie throbbing on my belly in the weeds, wondering am I lost. By then we both know he's my horse. I call him Plunder.

When I make my way back to them, the others have caught up with Pa and Tige. They're setting around eating burnt bird. Eustace's eyes on me stick and seem to focus for a change. He swallows and wipes his mouth on the back of his arm and asks, "Son, where'd you get that animal?"

I heat up and flush. I look at Pa. But Pa's busy eating and hasn't an eye for me. Tige's watching though. He ain't satisfied unless there's some commotion.

Eustace says, "I ast you a question, son."

I count my heartbeat in my ears. Open my mouth but ain't able to bring out a word. Georgia's watching. Earl's watching. Emile watches a minute, then lights his pipe. Eustace turns to Pa. "Loren, where'd your boy get that stallion?"

Pa's jaws work on the meat, but his eye ain't nearly so casual watching Eustace. He don't answer.

Eustace looks at Tige. "You say a relative hereabouts loaned you the hackney?"

Tige talks with his mouth full. "My sister's husband's uncle. He let me have the loan of it."

Eustace is setting on a rock, elbow on his knee. One of his fingers digs at the runnel beneath his nose, a habit he's got. He looks stern and just, the way he's always looked. I don't doubt he knows Tige's lying, but he don't so much show concern for Tige or for the stolen horses. He is, I see, troubled over me. Suddenly I could bawl, but I glimpse Pa and steel myself.

Eustace says, "Tell the truth, son."

This time I can't answer for the grab in my throat and the sting in my nostril.

He says, quiet, "We're all ready to be home. But we'll lay up here long enough for you to get it back to whoever it belongs to." I feel some loss I can't name. I'm torn ever which way. It'd be a relief to do what he says but I'm afraid of doing it, of what they'd do to me if they caught me. And I don't want to give up the sorrel now I've mastered him. I'm torn, too, over Pa in some way too rich to sort. And aware of missing something, something missing.

Pa flings a bone in the fire and says to Eustace, "He's my boy. I'll look after him."

Eustace says, "Do you know what you're about?"

Pa tells me, "Go hubble your animal."

So I hurry out to where I've tied him to a tree, but not so far that I can't hear Eustace say, "It ain't right to interfere between father and son, Loren, and I know it—"

Clearly he ain't had his say, but Pa breaks in, "You give yourself good advice, Eustace."

From the dark, I peer at them in the ring of firelight, Eustace and Pa looking at each other. The others set looking at the fire. They might be deaf, dumb, blind. All but Tige, who don't miss nothing. Strange, the look on Eustace's face—as if he *wants* to want to engage Pa some more but *can't* want to. Then, a little relieved it seems to me, he gets up and goes to get his blanket. Something more has happened than that Pa has won an argument. Something has happened that—though I want to keep my horse—I wish could be undone. Whatever it is, it's enough to hush even Tige as he looks into the fire, sneaks a look at Pa, then off toward where Eustace has laid down. Again it comes washing over me, some loss, something gone. Caught by some little movement, I glance at old Emile sitting there with Tuck. He's taken his pipe out of his mouth and sets there nodding his head. Just ever so slightly—you can hardly note it—he nods his head. His eyebrows crawl up his forehead. He overturns his pipe, knocks it empty on his hand. Then, rising, he goes looking for a place to lie down.

Earl says, "No moon till morning," and yawns. Georgia takes herself off and lies down in the lee of a bush. I finish my hobbling and still ain't in a hurry to return, hear a movement and with a start see it's only Isaac, creeping in a circle like a dog to find the shape of sleep, and I kind of envy him. Then what's missing fills my head. Where's Toliver? I hang at the edge of the light, counting blankets. I run out to the animals to see can I find Beth. Then stand dumb looking at the starcrop while it blurs and flares, thinking that's what it was, that's what it was all the time. I want to stretch out my arms and gather everything and, hugging, draw it all together again, but end up hugging just myself.

Georgia Gem Hite

Climbed all morning till in the early afternoon, exhausted, we fall into a declivity cut by a white river bucking over boulders and fallen pine logs, but here and there a dark pool where the current dives. We stop to rest and let the horses drink. Pa yells at me, "You get on aways off, Gem, so we men can wash."

I yell back over the river's fuss. "You can waller among mules and horses if you like, not me." I take myself upstream along the riverbank looking for a pool, till I'm blocked where the river curls round a limestone bluff looks like a wading elephant. I portage myself around it on a path snakes up the beast's behind till I climb out on a crest with the river below and see a litter of Indian cubs tumbling in the shallows, watched over by a boy squatting naked midstream on the prow of a wedge-shaped rock like a sturdy ark making slow headway upstream.

Never known they was Indians near. I follow the path, keeping apart from the river till it rounds another bow, then brush through stunted alders and look down a landfall to a sandbar. A good private place. I'm hunting for a way down when I see below me, up to her knees in water, naked as her cubs, an Indian woman bathing. Plainly Creek. Their braves are big manly things, but the women are uncommonly small. Her unbraided hair mantles her to the thighs. Her skin's a tawny gold, and the water beads on her like she might be tallowed. You hear some of them have gone into hiding and stayed behind, at the fall line, where navigation stops and roads peter out and we'll be spared a little longer the blessings of progress. I can see both mama and her brood from where I stand, though they're cut off from each other by the small oxbow in the river.

I'm about to duck back under the alders and find the path again, when something below me on the landfall moves. I peer down upon the numerous rock rooms where the face of the bluff has broke off and rolled down, making what slope there is. Time passes while I don't see a thing. But I always trust my eyes, so I wait, then catch another movement and this time I see him clear enough. I'm looking down upon his blond curly head but it takes me a minute to register it's Loren McElroy. No sooner do I recognize him than's he's springing bent-kneed down a goat path toward the river. Once on the sandbar, ten yards behind her he pauses and, to my amazement, unlaces his shirt and loosens his clothes. I don't see how she can hear a thing over the river, but as he moves toward her, she turns. I see what I ain't seen before, that she's come full moon, big around with child. She sees him. No, she's after something moving in the water, maybe a darting fish, for, bending from the waist, hair curtaining her face, she lazies this way and that, following its movements as intently as Loren, behind her, follows hers. Just as her hand darts to grab whatever she sees, he grabs too, and I catch sight of it sticking out of his trousers like a rod. Then the trousers fall down about his boots and lie on the water and he takes and bends her from behind and I see but don't hear her holler, him holding her easily with one arm and reaching under with the other hand to find her, spread her, put it in her standing up, horse-to-mare, except small as she is he's raised her out of the water, a frog on his gig, him crouched along her back, holding her and going at a gallop and her struggling. Looks to me like the struggling helps more than hinders, like she's just screwing down tighter onto what lap he's got. Pretty quick, he stops and draws back a little and her legs fall, but before they fall I see it, still big but limp like a gelding's. And I think he'll let her go now he's took his pleasure. But no. Waddles in the shallows onto dry land and steps out of his pants, gives a little kick that sends them into the air and, running, catching them in his free hand, throws them over one shoulder, and still carrying her in front of him heads back up that goat path, stopping once to look up, and I think for a minute he's seen me. Then he's made the lowermost of the

181

rock rooms and I see he means to do it again but take his time.

I ain't eager to tackle Loren McElroy, but it's ravishment, ain't it? Even if she is an Indian. And her a dam and fixing to whelp again any minute. I pick a good-size rock and strike out down the path, but stop before they've seen or heard me there. She's laughing. Can't hear it but I see it. Laughing. If she's being raped would she be laughing? I squat before they see me, half hidden by an alder. But they ain't studying me. Loren he looks amazed. But he goes about trying to get it in her underneath that mountain of belly that's come between them. Big as that thing a his is, it can't reach. So he sets there bare-ass with his boots on, stumped while it keeps its bead on her. And she takes and shoves him flat a his back, only his head up to see what's going on, and squats and straddles him, not touching yet, teasing. I see it under her where she hovers. And she takes and, with the fingers of both her hands, opens and spreads herself and tucks in her bottom, throwing it forward to show him. And he's looking, propped up on one elbow, sort of braced and holding back. Puts out his hand and touches her, surprise smeared all over his face, and she sort of moves, still squatting, and drags herself over and back and over and back and I soon see slime stringing from her to him like she's weaving them together in a web. Then squats lower, still holding herself spread that away, and curls a finger around that thing and dredges till it's buried its head but not its column and Loren sort of raises hisself to that elbow again and looks startled and disapproving, as if for a bare instant he wants out of it, wants to roll aside and fling her off him, but hesitates because that thing is of another mind and might desert him and stay with her, for no matter the look on Loren's face, there it stands straining, craning, a red Indian scouting this new abundant plain. And I could laugh at Loren so saddled and rode. Then he moans and his shoulders draw in and his head drops back and his brave is a peak and her a cloud, heavy and wet, descending, that finally swallows him up and sits down on his valley. They commence to rock and she takes and pumps herself in short strokes and him going after her, arching hisself, and hollers and falls back flat, and she hurries, all that wild black hair raining down on him, and gets herself in a frenzy till she stiffens and gnarls, and me throbbing with it to my quick, and feel it again and once again, but fainter, and it dies, leaving me wrung and soiled and consumed by a sudden loathing and for half a minute I doze because I've got to, if I'm going to slough that sick disgust. Then hear him cuss and scramble up. She's running surefooted along that goat path toward the river, her laughter purling like water. Loren's in his pants already, standing, whole face and neck engorged with angry blood. He yells something after her, picking up in both hands a rock the size of a watermelon and raising it over his head. He halts, aims, and on the downstroke lets fly, then turns and runs. I've sucked and swallowed all my breath. I see the minute it leaves his hand that it'll find its mark, its path so sure it can take its time. More like a bubble than a ball, it floats into the small of her back. She's a rag doll flung out in the air, limbs ever whichaway. She strikes maybe ten foot farther down and rolls, starting a small landslide that piles up against her, over her, when she comes to rest. Loren long gone, leaving me here with this mess he's made.

She ain't moved. I keep still and watch to see will she. Then something drags me out from behind the bush. She's maybe thirty yards below. I twist with the path till I drop

183

beside her, shoveling the gravel off her with my hands till they're bloody as she is. And, close enough, see a movement in her belly. She opens her eyes and looks at me, afeared, frowns a little, studying me, puzzled. Then caught by a pain that hangs the length of her on its spit, she crams her fist into her mouth. It's the size of a child's of maybe ten, and tiny feet to match. She's surely Creek. Her cry rattles in her throat, she bites into the fist like it's a McIntosh, drops off the spit of pain and looks at me again. Reaching up the hand with her own toothmarks purpling along the knucks, she strokes my cheek, then touches me lower down, and I hold tight, won't look at her, hotfaced till she's felt them and satisfied herself.

Then it grabs her again. Her fingers sink into my arm. I feel it as her pain flowing into me. When she falls limp, she's not one person, not just one wench, the pain ain't just her pain but one portion of a pain old as time. She's got my arm and don't let go. Her knees rise and spread, her feet leave the ground, and for a minute I'm shocked by this new obscenity, then see that pretty and ugly lie on a wheel and run into each other. Then a flood, part blood, that soaks into ground, leaving a wet pink stain on the shale. And the head, black hair wet, matted, stretches her, then one red temple. She's up on her elbow, dragging my hands. Seeing what she wants, I cup them so she can sink back and leave catching it to me. I've got its whole head, and she's bearing down, and more blood and then its shoulders and she collapses with a moan to lie like asleep and I'm left holding it, the cord from its belly disappearing inside of her. I drag on it till it's come out far as it's going to. Then—I've done it many a time with pups—I take and hang him by the heels head down till the slime strings out of his nose, out of his mouth, weaving them together by more threads, and minds me of her and Loren. He stiffens, his mouth yawns, and his first breath ratchets through him. She's watching, reaching for him. I take and bite the cord and hand him over. Lying in chiprock like it's her bearskin bed, she takes him in the curl of her arm and goes over him with her eye, then smiles up, holding the end of his cord to me. All thumbs, I knot it close as I can get it. She lifts her head, looks, nods, and says something sounds like thanks. So I nod her back. I see her kilt hanging on a willow, her shawl folded under it on top of her doeskin buskins. I bring them, folding the kilt under her head and covering her with the shawl and, laying the soft boots in the circle of her arm, make a nest for the babe. She's barked all over from her fall, so I rip off my shirttail and wet it in the river and bathe the blood and sand off her. She finds a clean corner and puts it in her mouth then dabs at his eyes till they're clear. While we watch, they open. She picks up her breast and shows it to me. I wipe it clean. At the touch, the tit turns into a wild raspberry. Which he commences to eat with a right smart appetite. I laugh at his nerve. "Ain't been here ten minutes and look what he's up to!" She laughs.

The boy appears from the other side of the willows. She waves him over, and he bounds from rock to rock to kneel beside her, scared, but she touches his arm and jabbers and he nods and rises, wide-eyed, steps back, bears his eyebrows down on me, then turns to run, I guess, for help.

"Are you all right now?" I ask.

She's sort of smiling at me, puzzled. Then she does it again—touches me—and my face goes hot. I never felt so big and clumsy. Then, smiling, she says something again that sounds like thanks.

I want to leave and I don't want to leave. I stand up,

back off a step but still don't go. She holds out the rag. I shake my head. So she waves it good-bye then, like a handkerchief.

All the way up the goat trail to the path before I look back at the two of them. A ligament of sorrow tightens my throat. What is she? A reservoir to be filled up and emptied? A sort of gin, a factory, the input and outcome two different matters altogether? In again—out again, thread to her eye, what she is, what they are? But that don't satisfy me.

Not halfway back to where I left them I come on Duncan sitting on a rock looking down at the river. He starts and turns, swollen and red of eye, dark lashes matted. His mouth works. He manages, "You seen Pa?"

Yes and something tells me you have too. But shake my head. He studies me, hiding something behind his eye, and I fear I can guess exactly what it is.

Emile

All morning climbed the fall line, almost home. Wind booming thunder in longleaf pine and air diaphanous, but all lines fracture, shimmering indistinct, till evening cools this firstborn land that still commemorates on summer days its heatrise when He said *Let land appear* and it came rearing, dividing the waters off its crenellated spine, shedding blue fog to settle in valleys or tower into fleece that rides its shoulders. And the young chief, preceded by his pipers—colored streamers off their flutes, small fluttering yellow birds fastened by threads about his fingers—the young chief, feathers in his hair, rode out upon the shoulders of his senators to meet the Spaniard, saying *Ask whatever you would have*. The Spaniard asked for slaves.

We're dividing a few fish Tige and Tuttle trapped in a pool and Tuttle cooked. "When I was a boy in Carolina," Loren says, "them things would set down on a stack of grain and cover it like a Joseph coat. Mostly green, a wingtip dipped in blue, and yeller-headed with red masks, they'd eat theirselves to death if you didn't stop them. Hadn't a lick of sense. They'd swarm over your orchard when the fruit was green and open every apple, every pear, for nothing but the seeds, and the seeds still milky things not hardly formed. They'd th'ow down the apple in disgust and move on to the next till they'd stripped a branch, then a tree, then your whole orchard bare that way. No matter how many they pecked open, they couldn't get it th'oo their heads the fruit wasn't ripe yet. No sense a-tall. Go after them with your gun, why every shot would drop a dozen and the live ones'd rise up shrieking then fall back down on the selfsame stalk of corn."

Ever since he come to and had that spell of vomiting, he hasn't been the same. All scabbed over, half his face like spoilt meat, just now beginning to slough off and show some junction hard to locate. But that's not it. Something you can't lay your finger on. Never had much to say, but now it'll come on him in fits and he'll talk. Can't eat for talking.

"Ain't hardly any of them left, they were so easy to kill.

You'd hear them coming. Hadn't the sense to keep quiet. Set up a racket to tell you they were on their way so you could set the table. Easy to bring them down on the wing. They'd never change their course for nothing short of a bluff or a treetrunk in their path. You could be blasting away at them, they'd never even swerve their course. Hadn't a lick of sense. They'd settle down right on top of you, on the smoking barrel of your gun if you laid a cornstalk on it. And if ever you glimpsed a vanishing flock the trick was to take and wing one. Let that one set up a cry it'd bring back the whole foolish herd and you could kill them by the hundreds. Not a lick of sense.

"Pretty things though—the way they'd fly, dipping one wing, then the other. You'd see the underside, then the back, like a star will shiver, like some leaves sparkle in a wind if they're different colors above and below. But wasn't much pleasure in the killing, except that as a boy you could waller in it till you stood there like a tree and your gun your limb and dead parrots all around you on the ground, like leaves. They were good eating. I've set down to platters stacked so high with them if you wanted to know who was down't other end of the table you'd have to send a message astin. But all gone now. Ain't hardly none left."

None left. For Alick McGillivray—born to a daughter of The Wind to sit with presidents and kings, a king himself by birth and by his nature—Alick McGillivray died young, and with him what was vital of the whole Creek Nation. Driven west, and west in their worship is the shadow country that blows the wind of death. All gone. None left. Fallen not as leaves fall in their season, but as the parrots. They were pretty things.

Georgia Gem Hite

No telling what he seen, how little or how much. And where is he while we lay up waiting on him? And Loren sleeping sound as a man with a clear conscience. Setting there eating fish when I got back. Talking about parrots! Looklike to me it'd take some advanced form of maniac to lob that boulder. Meanness. Just meanness. Way they are. All a them.

Well, not Eustace, not Emile. Not Toliver. Poor Toliver.

Jay Dubya, there's another story. Well, but not on purpose. Just what it comes to. All taken up with God. Some God is all I got to say, if that's what He requires. He ain't a going to get it from me. I'll hike to hell barefoot first.

Yonder he comes. About time. Where is there to go for two hours, way out here? Would you look at him! Slugging across the river, blood all over him, shirt torn half off. Tige punches Loren and Loren shakes hisself awake and rises to look at him there where he's fell by the ashes, head on his knees. "Where've you been?"

Duncan don't raise his head.

"What got aholt of you?"

Boy don't say nothing.

"I ast you a question."

Earl looks up, frowning with sleep, but Duncan don't move.

189

"I'm talking to you."

Not a peep. So Loren gets up and walks over and with one hand lifts him standing. Duncan hangs a minute, then brings up his eyes. The muscle along his jaw sets. The gash on his shoulder's not clean enough for a knife, too clean for a fall.

"You going to answer me?"

Duncan mute. So Loren swats him across his face. Duncan startled.

"Are you?"

No, he ain't. I think Loren's about to knock him into tomorrow afternoon, but he don't. He says, "Turn around." Duncan turns. Torn pants hanging off his bloody bum. "Did you wash that?"

Duncan nods.

"Go wash it again. Wash it good."

Duncan walks back into the river and sits down in it and after a minute lies down and lets it travel over him.

"Then saddle that dickens," Loren yells, and kicking Tige, "let's get out of here."

By the time I get the horse saddled and start looking for the mule, Duncan, wringing wet, is hoisting the girth on Plunder. Loren picks up the Isaac rope, ready to go, but twists around in the saddle to watch Duncan mount up. When Duncan's ready, Loren throws him the Isaac rope. Taken aback, the boy barely catches it. He turns wonderingly to look at Loren. Loren waits for that, then kicks the Eagle, and him and Tige start off.

I expect to hear Eustace's "Earl." I wait on it, wanting to see Earl take that rope off Duncan. Earl is waiting too. But Eustace don't say it, just moves on after Loren and Tige. So the rest of us follow. Duncan, high on the brute, loops the rope in the crook of his arm like his Pa's done all the way, his face, as he glances back at Isaac, stern, all sign of whatever he's feeling smoothed out of it. Then he prods his horse and the horse spurts, lifting Isaac's hands head-high, making him step out in that little shambling trot that's become his habit.

We wade through the river and cross some sand and commence a steep climb out of this crack in the mountain. The way, paved with loose arrowheads of knife-edged shale, gives uncertain footing for the animals. All along the washed path, the sound of sliding, of shod hoofs clinking, striking chips that fly into a horse's leg, of snorts or whinnies, of broken rhythms as the animals try to find their footing.

All Duncan can do to manage that spiritus he's riding, no attention to spare for Isaac. So Isaac is pulled and yanked ever whichaway up that knob. Gaining the top, we see another valley. We're moving toward the dropoff when Duncan gives a cuss. I turn.

Isaac has set down. Duncan yanks on the rope. Isaac tumbles onto his knees, head falling back on his neck. Another sharp pull, and Isaac falls down in the grey chip-rock.

Duncan says, "Get up!"

Nothing. Just lies there. Tuckahoe up ahead has turned. Calls to the others. They look around. Duncan kicks the brute, who steps out smartly. Isaac grabs for his rope, but he's dragged maybe a yard before Duncan, with a curse, yanks the red horse's mouth and manages to stop him.

"Pick yourself up!" he says.

Isaac lifts his face but his eyes don't focus. Duncan takes and reaches maybe two foot of the rope and yanks on it.

"Hod damn you, I'll drag you on your belly, fool with me!"

Isaac falls.

Emile is off his pony and grabbing the rope, saying sharp to Duncan, "Behave yourself!"

Duncan scowls and yanks the big horse. Forehoofs off the ground, it spins. He catches the rope and pulls it out of Emile's hands. But the Frenchman, life in him yet, springs for the bridle, then hauls the Isaac rope off Duncan's arm. Duncan's face goes black and sullen.

But Emile has bent to Isaac, lying in a heap, his whole huddled form lifted by each breath. Emile turns him. "What is it? Do you hurt?" But Isaac ain't focusing. "Where? Show me, Isaac." He touches Isaac's head, his chest. We can count them carved ribs, coppered as an Indian's. But not a movement, not a wink.

His stomach? Emile feels it all over with his fingers, watching for a sign, the way you'll go over an animal looking for a hurt. Emile's hand runs down trunk and thigh, feels his knee. Nothing. Then starts down the leg.

The sign he gives is the negative of a sign. He looks more frozen than before. We're all focused on the hand that moves down his leg toward the top of them brogans she sacrificed to keep him in. I imagine I see his jaw set. That's all. Emile sets to worrying at the knot, and startled, I see it's still the double knot she herself has tied way back how long ago? The morning he rose from his bed and went out to the pasture spring and there waylaid and killed her. Still tied in their double knots the way you tie a child's so it can't come loose and trip him up. I'm staring and wanting to look away. Emile can't get it loose, his fingers urgent. I reckon them knots have made their impression on him too. Takes out his knife but can't open the blade. Cursing, wiping his hands on his pantsleg, he tries again, in too much of a hurry. Then it's cut. The whang lace too

192

often wet and dried, shrinking more each time, has bit into the leg above the ankle.

Emile takes brogan in one hand, leg in the other, and starts to pry it off. Isaac throws back his head, eyes wild, mouth yawning, and shrieks—only no sound but the sound of breath. Emile's fell back. We're all shaken. The shoe has come off in his hand.

An inch of rag, all that's left of his stocking, still circles his leg above the ankle. Emile is staring at what you wouldn't call a foot if you didn't know it to be one, not minding the brogan. But me, I've had to turn from the sight. I look instead at the brogan upside down in Emile's hand. A sickening stuff—part blood, part pus, part river—strings out of it. Make myself look at the foot and try to judge his pain by what just the sight of it gives me, but I've hit on an impossible measure. Ankle speckled blue with dirt, what looks like mud but might be blood clotted about the nails, too long, curled down over the ends of his toes like claws. Then see the sole—hanging in shreds slug-shaped, slug-white, shriveled from the swash, but the new blood startling red. The circle wounds from the brogan's bared nails look like the mark of ringworm, but under the skin the palest yellow of trapped pus. I never seen nothing like it. Never seen nothing like *him*—how he'd of had to separate hisself from his body to walk that way, lifting a bed of nails each time he lifts a foot, and setting it down again under him. And never give sign of feeling it, not once, his body a house of flesh he lives inside, no more connection between him and it than between an Indian and his house of skins—a break, airspace, fissure, between his body and hisself. And recall one time Ma's sweet old dad looking in a mirror, saying "Ain't it strange. After a certain age you never feel no older, but see your body changing, going its own way toward the grave and taking you along with it." And feel a shiver. Two selves. Strange. Sloughed his body the way a snake will slough a skin. Don't even feel his body. Without it, what can he see, hear if he does hear, feel, taste, touch? He has in another way taken leave of his senses who years ago taken leave of the other kind. Not just will. He don't feel it. How'd he accomplish it? Is it suffering allows you, suffering so great you've got someway to seal yourself off or else die of it? And what a will to live, regardless. Wills life so hard he's willing to die for it?

Them feet might a been hoofs of some beast that bore him, that he never known had anything wrong with it till it foundered and wouldn't carry because it couldn't. Not one step farther. Then can they kill him? How can he die? Ain't he dead already? A suicide because of wanting so bad to live? How can they kill him when he's made this separation? Is that what they call *life everlasting?* Then how's it different from death? Lord, what a thing to dwell on.

Tuckahoe's had Tuttle's bladder bucket. He's worrying the knot loose, beside Emile, when up come Tige and Loren. Emile, catching in his hands the water Tuck savingly pours, washes it over them feet. Tige dismounts, takes one look, rears up, swelling like a frog, and busts.

"Nursed them sores till sores are feet and feet are nubs and never let on! Saved up on us till they was overripe. And ay-God, you're letting him do it! Stand there, all a you, ashamed! He's satisfied. You're giving it to him! Saved up on us, let it happen, not a word!

"It's his own fault! Serves him right! He done it to hisself wanting to do it to us! Fools! Stand here and let him put it off on you. Well I ain't taking it! Nosir! You can if you want to. Not me!" And leans over Isaac and spits. "You turn my stomach." Prods him with his toe. Tuck knocks him away. Tige shaking all over, shivering, freezing with the heat of his rage.

"She had to keep him in clods! Sacrificed to put them on him! Nothing too good for him! Not a one of us knowed what a shoe was till we stood barefoot on the sill of our manhood! And not a one of us but could a walked it barefoot all the way! We been properly cured by some knowed it takes starch to stand up to it. But not him! Coddled, spoilt ever waking day of it. Shoes! I never had no shoes! I member once't standing on the edge of the hoglot, one bare foot atop the other, and Pa seen me not wanting to walk in it and knocked me sprawling face down in it to show me! Snatched up by the hair a the head. Razor strop hung on a nail on the back porch in easy reach and they used it too. Not a lesson but was burnt into me so I'd never forget! They serve me to this day!" Spit bubbles on his chin. "Tough!" And prods him again.

Emile goes on pouring them little soothing streams of cold water. I never saw Isaac's face so open and so closed. Lids like thinnest china, closed but you can see his eyes through them, round, centered. You can see them.

Tige muttering broken stuff, then breaks out at Isaac. "They say you cain't hear. Then howcome I so often see you listening? Cain't talk. And right now I see spasms in your throat. Ay-God they say you're struggling to give utterance, but I say you're struggling to keep from it! What a will he's got!"

And prods him again, then, shivering, jams hands in pockets and flings off away from us, shoulders hiked up

195

around his ears, all huddled in on hisself. A minute later he shouts, "The Dog!" Pointing, his whole arm rattling with it. "Hod damn, I can see it! Yonder! Over there!"

I step over and look. We couldn't a been a whole day outside of Culloden when we come on that eminence. Shape of a hound's head. Duncan he christened it. Earl steps over.

"There!" Tige says. "What'd I tell you?"

Loren steps over and after a minute points. Looking off, I see—woods crowding in on it—a short fall of river that from here looks like a tin shaving. "That's the Coosa," Loren says.

"What'd I tell you!" Tige says.

Me, Tige, Earl, Loren, And one by one the others come and line up with us, doubting: Duncan, Tuck, Jay Dubya. I point for Tuck. He nods. Jay Dubya's lids close and he jabbers. Then Emile stands with us whispering, "I know this place."

Then Duncan says it. "Home."

Another movement and we all look down. Isaac has crawled, dragging hisself, till he parts a little space between Emile and me and also looks.

Emile says, "We'll stop here tonight."

. . . and waken slowly, unwilling to give it up or own to it either, pulsing in slow rings that I somehow know have passed their zenith and already commenced to diminish from the whole of me, drawing back toward the quick where they began.

I dreamed of Loren and the squaw, only Loren swelled and become the babe as he came out. And I bit the cord and tied it. And then a babe's petal mouth and a breast

196

and I'm not in it I'm not in it. Rings widening widening till they reach my shores. And waken slowly, unwillingly, as they weaken, die.

Yet soft fingerpads like blown petals still, but just, cling to a raspberry bud though I'm awake. I don't know I'm doing it, do I? So I ain't in control of it, am I? So it don't count, does it?

But still it ain't softened, still stands hard and I feel the blown pink petal fingers tender.

Then wide awake. A hand not mine still cups my breast, now and then moving a little. Afraid to move, to reach and see, to open my eyes, I lie feeling my heart run away with me. It moves, the least bit of a stir—me not even willing it. I feel warm breath on my throat. I reach, touch, feel hair, a head.

I leap up. His eyes open like a child's with sleep in them, startled, and look at me. Why me? I want to know! Why me? Just looks at me. And I know why and want to scream *No! You make me sick!* I jerk my blanket out from under him. His eyelids fall. He puts his thumb in his mouth and sucks on it. I hang there, the voice in me yelling *No!*

Then settle down a good ways off from where he crawled to nest in me like in the mule. Drowned in my own anger. Wide awake. In the moonlight I keep an eye on him. Then doze and see the Indian woman give her jug. And, shaking all over, curse the cold. Night full of shadows. Wind speaking tongues.

They sleep around me in the moonlight, strange, abandoned shapes—the night scene after some battle fought and won and lost. And I'm alone and know I've always been. Tears rise in me. I mourn the dead. Such strange forms it will take. I look at the shadow of Isaac, the killer of the

girl, and startled, feel a curious pity. Then pull myself together and roll over on my side and later dream. The
trunk buried under hay in the loft so long now open. I'm
standing by it, something in my hand, something belongs
to me, something I've always treasured and lost I've found
in that trunk. It's all familiar. *I am going away,* says someone. Not clear who, but a voice I know as well as my own.
I break down and bawl, then wake with tears on my face.

She was an angry woman. Grumbled at us day in, day
out. "No mind for nothing but hisself and God, and God
to him is just a form of lunacy." Always at me—do this, do
that. I was stubborn. I'd demand to know *why.* She'd fling
at me, "Because!" I'd fling back, "All that answers is what
does b-e-c-a-u-s-e spell." Made her furious. Washed my
mouth with soap. But I wasn't sassing. When she come at
me again and I come back with *why,* she'd say, "Because
you got to!" So I turned it over and looked at it till I had
the answer: *All I got to do is die.*

"You won't be happy till you make up your mind you're
a girl and nothing whatever to say in the matter. You
won't be happy till you've got your own sweet baby at
your breast." Turning me hot and sick with shame.

I see the redskin with her babe in the crib of her bloody
arm, that other blood diluted, soaking in the sand, and
smiling, having me wipe her breast so she could give it to
him.

"Woman!" she'd say, *woe-man* she pronounced it. "Just
a form of mankind with the woe built in. All she is."

Then pronounce that doom on me "Because you got
to!" *All I got to do is die.* Isaac's gone back to sleep, sucking his thumb. Almost morning, almost home. Listen to
Jay Dubya jabber!

J. W. Hite

Never seen you, never heard your voice. Howcome you don't show yourself to me? Never known nothing of you at first hand but your hunger. First fed on my
heart, then my brain, then gnawed on all my organs till
even as a youth I was afire with you. And you the parasite
in my liver, in my bladder, in my groin. Hunkered down
like a turkey buzzard on my dying will till you'd ravaged
that. And nothing left for them that belong to me, nothing
for Gem, nothing for her sainted mother, may she rest in
peace. Nothing for myself. I stagger and thirst and faint
and famish, while you—the paraclete—ride the easy barge
of my veins. You are a sickness nourished on my health.
My body! *My* blood! After what all I sacrificed looklike
you'd show yourself to me. Showed yourself to the one who
doubted, but not to one who never wavered once't. Spoke
to the prophets but never once whispered in this ear. I
don't ast it as proof but for the exultation, to feed my
starveling's hunger, to know you recognize this vessel of
myself that's weak of supporting your habitation.

But no. Never seen you. Never heard your voice. Never
known a kiss at these here lips, enabling them to talk with
tongues of fire laying claim to what they touch. For you.
Nosir. Am I the stepchild of the Lord? Take take take. I
don't say nothing. But howcome you don't show yourself
to me?

Duncan McElroy

She lied. I known from the look on her face.
She seen him all right. Watched her out of sight down the
river path before I went headlong down the bluff and fell in
the river and for about a minute felt clean. Just an Indian.
Nothing but an Indian. But the flung rock! Swam across,
dragged myself out, upstream the little Indians watching
me. And I set and pant a minute, then take myself up and
run so bent I almost could a been on all fours. And hungry. All kinds of hunger. Swollen with it. I come on the
flock, backs of some of them raw where they been too close
sheared. Naked looking. I draw a bead on one and throw
myself at her. She gives a start and leaps the way they'll
leap from a standstill, flat-footed, right out of the circle of
my arms. Her lamb bleats, but I'm on her again, and got
a hold and trying to find her *(and she bent, waving this
away and that, watching something in the water, likely a
fish hovering in the current, then him upon her, clasping
her, lifting her off her feet, and fumbles her, spreads her,
sinks hisself up to the hilt.)* Then overwhelmed, swarmed
over, not a sound out of him but fangs seat themselves in
my flesh and hang on. I let her go. A silent stampede all
around us as we flay the air, me tearing loose, shredding
the flesh of my ham, my shoulder, blood flung out on the
pitiful shorn things milling close. I fall on him as he goes
for my throat. Color of wolf, but shaggy, tannin on him

here and there. Marled. I fling him off me and leap out of reach. He thrusts again. But I've got him now, my knee in his throat. His growl comes out choked. I'm throttling him. Right's on his side, but what's right against my advantage of weight? His eyes glaze, throatbones like a string of beads under my knee, a mossy bank, a pasture spring in green light, hands grubbing at a pale throat. I let go, leap back off him while he's still stunned—eyes slit, a little blood out the corners of his lips, down the sleek jaw with its long single wart-grown whisker hairs, black. Flock watching with a single eye. Then I'm running hard as I can and think I'm homefree when, slowing, I look over my shoulder, and there he is, silent, at my heels, lips drawn to bare them fangs, about to spring because I've slowed. And leaping grab the lowest limb of a jack-legged tree, swing out of his reach, pull myself up and climb. Trying to growl in his injured throat he whistles, prowling around the trunk, pawing the bark like a cat, prowling again, whites of his eyes bloodshot, showing me his teeth. Treed like a possum or coon I sit whimpering under his accusing eye till by and by one sheep baas and then another. Restive below me, he paces. Then, the whole flock noising at some danger, he turns and trots away.

I leap down running and don't stop till I fall in the river. Dragging myself up, I slug toward them thinking I'll say a wolf. Lies. Pull out again on the same side, fall sobbing behind a bush, nose stopped, breathing through my mouth. Then drag myself up, quit bawling, blow my nose, and go on across. And glad he knocks me around. I don't have to say nothing—it's a revelation—and makes him knock me around some more.

Our last night. I don't want to get home no more. Do you come to be what you do, what acts you commit and aim to commit? Do they come to be part of you like a sight or sound your mind stores to fetch up on an instant when something recalls it? And am I that? Already changed by it, the fang marks the least of it, so it won't be undone? For the first time in my life the night sky can't make me small, the bigness of that star-sown field can't lose my sins for me. All right. And hitching my blanket higher, rolling over, remember Toliver. Too bad, Toliver. You didn't make it. You wasn't tough enough.

Part Six

Toliver Pullen

"We'll take our leave of you."
Oh not of me I've nothing to spare.
"We can't stop here."
"Reckon I'll be staying too."
Never knew silence to be so grey!
"You can find your way alone?"
And moving! If everything moves, by what still measure do I know it?
"You cain't fault Toliver on directions."
And into the moving silence the weathergrey wagon of time with its tireless horses and stiffnecked driver in sprung top hat, a bite out of its brim neat as out of a sandwich. The canvas blows, disclosing unwilling passengers jammed on the moving stage, here a limb, there a head, stuck any which way on the wagon that will not stop for those who get off, those who get on. Lining the road, shaking fists, they shout:
"Early!"
"Late!"
"Stop!"
"Wait!"
But pewter driver on pewter sky (it's done nothing

these past days but cloud up and weep) shouts: "A frontier gained is a frontier lost!" And *crack!* The whip. Some leap on, others drop off, but the stiffnecked driver will not look over his shoulder.

Dust. Dust in the wagon of time with its pewter horses and knobnosed driver who only looks ahead. Bump, sway, rock, through passage of greys nights seasons constellations not marking change—no more change than in the look on a clock's face, marking time. Round, mill, repetition. Grindstones. Big wheel the world, little wheel the wagon of time. "And we the threshed grain! Stop!" they cry. "There's no more time! Stop!" they plead. "There's nothing to fear!"

Dust in the wagon. Dust that slips through a crack and falls from the wagon of time that continues without it out of sight. Then swept by a wind that churns like smoke and thins like rags of mist into a pewter house, poor but complete: floor, wall, roof, hearth, door, window, odors, drafts, squeakings, sighings, furnishings. This bed. A company. The driver!

"I'd know you anywhere! There are no lines in your face! Where have you been? Where were you going? But not before strangers."

Better with strangers. They won't distract you. This will require your whole attention.

"Oh let me have light!" and let it be yellow, no more of this shroud of fog blanketing blanketing. "Where are my gentlemen?"

As you left them. They haven't coughed nor sneezed nor spoken nor moved since you abandoned them, one pulling his beard, one tugging an ear, one caressing the arch of his foot in its patent leather shoe.

"Did you speak? What did you say your name was? Put

down your whip. Come take a chair. Make yourself comfortable. There's no more time."

You won't get home, won't see her again.

"But I can't stop here, alone, in this wilderness, unfinished, it won't make sense!"

You'll never have what you wanted, the one thing could have made you happy. Not by any means. Not by effort nor excellence nor desert, not by trial and not by error, not by theft nor as a gift of what must be free and can only be a gift. By nothing. Do as you please, gain higher prizes. That one, you must do without. That one, you may not have.

Oh pity please pity my pretty! I've known it before. I've read it somewhere. "This is nothing new! Who kneels by the bedside?" Face like a morning sun over the hills of coverlet?

She's going and he knows it. Abandoning, deserting him. She's going with this new rival whose arrival . . .

"Impatient, impertinent, he didn't even wait for her!"

She leaves without reluctance, look at her face. If you'd hold her, hold air in your hand. She's going without a word because she knows as she knows everything the depth and fury of your rage. Storm, rail, you'll only drive her farther. Can't you be quiet? You know she's driven because it grows and as it grows this storm of yours that twists and howls and whips thorn fingers to tear her hair and clutch her clothes as she tries to escape with the help of accomplices to follow the nameless serene and saintly babe lying naked in death there on a cloth. *You* are the drover who drove her!

"No! Innocent! I tell you it's the babe! She was attached to it!" Held it in her lap inside her while I . . . couldn't get warm enough, close enough, couldn't lie dozing on her lap before the fire in the hearth there opposite the bed across the square room, its ceiling lost in shadows that hide the quilting hooks.

"Lies!" In a mummy-shaped box with the babe in her arms. They seal them in for their long voyage and tell me for cruel comfort the two of them are happy together forever.

Then why weep bitterly? No wonder she turned from this jealous, idolatrous rage toward the boy wrapped sufficient to himself in his swaddle of death, coldly spurning her love though its strength impels her after him into . . .

"Unthinkable!"

Who kneels by the bedside so lonely alone in the desolate room the fire out, abandoned to life and cursed: henceforth stranger, for she alone knew him?

"The mourning son."

You must live this way.

"Naked? Alone?"

If at all.

"There's no door. No way out, no way in, who'll feed me?"

Feed yourself.

"Impossible!"

You can find your way alone?

You cain't fault Toliver on directions.

The path is marked. You can read a life in these lines if you take the time.

"There's no more time!"

Homefree! Homefree! flies past and down the dark.

The lecturer mounts the platform before the worthy gentlemen: "I show you The Book of Transmitted Truths. You'll note each page comprises a system such as The Book of Law, subsystems of: God, Nature, Society, Reason. And each subsumes subsystems till each one is a constitution or a commonweal. Gentlemen, observe. I tear them out, all of them, one by one. Worthless. Worse than worthless. I go. You may follow by means of these bits of paper. To here. This is the end. Go no farther, you'll be lost, the way from here unmarked. You're on your own. I leave you with a paradigm: I saw a gentleman put down a horse and tether it. First hobbling its forelegs and its hindlegs, he dragged it to the ground. Then tethered its forelegs to a stake till they couldn't move. Then the hindlegs, likewise to a stake, till they couldn't move. Then haltered its head up short to a stake and likewise fixed it thoroughly until it couldn't move. Then he said to the horse, 'Now you'll do as I say.'

"Gentlemen, I give you your philosopher and his horse —his vehicle of words. I leave you with your tethered horse, your beard, your patent leather shoe. Good-bye!"

What will you eat? What will you drink? Take something hot! Something cold, something lukewarm, Hot Cold Luke John! For what is the meaning of *poet?*

"Gentlemen, a poet is a little po."

I give you a riddle: his mother had a child. It was not he.

"Impossible. Unfair. No answer to a thing like that."

You think you've gone through them all! You think yourself quite done. Look what you still hold in your hand.

The cardboard back of The Book of Transmitted Truths, inscribed with one word: OUGHT.

You have said to yourself *There is no,* and your heart cried BUT THERE OUGHT TO BE. *There is no, there is no,* BUT OUGHT TO BE. *No order no absolute absolutely no law nothing nothing nothing.*

"But I can't die here! Alone! Unfinished! There'll be

no sense in it!"

There's your OUGHT TO BE. In your bitterness OUGHT TO BE. In your rage OUGHT TO BE OUGHT TO BE. In your fear OUGHT TO BE. If you'd leave us, swallow it whole, chaos, sickness, and old night, relinquish OUGHT. But you still clutch it in your hand.

Not fair! I didn't know it was there! And throwing it down feel some abandon. "At last—to reach the end, to be free, and free only to die. Is that what it means? Why are you laughing?"

In your irony OUGHT TO BE! Looking for order even as you say there's not any!

"But damn it there sometimes seems to be. Take, was it Wiley? It must have been. Isn't there order in that? Had I not swapped my mare for him, then let him go, he wouldn't have been there to . . . and so—"

No, quit it, tear it out, throw it up, discard it, you can't have it. If there's order in that it's only the order of one man doing a good turn for another who then returns it. That's no order—another man some other time might as he's free not choose to. Let go, give it up, throw it away. Orders may be, but never an order of being. Disorder the order, change the immutable. Freedom, chaos, death—the certainties. Follow me!

"Coming!"

The air is light. Can light be air? "I'm too heavy for this bed!" And sink and sink as feather mountains rise. The air is light and—growing growing—I'm a world. If I'm a world in throes of creation would I be light and light be parts and they particular and, moving, still and still be Toliver? If I were the world would I, still, be spinning?

"Everything changing! I'll fall in despair!"

In a featherbed.

"In a fever!"

In a house.

"The poorhouse!"

Rich. In the certainty of food at intervals corresponding to your hunger, and if you can't lift your head it's lifted for you, and if you forget to swallow a hand strokes your throat, reminding the muscle to do it.

"Out! Cross that sill I th'ow up my hands! You brought him to me, didn't you? Then he in my hands and on my conshunt. Do like I say or I wash my hands—and if I do I can tell you rat now he a dead man.

"Ague. Ain't ague! He got the complications. In the old days they call it conjure. Thought somebody planted the ball on you to roll yo life away. But ain't conjure. He all bound up like a fodder bundle in a piece of hisself. No more use to hisself than a limb gone to sleep. I know what I'm talking bout. I seen it befo. Oh yes. I been midwife, waterwitch, black medcin, yerb doctor. I haves the power and practice of yellow root, ginseng, dog hobble, horsemint, mullein, boneset, bitters, balsam, pennyrile and everthin else besides. I haves the power to birth, say where to sink a well, I can cure and curse. Now Turtle, if you think I am free *because* I haves this power, you are wrong. It the other way round. I haves this power because I is free.

"Tole you I *maught* kin. I ain promise. He got to worry loose that string, do that much hisself. We'll see kin he. That *the one thing,*" swinging the kettle out of the hearth, bending, lifting its lid, her old breasts hanging away from her body to inspect the pot like a second pair of eyes.

The one thing could have made you happy—not by any

211

means, not by effort, excellence, desert, not by trial, not by error, not by theft, nor as a gift, though it must be free.

Duncan McElroy

When we woke up, the swelling was down, but he couldn't walk on them. Ignoring Emile and them, Pa'd set him on his feet, but he'd just sag. So finally they won and Pa told Tige, "Th'ow him over your horse and climb up behind." Tige was a sight trying. When he seen what Tige was up to, he used them bound hands like a club. Tige come out of it battered, hopping mad. I made the mistake of laughing, so Pa told me if I was so smart to show Tige how to do it. I'm taller and heavier, but when I got him next to the horse and reared back to try and shove him up feet first, using them ruined feet against the saddle he recoiled into me like a gunbutt and fell on top of me, rolled off, scrambled up, and *stood on them*. Clearly he didn't aim to be rode in. Pa got that pleasure in his eye he'll get when he sights his game, just before lifting gun to eye and drawing his bead. "Walked this far, let him walk all the way."

So Emile unstrung his doeskin mocs off his saddle and knelt to put them on him. Isaac rested his tied hands on Emile's neck and, obedient as a child, lifted first one foot, then the other.

It's been slow. We've had to stop a lot. Nobody says

nothing but looklike we divide up just the opposite from the way we started out. Me and Tige and Pa, who wanted to make him walk, want to see him give in and let us ride him in, but Emile and Earl and them, who wanted to carry him, now want to see him make ever last step of it on foot.

Earl

You wouldn't take it for a fresh one. Grass thriving, moss undisturbed on the big flat rock at the head, the small one at the foot already sunk. Of course all this time—you set your mind like a clock and long or short matches that. Thought days, been months, like years. Eustace's face—so long like the face of a vacant house—lights so you think somebody's home after all, but the light fades and you see it was just the sun reflected in the windows on its way down. And Isaac, who planted this plot, don't note it at all. He stands beside it waiting to go on.

A woman we never laid eyes on before comes out to sweep the stoop of the church we built ourselves and eyes us like strangers. Duncan moves on over to the crest, his brute dancing, snorting, tossing spume. One by one we all draw over. Sky a field of sheep each with its lamb, valley that yellowgreen comes in a storm's wake. I could eat and drink it but Loren prods his horse into the falling road and Isaac dumbly commences the final time to walk.

A figure too far off to recognize walks toward us, sights

us, halts and stands looking. Before we're halfway to where the road angles, cuts steep between claybanks, the lone figure in the clearing by the dripping spring's become a cluster.

Emile

Let them go.

To this hill came the Muskhoghe with his pipers to greet the Spaniard, through this gap Old Hickory with bloody hands on his way to Horseshoe Bend. I climbed this road to see the stars fall, that was thirty-three, and again to watch the last of my Indians go.

Eily, you gave me your featherbed, let me climb down and rest on your stone. Earth your womb and all your babies, the bad things never will grow up, you're delivered never to be delivered.

You burst into the den and the old brute embracing his final hibernation groaned to open rheumy eyes upon another spring. But you shook me. "Aimyul, don't possum, you've only got the croup, like a baby. Look what I've brought." Your rough thumb hoists my lid. I growl. You've brought me your featherbed.

Dropped the tick-and-feather luxury to run outside for water and give me a chance to pull on pantaloons. "Pa gave me the set of eggs when I was little and I hatched the goslings and raised them and drove them with a stick all that long way down the back country." And each late spring flopped each squalling one on its back and plucked its netherside into your apron against a featherbed—"for my dower" you'd explain—then gave it to me to cradle these brittle bones.

I'm three times widowered, children all taking the Indian way as I would have them, I've grandsired many older by far than she. Yet she draws the sap in me again and the devil and saint in her both know it. A girl still a child and a rancid old man, between them that bright riddle too soon for one, too late for the other. Nothing to do but laugh.

Then after a while there's always Isaac, his sungrin tilted to catch light at the tip of his long upper lip.

Now awful trouble befallen the two of them.

Well, Isaac, I said you wouldn't have to be alone. Rain? From a clearing sky, big single drops. Well, it can't last. I'll go in their church.

She's locked the door. Harder. Still coming down and me with the valley to cross, and tired. "Come! Come here, pet! That's it. Let me drag the saddle off. Go find yourself a tree." I'll crawl in under their church and wait for the rain to stop.

Georgia Gem Hite

As we break into the clearing at the old place, Tuck says it reeks of Indian.

"Here's where the Old Town stood." I tell him. They'd

all live together in a town, houses clustered around the council house and the whole surrounded by plantation like a family with the farmhouse and outbuildings surrounded by their fields. "Andy Jackson burnt it to the ground, they say, on his way to Horseshoe Bend. They was Creeks here twenty years or more after that, but that was their finish. They say he routed them out from under the bluffs along the river where it bows and slaughtered them. They say the Tallapoosa run with blood."

Loren: "There was a man known how to deal with Indians."

Tige and Duncan laugh.

They wait under the pasture oak, the only tree left in the old place, sand beneath it dry in a great circle. In spite of the drizzle on its turning leaves you can hear the dripping springs. Roots like crippled fingers reach out of the limestone ledge to try and catch the water.

"Said to be blood of slain warriors and never will run dry. Drink it, it'll make you strong. Colored that way by the dye rock it runs through," I explain to Tuck.

Duncan says, "Indians say dye rock. It's iron."

Under the pasture oak, they wait on us. I think just ridgers coming after water, then I see her. Stood then like she's standing now. They wanted Eustace to say no to her, come to him asking who'll fix her wagon when it breaks down on the way? who'll hope her raise her roof once there? who'll do her plowing? hope her harvest? take on her heavy work?

Stood waiting—her two hands carrying on their mute powwow—not even stating her case, much less begging. That time, Pa settled it. "Who's Eustace to say no to her? The roads ain't his, the land ain't. By what rights say no to her?" They listened for once in life the way they'll listen to him in church. Stood then as she stands now, her poor diseased eyes brewing their tears so you can't say if she's weeping. And these with her—newcomers among the Saunders and Colliers. They're flocking in. They'll settle on top of us, on the slopes, and clear hillside fields that'll only wash their topsoil down to our increase in the valley. They'll set up there while surprise turns to envy and envy to hate and say they never had no luck and we're favored by God.

Nab Saunders, head ducked under his shoulders like a hunchback, cocks up at us. "We never give you up. Still— Indian trouble, bands of predators, plague, woods fires, flood in August . . . Found him, did you!"

A stringy stranger says, "Ain't much to him, is they. I'd a thought— I declare, and do a thing like that."

"Hushup," Nab says, jabbing him, winking toward her.

Isaac gives no sign he's seen her. She looks at him, mouth working. No lips, just a drawstring edge. What can she make of the change in him? The drizzle lets up and the instant before setting the sun points a red finger and softens the hills. The duskdark draws a fog up from the bottoms and a little chill off the mountain corridor to the north. All the horses sniffing the barn. Eustace sets still, features indistinct in the purpling light, watching her go up to Isaac and touch the top of his wrist. Isaac looks at her like he wonders what she wants.

"Undo him," Eustace says to Loren. "She can have him for the night."

Loren nods to Tige. Tige says, "Are you crazy?"

So Loren tells Duncan, "Get down and undo him."

Duncan eagerly swings a leg over the brute's poll and slides off. Taking the garland off Isaac's shoulders where it's so long lain, he tosses it to Loren, then cuts the binding off Isaac's wrists. Them long splayed fingers wonderingly stroke where the rope has rubbed. Loren says, "Stay here tonight, both of you. I ain't running back to Texas."

Tige sighs and nods. He's got nobody anyway. But Duncan, the light of his ma's eye—you'd think he'd be less eager. But he picks up his reins and turns on her and Isaac. "You heard him. Get on't the house." The ridgers look modestly down as she takes Isaac's hand. He turns and looks back at us.

The dark thickens. They offer Eustace a calabash lantern but he shakes his head. "All right," he says. "In the morning." We set another minute, surprised to think we can part now and go our own ways home. But Eustace is riding off. Pa, with a twitch, starts the way you'll start awake and follows him, calling, "Eustace."

Eustace don't seem to hear. Pa jogs after him, coattails flapping. "Eustace."

Out of the clearing, Eustace is lost to us. I come abreast of Jay Dubya and tell him we'll miss our path. He stops, bewildered, looking after Eustace. I go ahead on R. Mule, knowing he'll come on behind me.

Hedy McElroy

No sooner hear hoofbeat than know it's the Eagle and it's a lone horse. At the well outside the kitchen house, bucket in hand ready to be dropped, heart running away with me, I hark if Maud's lagging. But no horse will lag that close to the barn this time of night. The tide on the swell fills my throat. I see him in the dusk ride through the gate and keep on toward the barn.

Set down the bucket and sleepwalk to the gate, straining back the dark, looking down the ribbon of sand for him. Empty, a crevice the tree banks on either side slowly close. I'd never of let him go. He'd a had to been torn from me a second time. But sneaked off after him. . . .

He's at the corncrib, taking feed. Then pretty soon footsteps halt by the well, at the door to the kitchen house. Now in the dwelling lamplight. Steps cross the dogtrot, enter the other room. Light climbs the ladder to the sleeping loft, steals through chinks in the shingles. I shrink against the tree. But never calls my name. Light descends, and out the back, across again to the kitchen house where I was churning when the cat complained of an empty water pan, sending me to the well.

His form in the kitchen door cut out of the light behind him. He'll see me here in the moonshade of the tupelo. My knees give, set me down on the mounting block. He turns back for the lamp, then comes toward me, pausing by the well to note the bucket off its hook, then strides across the yard fretting the chickens in the fruit trees. Turning, I cross the road, clutch the low branches of the pecan, swing up as his stride lengthens behind me, and hold my breath, keeping still. But he lifts the lantern and all exposed.

"What do you think you're doing?"

Search his face to see can I find a sign.

"Will you answer me?"

Nothing. My mouth works but can't bring out my question.

"Will you get down out of that tree and get me supper?"

I slip down and hurry around him to the kitchen. He enters behind me and sets the lamp on the loom. Bending to lift the cellar hatch and go for meat when he catches my arm and lifts me. "I'm your husband, I might a been dead."

Move my lips and make his name, then say it: "Duncan."

Hand on my arm hardens. Shut my eyes, brace myself, slammed all the way to the wall. "Duncan!" Lets go of me and walks to the table and drops in a chair, hand up to shield his eyes from the light. "Duncan," like a curse. Drops his hand, looks at me.

"Where is he? What have you done with him?"

Hand falls and slaps the table. Wearily answers, "Can't you see I'm hungry?"

Earl

"I'll take him for you," knowing as I offer it ain't generosity. He climbs heavily down, holding onto the pommel a moment as if once on his feet he's lost his bearings. "Thanks." Steps toward the lighted house. "Thank you, Earl." I lean down and pick up the reins he's forgot to hand me. "Stop in and eat a bite when you've done." I don't answer. Maybe I'll find the will to walk on by and go home. Leading the horses past the window, I see her in her wrapper before a little fire, patching together a

220

quilt, a regular Joseph coat. All the mingled reds and blues spill down her lap. Her hair, undone, spills down her breast. She looks up toward the door, hand poised. Thimble finger sparks. She's heard his step. I hear him close the door. Then with her awkward grace she goes to meet him. I turn downhill toward the barn. Scudding clouds, moon up—a bubble off the cone of mountain. My hand snakes higher on the reins to feel the breath of the horses. Down the gullied path past corncrib to barnlot, water them at the trough. I unsaddle Eustace's gelding and spank him into his stall. My own nag stalled, feed them millet tops and hoist the saddles on a rail and hang the bridles and go fetch them each two dozen ear of corn. And, taking my time, walk back up the gullied path, meaning to skirt their yard and make for my own shack down the fenceline beyond her salad. But no more will than the boy who learned to live in Eustace's fields, sleep in his loft, take his kindness and hers, waiting always on evening when he'd sit at their table. Long before the Colvins left me, I'd rarely go home after chores. I'd climb to the loft to wait for the sight of her on the path, pails dangling from her shoulder yoke, stepping round washes and cowpats with her graceful clumsiness. She'd reach down her milking stool, the white of her underarm lovely. She'd lean to her milking against the cow and, finally, rise and go again, slowed by her bowed yoke. And Eily a little thing, dancing round her. Never even saw Eily till she was growing up and I saw her mother in her, that same strange grace. Now, walking this path, remember the path she walked in Carolina, the boy in the hayloft. Look over my shoulder, I'll surely see him there, a burning eye in a hungry face obscured by shadows. Almost as if, though

221

I escaped the loft, he never did but lies there still, counting the stars like they might be apples hoarded against the hunger that gnaws him awake in the deepest part of night to lie thinking of the houses and sleeping folk, wondering that he's so singular.

The eye of the boy watches me top the rise and turn toward the house, a scornful eye that fears I'll discredit him. But he can't escape the loft. I can leave him there and softly approach the lighted house.

Eustace, on the square back porch that fits the L, cranks the bucket up. Water splashes the basin. He walks with it into moonlight, sets it on the bench, and shrugging his galluses, removes his filthy shirt to bathe. In the moonlight he might be chalk. In the spring we'd shuck our shirts and plow half naked to the thin sun, him a lean-muscled man, ribs showing above the hair-grown navel, flat-muscled stomach. Now in the moonlight—not flesh, chalk. Buttoning his clean shirt, walks back in. As he reappears in lamplight, I'm startled by his grizzled hair.

I squat in the yard and, hungry, watch Eustace eat. Their lips move, but I can't hear. I rise. Among the fruit trees wind worries roosting fowl. A wing beats, a pear drops heavy.

On the stoop of my shack, I look up at the moon, higher now. Along the fence and past the orchard, down the path round the corner of the forge comes hurrying my old companion, loneliness. I think of Toliver dying among strangers. I think of Sidney Pullen. Will anybody think to tell her? I could go myself. Standing, I stretch and look toward their place. But who am I?

222

Toliver Pullen

Follow me.

"Coming!" through dappled woods, turning leaves. "Coming!" through scarlet oak, black gum, sweet gum, poplar. Chestnut, chinquapin, buckeye, maple.

"Here Het now."

"Coming!"

"He sho do tawk. Law, look what you got. Ain he somethin. Rides that hip like a donkey. What ah'm own do with him?"

"The leaves are turning! Too soon to be read! Coming!"

"Turtle! Git him, Het! Hold him down! You ain going no place!"

"Coming!"

"Heah, Turtle, take this bucket and see can you find my hot spring in the dahk. You'll heah it boil. Now then, Het, how you gone do with him riding yo hip? Look at him. Just picks it up in his two hands! He got a thirst, that boy!"

"What child is this?"

"He so hot, Lottie."

"Set it inside and shoo fly, don't pester Lottie. Now then, Het, he don't want nothing cold. We gone bathe him with the wahm bubble. You feel strong? Lottie ain got the strength no mo. Give him heah. Let me take him. I'll put you in dis basket and hang you up on a rafter and give you a shove. Theah now."

"What child is crying?"

"Jes listen. Bofe ob'm. Hush. Go to sleep. You awright. That the way. Now then, Het. You looks tared."

"Half hand today. Big harvest. No mo quawtah hand, an him still nursing."

"Feed him cawnbread. You gone nurse im till he big enough to say no thanks mammy? That's rat. That the way. See? He like it wahm. Burning up with fevah, the least cold they'll shrivel up, die on you. They don't want it. They likes it wahm. Like this now. All over. That's rat. Sole of the foot, parm of the hand. That the way."

Women and winding sheets and this poor body, naked arms, legs, belly, member. "I've never been so touched!"

"Listen at im. That's rat. All over now. Roll a little over him. Th'ow it like dice. Heah it hiss? Look at im. They'll git rat quiet to listen at it hiss. Parm of hand, sole of foot. That's rat. Bathe his face. That the way. Less turn him. Turtle!"

"Never so moved!"

"All boun up. Seen it lots a times. I was free befo I was free. Ain no man living could give Lottie Petrie *to* Lottie Petrie. Naw. They had the papers on me but I never was slave to nobody. They knowed it too. I let them know it. I seen many a slave white as you. White as this boy in my bed. One to drink, one to craps, one to pride, one to the table, one to a woman. One to Lottie Petrie. You know how I got my so-call freedom? I tell you. I walk in his office—guns lining the walls (this particular one a slave to killing) —and say I'll take them papers now, been round here long enough, want a little rest and peace off by myself someplace befo I die. Naw, I tole him, I ain just talking, come on, givum heah, don't want em nosing round astin who you belong to, Lottie? I tacked em up on the wall there where I can hike my thumb and tellum there they is but don't mean nothing, nevah did mean nothing. I was free befo I was free. Ain no man living can give *me* Lottie Petrie. That's who I is. See what I mean?

"But him—he got to worry hissef loose. That the one thing."

"The one thing not by any means!"

"Listen at him. Oh I seen it a heap. People gives themselve away fo nothin. If it wadn't fo nothin wouldn't be give-away. I seen it plenty, and I seen lots of people stolen from theyselve. Oh yes. Hit ain uncommon. You take women. Women get raped. Oh yes. Known plenty ob'm. I was. Befo I was old enough to call myself a woman. Twice't. Once't by white, once't by black. And in that Christian brotherhood let me tell you color don't make no diffunce. You take, I known one woman—young woman too, with a man and chile—and she was rape and she die of it. Not from the hurt—naw, though she *was* hurt, all tore up—but the *idear* of it. She didn't want her body no mo, couldn't live in it. It was like some old abandon house —shutters sagging by a hinge, winders broke, door that cain be shut, and she walk through all that desolation clutching herself from cold, and cain live in it, cain live in her body, don't want it no mo, ain hers, just this old abandon house the tramps and vagabonds and outlaws use —piss on the walls, shit in the corner, wrote all over, joists jimmied out to build a fire in the pried-up floor. She don't want it, don't reckonize it, won't have it, don't belong to her no more. So she ain got no place to live. You got to live in your body, ain't you? So she die. But me, my mam told me say Lottie, when it happen—not *if, when*—remember this: they try and get in me that away. Done ever thing they could do—hahm me, hurt me, nearlybout kilt me, and I let them climb me, mine me, do all they can do. I turn myself into a worm and they went rat th'oo me like the dirt they was, and all I done was keep on moving, moving along—using them to move on too—till I was shut of them and they wan't nothing but my castings left behind."

No choice, out of your hands, give up. "Never so touched!"

"Spread them. Hot in there. That's rat. Now roll him back ovah, Turtle. That the way. All over, Het. Circle on the belly. Keep him pleased. That the long and short of it. Git his sides. Under the arms. That's rat. Parm of hand, sole of foot. Th'ow some on. Let it roll! Heah it? You haves to take the fevah when it reach the skin, wash it off, make way for more, it'll come. Then the same thing all over. Don't let it pile up on the skin. More water, Turtle. Take the bucket. Take this rag, Het. No, don't wad it, let him feel the shape a your hand. Easy. Up the ribs like a swimming bird. Nice flat belly. Pick it up, pick it up. Law, it be a shame to lose thisun!

"See him laugh? Yes he did. Heard me, didn't you? This Lottie tawkin, Lottie Petrie. Part them legs, bathe the thigh, inside, inside, that the way, all rat, wash his face, get the ears. He rat pretty. Sole a foot, parm a hand."

Oh never so touched, never so moved, I swell and swell till I'm the earth in throes of sensation, all over me feel the barefoot rain, the scampering life with fingertip feet nestle of fur petal of breath. Down in my pores the hair-root carrot root tubers that press grow and wither down tunnels of air. Never so touched, rolled by oceans that hiss cover bare, and seasons that pass and licking my bowels

226

flame tongues eat away shape away tunneled by caves where clear rivers rise, spring vapor steam off me cooling and leaffall strawfall starfall footfall, circled by clouds that brush my high places. Never so touched. Oh let there be life and let it be this and this be Toliver.

You are the driver who drover who whipped wily Isaac who weak and despised must die for she left him despised him who drover tormented her killed her can't live, he must die, let him go. Oh weep for the poor thing despised thing dying oh weep for yourself. I! Sick! Isaac!

"Coming!"

Dappled woods, fallen leaves, fall on them crying, one by one take them up, bind them, inscribe them *Toliver*, look up, see myself.

"Coming!"

Part Seven

Earl

It wasn't good daylight when Eustace whistled for me, Mister Hite already dogging his tracks, sputtering, spitting, making great big figures in the air with his hands, jackknifing to get the last deep pocket of air and swollen-faced having to shut up a minute to reload before setting out again till by and by I lost him. Eustace would nod, polite, but went right on with what he was doing. He thought we could use a trough he'd put together in mid-summer, though it don't require oak. So we went down to the barn and took its measure. A mite wide, too short, but Eustace said, "It'll have to do." So I went to the pasture to get the young mule. He was grazing way off by the spring. When he heard me coming, them jackrabbit ears swiveled and he commenced to move off, grazing as he went. That way I walked him into the fence corner. Stood there backed up to the corner post, eyeing me head down like a billy goat apt to use his horns. I been bit, throwed, kicked by him, so I kept an eye on him and, halter behind me, walked in slow, sweet-talking, "Just stand where you are, you little sonabitch." Ears swiveled, pointing at me like hearing horns. But he let me walk up and pet him and draw the halter on.

Like to never got him in the traces. Eustace striding, Mister Hite running alongside him, already halfway up the hill again when I climbed the front wheel. The plank seat was missing, so I drove standing up. After not working for so long, the mule resented the bit. We made a racket bumping up the hill. I pulled up at the forge and found some horseshoe nails that would do and put them in my pocket, then went and tied up at the black walnut in the yard and Eustace and me went to the shed. I picked up a wide board from the lightning-struck tree he's had sawn into lumber but he said, "Let that alone. You got all the oak you can handle as it is." So I picked out two pine boards and chunked them up in the wagon and climbed up and measured them in place, marking them with the scratch of a nail while Eustace went to fetch the saw, Mister Hite wild and getting wilder.

Looked like the beginning of a cold snap. I welcomed the sweat I worked up sawing. The rasp of the saw tore his voice, but that never stopped him. He had a wad of sweet plug he kept switching from jaw to jaw—gummy old black molasses, it'd do for a sugartit. All that talking, he worked up a tar rim to his mouth. Now and again a fleck landed on Eustace and he'd brush at it, sternfaced with distaste. Mister Hite's a grand preacher but he'll get enthusiasms.

Along about nine o'clock here come Georgia on foot looking for him. Kate Jurdin come to the door and stood and listened to him, fixing her eye on Eustace. He looked at her once, didn't look again. She nodded at Gem, but Gem never noticed. Never has had much to do with the women.

Kate, arms folded, hands run up her sleeves out of that touch of cold, said, "Is it eye for eye?" She was speaking

232

at Eustace's back. "Is it a transaction?" He acted like he never heard.

Seeing she couldn't do nothing with Mister Hite, Gem she come on up in the wagon and spelled me, tapping me out of her way to fit them boards like the halves of a walnut. If you want a nice joining, get Gem to do it. Then I took the brads and toenailed them. Of course they was too long. I had to clip them and hammer them flush. Then I laid it in place and seen it would do.

Before long here come Loren, Hedy trailing him, arms folded in a shawl, eyes lowered, an ugly red mark on her face to match the fading one on his. He had the rope coiled on his shoulder. He give it to Eustace, who taken and tossed it over a limb of the walnut tree and swung his whole weight on it. It held.

She'd come back to stand in the door, looking out at us. Hedy spoke to her but she didn't note it. Said to the back of Eustace's head, "Can you barter her back?" Eustace acted like he didn't hear. "Eustace?"

"Put blinders on him," Eustace said to me. "I don't want to have the aggravation of a testy animal." I nodded, trying to think what I'd done with them, worried that Tuttle never brought them back.

"Didn't Tuttle borry them?" I said.

He looked like he was listening, but he never heard me. He said it again: "Get some blinkers on him."

Do this, do that. A good thing I early got used to doing what you ask, whether or not it's possible. I'd a been too old to get in the habit now. I can see them just as plain, hanging against a post on a nail. But where's the post?

"Looks like a little cold snap," Hedy McElroy said. Loren thrown her a look and she hushed. A frail thing—

hair unseasonably grey, a white-headed child, skin pale, eyelids transparent as some leaves that you can see their tracery. Contrary. Nothing she says seems fitting. Like she ain't quite in the time or place or circumstance but is somewheres far away where something entirely different is going on. They say she was a pretty girl.

Eustace and I went in. Sat at opposite ends of the table and had some breakfast. She would set things on the table and pour our coffee, but never sat with us, just leaned in the door and watched us eat, not saying anything. Eustace kept urging me, "Take a slab a that ham. Put some of that fig preserves on your biscuit." If I'd a listened to him I'd a stuffed myself like a sausage. Something absent in his eye. As we were leaving the table said to her without looking at her, "Kate, would you get me one of your nightdresses."

She looked at him but never said nothing, just walked ahead of us out of the room and come back with it over her arm and handed it to him. Like she'd be durned if she'd ask what for. He said, "Thank you," folding it, and we passed on out the door. They'd gone on, the Hites and McElroys. And Eustace coiled the rope and laid it on the trough and slung the nightdress over them, then backed off while I climbed the wheel and untied the reins from the brake and stood up there waiting for him.

"You'll want to put blinders on the mule," he said, like that was the first he'd thought of it. Then said, "You go on ahead and pick him up, I'll be along." I stood there looking down at him. "You go ahead," he said. "I'll beat you there." I just stood in the front of the wagon, the coffin and rope and shroud behind me, looking down at him. "Do as I tell you," he said, "and I'll be much obliged."

I finally got my mouth open and got up wind to say

something, but he'd stuck his hands in his pockets and looked up at the ridge. "I declare," he said, "the shumate's turning."

Loren McElroy

When we walked into the clearing, some of the ridge folk was there, squatting along the tree line murmuring, drawing idly in the dirt with sticks.

"Sometimes I'll see them Indians," she said, kneeling by the dripping spring, leaning over to see herself in the pool, "like pictures lightning'll leave inside your lid. Just as plain, sitting in a ring, passing their pipe, them old sagamores, drinking tafia, all that bright calico. . . ." She trailed off on the calico.

I said to the ridger with his brats dipping drinks out of the other side, "She'll see faces in clouds and her pa, dead twenty years, in water. Not every man has such a wife." Polite, he didn't say nothing. They walked off.

"All in the wink of an eye. Then gone." She hadn't let go of it.

"When will you go to talking sense?"

"When will you go to hell?"

"A pretty way to talk!"

"Pa'd a beat me for it."

"You're trying yourself."

"Where's my baby? What have you done with him?"

"Made a man of him."

"No!" she wailed.

"Hushup, they're looking."

She spun and hollered at them, "Look!"

So I pulled her into the brush and slapped her. "Take holt of yourself, Hedy. A pretty come-off!" I had her arm behind her. I give it a twist. "Will you behave?"

"Yes," she said.

"Say it!"

"I'll behave."

I let her go. We walked back into the clearing as Tige dismounted. He tied the hackney to a tree and walked over. "They're coming now," he said. "I ain't slept a wink. Halfway to California and back to get his lordship home in time for his bath and dinner and featherbed. If we had a trimmed some Texas tree with him it'd all been over and I'd a got some sleep. I didn't see nobody bustling to get my supper, much less bath and featherbed. I was privileged to set in a straight chair all night and watch him sleep."

"Calm down," I said.

"Cahm down! You think he's the crazy one, but ay-God, she does him one better. Stopped in the yard in plain sight a the road and stripped him buck nakit. I like to choked. Then set fire to them. Taken him in her kitchen and poured a bucket of cold and a kettle of hot in a tub and lathered and scrubbed till I reckon he'll be the cleanest jaybird ever to decorate that tree." He'd got a plug someplace. Offered it to me—black, gummy-looking thing. He took a bite. "Clean, he's still black as a nigger ceptin where his pants were. Little frail-looking baby butt, dong more like a ding. I wonder is it good for anything but to pee."

"Watch your mouth."

"Duncan had a spell or something. He'll be along."

And here he comes, walking, green round the gills, leading the brute. She moaned and it looked to become a wail. "Hushup." She hushed. He'd seen her. Lips loose, looked like the idiot. Before the two of them could get together and act like fools, the sound of a wagon rumbling, Earl yelling at the mule. They hurtled into the clearing, Earl standing up, reins round his wrists, hauling back on the mule so hard he slanted, Isaac behind him seated on his coffin.

Duncan McElroy

Hung back to walk with her but she didn't want my company. I'd of left Plunder in her barnlot but she wouldn't have it. I went and got him and thrown on my makeshift saddle but left the girth loose. I couldn't a rode him. Wagon already out of sight but not out of hearing, and still in my mind's eye his face lit up to see Earl motion him into the wagon. I never looked Earl in the eye nor him me. He spoke gruff to her: "You can ride with him." She just looked. Earl climbed the wheel and undid the reins from the brake and yelled, "Giddy-up" like he was mad at somebody.

I got there just behind Earl and him. I seen Ma. I didn't want her to speak to me, touch me, nothing. I kept away. Then here come Eustace on his gelding. He was there before she come down the path behind me, carrying her calico. Cat looked fierce in the eye and coiled the way she held him, tight as a child will, her head bent, bonnet hiding her face. Stopped at the edge of the clearing. It was mostly ridgers. No Toliver. No Tuttle. No Emile. No Tuckahoe that I could see. Some of the ridgers had climbed onto the ledge over the dripping spring where they could get a good look. Bunch of ragtag. Got to be in on everything. Way they are.

Then along behind Eustace, kind of running, rolling on the outsides of his feet like a cripple, flinging his arms, coattails flapping, and you couldn't make out what he was saying, let alone the sense of it, Mister Hite with Georgia sort of bashed, following on the mule, leading the horse.

All eyes on Eustace. Taking his own good time, he dismounted and carefully looped a limb and tied a slipknot on the bridle and turned and looked at the wagon and Earl standing up in it with the lines wrapping his wrists, looking angrily at the woods. We watched Eustace—bareheaded, grizzled—walk up to the mule and in the quiet heard him say to Earl, "I'd a thought you'd a put blinders on the mule." Earl—face swollen, angry—never looked around nor said nothing, just stood in the front of the wagon that way, waiting. Eustace looked at Isaac sitting on his coffin. Stood there a minute and looked at him. Then hands in pockets he strolled to the back wheel. Took his hands out for balance and put a foot on the wheelhub and we could hear his grunt as he swung up onto the wagon bed. Stood there looking around before he said, "Pull up a little, will you, Earl." And Earl stood there a minute like he didn't hear before he taken a better grip on the lines and clucked angrily to the mule and slapped the lines along its back. The mule lunged and Eustace like to lost his balance. The wagon lurched under the pasture oak and Earl yelled, "Whoa" and called it some names and stood there, lines round his wrists, glaring at the woods. Eustace turned and looked at Isaac again.

We all waited, even Mister Hite. I thought *Eustace ain't a-going to do it!* I was surprised. Then more surprised that I'd ever thought he would. Suddenly it didn't seem reasonable to think it was a thing Eustace nor anybody there could really do. And if Eustace didn't, him the next-of-kin, it wouldn't be done. Looked like the same thought was in everybody's mind. Some it disappointed. Trash.

We all heard Eustace say, "Stand up, will you, son."

Isaac sat looking up at him. I turned and found her face. Face out of dough, eyes burned pure of all expression.

Heard it again. "Stand up, son." Spun to see Eustace reach and take his elbow and help him to his feet. Then Eustace picked up the coiled rope Isaac had been sitting on and slowly played it out and, taking his time, squinted up to get the height of the first limb, then swung and missed.

Mister Hite flew at the little knot of us, shouting something you couldn't make out, wheeled and would of stormed the wagon but Pa stepped in front of him and, when he moved on, Pa straight-armed him in the chest and the old man bounced, sat down, looking startled up at Pa. He staggered to his feet yelling, "Not a man? Not one?" Clambered up the rock ledge over the dripping spring crying, "Spectacle! Are you Romans?" Eustace turned and looked up at the preacher crowding the ridgers. Some come on down. But then Eustace thrown the rope easy and a little ripple ran it up. The end, knotted for weight, dropped over the limb and he sent another ripple and it slid on down to where he could reach it. Mister Hite, yelling, run at the ridgers like a rabid feist, clearing the ledge. Eustace pulled the other end through the loop and looked up at the limb. We all looked up. He pulled till the loop slipped tight around it, then reached both hands over his head and taken a good grip and in a seemly way lifted his weight. It held. Both feet back on the wagon, he went to fashioning the noose. I couldn't move my eyes, I watched like learning how. I could a done it after him exactly.

"Eustace!" It was Mister Hite. Eustace, startled, the noose in his hand, turned and looked up at him. "You cain't take this boy's life!" Mister Hite cried.

Eustace waited.

"Why cain't you? I'll tell you! Are you ready to lose yourn?" Silence. Eustace waiting. "Are you cannibal? He ain't a chicken or a fish that you can eat him!"

Eustace paused another minute, but I could tell it was manners. All it was. Then turned and put the noose over Isaac's head. In such a gentle way he pulled it tight. Then taken a heavy cord out of his pocket. And when he seen it, why Isaac held out his hands and watched Eustace tie them together at the wrist.

"Eustace!"

This time Eustace gave no sign he heard. We saw his lips move and knew he'd said something to Isaac, but we never heard it. Then he took Isaac by the elbow and helped him step atop his coffin.

Mister Hite shouted, "God said let him go!" Nobody looking at him.

Eustace walked up the wagon bed and touched Earl on the shoulder. Earl spun around like taken by surprise and ready to fight it made him so mad.

Mister Hite flapped around the ledge, a great awkward bird, nobody looking at him, just an embarrassment in the background. Eustace unwound the lines from around

Earl's wrists hisself, taking his time, while Earl looked down, startled, and watched.

Mister Hite on the brink of the ledge bent into his yell. "God said let the live goat go! Put on his head all your sins and send him into the wilderness! But no! You brought him back from the wilderness with *your* weakness, *your* darkness, *your* night of fears on him, and you think destroy him you destroy them! But that ain't the way! They *leave* the dead like mites leave the skin of a shot bird and come to rest again in you! You ought to've left the live goat in the wilderness! He is your innocence. Don't destroy it!"

Turned loose from the lines, Earl fell back off-balance, face white and somehow shapeless, arms long, palms up showing theirselves empty, held out as if to Isaac. He fell back a step, another, past Isaac, face toward him like Isaac was someone he had to keep an eye on.

"Is he a sin offering?" Mister Hite, at the top of his lungs, wanted to know. A crow flopping around on that rock. "Then it's your sin!" Earl like to fell off the tail of the wagon, but landed crouched, on his feet, still staring up at Isaac, mouth open. "But if he's the other'n, then shall he be presented live before the temple! And a fit man shall lay hands on the head of the live goat and confess over him all your weaknesses, all your sins and put them on the head of the goat, on the live goat's head, and send him *away!*"

Eustace winding the lines about his own wrists now. "By the hand of a fit man! Is they a fit man?" In one leap, on top of a waist-high rock up there, railing like an incubus. "The live goat shall bear on him all your iniquities into a not-inhabited land! Said the Lord let go the goat into the wilderness! *I am the Lord!* And he that let go the

241

goat shall wash his clothes! And bathe his flesh in water! And what man soever that *killeth* the goat, *blood* shall be imputed to that man and he shall be cut off from among his people!" Eustace holding the lines now, ready to slap the mule's rump but waiting for the preacher to be done. And Jay Dubya leaping, bounding, flaying the air. And suddenly it's in Jay Dubya's voice and out of Eustace's hands, it's Jay Dubya's voice that's the beginning and the end and Eustace just waiting, obedient to it. If it never stops Isaac'll never die. Us listening, watching Isaac's living face. "And that man shall be known as a blood eater!" Isaac bewildered, casting around, looking at us, at the preacher, turning to look at Eustace, look up at the tree. "And the Lord said, I will set my face against him and cut him off from among his *people! I am the Lord!*" Eustace waiting. Jay Dubya must hisself know it's his voice spreads a shelter over Isaac and, hoarse, he spews and breathes aloud and screams, "It is written! Unto an uninhabited land let him go! But no! You drag him the whole long miserable way back from the wild and now—would you send him to the vast inhabited land of the dead with your sins upon him? You! Sons of Aaron! You err! I am speaking to you of things which ought not be done!" Panting, face wide open like it reflects and you can see in it what he sees. But he's stopped. We all watch Eustace. I've found an angle where I can fix my eye on Eustace and just see Eustace without seeing Isaac. Isaac's just a darkness at the edge of sight. I can tell he's there and keep track of him fixing my eye on Eustace. But while I watch, Eustace lifts the lines. I've fixed my eye on him, but when I see him lift the reins, at the start of that movement—see Isaac or not—I can't work it that way but have to close them, not just close them, clamp them, not just clamp them, put hands over them to shut out all of it and daylight with it. I hear the reins slap, the mule lunge, rattle of chains, wagon creaking like it'll fall apart, can hear, feel, know, but don't have to see.

A shriek, and then: "Blind! Broken! Maimed! Wenned! Scurvied! Scabbed! *Cover* yourself with risings! You are *blemished!* And *never* shall go before the throne! You shall not avenge! I am the Lord!"

And don't know if the shriek was hers or Mister Hite's or maybe the calico cat's. It wasn't Isaac's. All eyes on him when I open mine. Still moving as if stirred by the faintest wind, turning a little at the end of the rope, his dangling feet in Emile's old mocs. It's them toes without nothing under them, like they been failed some way, that pull my cord. Eustace still wrestling with the mule. Finally stops him, quieting him when Mister Hite, his voice louder now it's so low, standing there on the rim of the ledge looking down at us, thickened from below, hands heavy, long as an ape's, way out of his sleeves. "Oh how shall ye be cleansed? With running water? With scarlet? Hyssop? Two birds and cedar wood? Don't believe it. Oh don't you believe it!" The spring drips in the silence. Then making a sudden leap like wrath has burned off all his age, he lands by the pool and wades in under the dripping spring, his hair that was smoke becoming a different matter, dripping down his face, molding the shape of his head. Makes a shell of his hands and scoops them before him full of water and rises up coming toward us holding them cupped out to us full of the stained water, and coming at us up out of the spring—Isaac's turning feet graze his ear—cries, "Blood. Blood. Blood." And flings it all over us. Rained on, baptized anew with red water, we fall back. "Blood!" His voice shudders, breaks, and hoarse and whispery, "I am he and no other with me, I kill and I make alive, I wound and I heal. None can deliver out of my hand and I live forever." Eyes burning. A shudder travels my track. "If I whet my sword and take aholt of judgment, I'll make my arrows drunk with blood from the beginning of revenges!" And moves on past so I see Earl walk toward Isaac and reach out and still them feet. And Eustace, sawing on the lines, backs the mule and the wagon till Earl can leap up in the wagon bed, then fixes the lines to the brake and turns. I see him look for Isaac and find him, and —I don't believe it, don't want it, won't have what I see. Eustace is crying. I want to scream, shout filth, damn and bless and laugh till I die of it. If you're a killer, how're you different from Isaac? If you're a killer, is everybody, the only difference what lets you? If someone like Isaac ain't got the control but lets go and kills then he's fair game outside the circle, releasing us all to step out of the circle and kill, only no one but the killer, and the circle nothing but a line drawn with a stick in sand? Oh Lord pity the kilt and pity the killer, in a desert without shelter or hope beset by the pack, their checkreins broke, utterly free.

Earl says, "Come hep me." I walk closer and stop. "Come on. Hep me," Earl says. I climb up in the wagon and Earl cuts him down and I catch him. His weight comes as a shock—not the weight but that it's dead weight. I look down. His head lolls on my chest. His eyes ain't quite shut. His chin's turned blue. The rest of his face looks black under the film of skin, the way water looks black under a skin of ice, like the beginning of a green, not like a new bruise, like an old bruise fading. And look and as I look back off and see myself holding him and inside my head an amazed voice says *Me*.

Earl's doing something with the coffin, shoving it toward the tailgate. He's taken off the top and set it aside and turns back to me and reaches out for him. I give him to Earl. He carries him on back and lays him in it, grunting as he lets go. Squatting, he looks at him for the longest, then says, "Reckon why he done it?" I can't think what he's talking about. I leap down, it feels like escaping just in time. She stands there clutching her cat, head bowed in its old bonnet. Earl clucks to the mule and turns the wagon and pulls out of the clearing. They wait, then walk behind it.

The only one left, I turn and run, leaving horse, losing hat, run hard as I can run till lungs burst, eardrums split, and heart a melon grows and bursts. That's all I can remember.

Earl

She set its ends on two chairs, a candle at the head and another at the foot. And everbody done as they always done—come by and set with her. Most stayed the night—us squatting out in the yard, watching the women and their outsize shadows on the porch, inside, everwhere. She wouldn't let us in, except to bring him and go get him in the morning. We built a little fire. Not good fall yet but the night was long. And chill. We were into that little cold spell'll sometimes edge in ahead of Indian summer and we could see our breath. Off across her yam patch

Poor Will mourned out of season. Tige he'd got hold of a batch of corn. It was something to warm us. Wasn't as if the fire thrown any heat, just shadows we could a done without. Duncan stomped his feet and hugged hisself and now and then went "Whoo-ee!" after he'd had a nip. Then Hedy would come stand on the porch peering into the dark and Loren would tell him to hush up. The Poor Will come in on the chorus.

"Seen one a them once't," Gem said, "whiskers like a cat, all hunkered down in a little nest of sand, asleep in the wagon trace."

"They'll do that to get rid of mites," Loren said.

"I was *that* close before it flew. I was carrying a calabash and got a good look at him."

"You don't often see them," Loren said.

"They say if you get a look at one by day, they eyes are little bitty slits. But when he woke up and flew, them night eyes was big as owl eyes. Only one I ever set eyes on in my life."

Loren said again, "You don't often see them."

"Hand me that," she said to Tige, reaching.

"I ain't th'oo with it," he said.

"Hand it here."

"You had enough to float yourself. Mor'n the rest of us."

She honked in her hankie and stuffed it in her bib, then swiped the jar out a his hand. "I require more. I'm bigger than some I could mention."

Duncan giggled.

Tige said, "Woman."

She lowered the jar and looked at him. "Watch yourself." She drank and coughed and swiped at her eyes with her sleeve.

"Nothing but true," Tige said, looking around at us. "All she is."

Gem got slowly to her feet and loomed over him where he sat, and said, "You want to try and prove that?"

Tige give a hoot and somehow stood up. "I'll be obliged," he said, commencing to unbutton his fly.

Eustace wasn't there. Loren wasn't apt to say nothing. Gem stood with her face raddling while he went on unbuttoning. She thrown down the empty. "All right. Let's see can you get it up. I'll use it as a handle and scythe them woods with you, runt!" But he kept on smirking and kept on unbuttoning. Duncan sat cross-legged, giggling, rocking, holding onto his ankles. Tige wasn't going to stop. She lurched off angrily into the woods.

"Put it back," Loren said to Tige.

"Works like a charm," Tige said. "Let her go. What we want with her? Let her go on in yonder with them whur she belongs."

Duncan giggled.

"Put it up," Loren said.

Tige took a step backwards and sat hard. He looked down at his limp peter. "Gitchee gitchee," he said, chucking it under the chin.

Duncan fell over backwards laughing.

"Did you hear me?" Loren said. "Put it away." And rising, he picked up his gun and walked over to the big dead tree standing alone some yards before the woods and taken a tenpenny nail from his pocket and pounded it in with a rock till maybe two inches was left showing. Then he stood back and handed the gun to Tige. Tige taken it and put it to his shoulder, laying his cheek along it and, closing one eye, fired. The gun knocked him down again.

The shot ripped through leaves, never even hit the tree. So Loren handed the gun to Duncan and Duncan fired and sent up a little rain of bark. I shook my head and passed, so Loren he taken slow aim and bam! drove the nail. I went over and felt of it. Hot. Maybe an inch still showed.

"Give it here," I said. "Let me finish it for you."

And shot and missed the tree. Georgia come back out of curiosity and tried. She bent the nail. Then Loren's Hedy come out on the porch and said, "Have you not one ounce of pity?" So we quit.

Then Tuckahoe appeared inside the wheel of firelight.

"I be dog!" Tige said. "Looky who's here! Where you been?"

Tuck said, "You could have kilt me, banging away like that." Had a little trickle of blood on his temple that he kept swiping at.

"Lord," Tige laughed, "you couldn't a grazed him like that if you'd been trying. Reckon whose shot it was? If it had a kilt you, we wouldn't a known who to—" He didn't finish.

Tuckahoe walked up to the fire, took his hands out of the pockets of his leather coat, and held them out to warm them. Seeing the bottle in Georgia's hand, he reached for it. "Where you been hiding?" she asked. She let him have the bottle.

Tuck drank and coughed and wiped his mouth and stood there looking at the house, then drank some more. "You hung him." It wasn't a question. It was and it wasn't. Still hadn't looked at a one of us.

"*We* didn't," Tige said. "It was Eustace."

"It was Eustace," Duncan said.

Tuck replugged the bottle and drove it in with the heel

of his hand and handed it at arm's length aside to me though I never asked for it and he never known who he was handing it to, and strode off toward the house. "They won't let you in!" Tige yelled after him. But he kept on going and made the steps and crossed the porch. At the sound of his heavy footstep, she come to stand blocking the door. We watched him brush her aside—not rude or rough—and go on in. After a little he come out and stood still on the edge of the porch a minute, then come on down the steps and crossed the yard in about three strides. I handed him back the bottle. Everbody kept quiet but he never let on how it was in there.

Poor Will, closer now and holding on longer. *Whip! Whip! Whip*poor*will! Whip*poor*will!*

"They're something like a nighthawk," Georgia said. "Flat-headed."

Loren said, "It's a goatsucker." He took and threw a stick of kindling into the woods to try and shut him up. It did for about a minute.

I kept coming back to Tuckahoe, that little twist of a smile at the corner of his mouth. And heard myself say, "It's all the same, ain't it?"

He looked at me. That little twist of smile. Never said nothing.

Then Will again, begging for his punishment, I would of sworn still closer, in a frenzy and never paused. You couldn't see how he could get breath enough to make all that racket. Right in your ear. *Whip*poor*will! Whip*poor*will! Whip*poor*will! Whip*poor*will! Whip*poor*will!*

"There he is," Tige yelled. We all seen the branch move at the edge of the woods. Duncan grabbed his slingshot and let go. Something hit the ground. Then for an instant the firelight picked up a glowing eye. "It's a painter!" Tige yelled. Duncan took aim and slung a second rock. The eye went out.

"I dog!" he yelled. "I got him!"

Loren walked over to see. He laughed and looked up at Duncan and said, "Painter!" He prodded it with his toe and bent over and picked it up by the tail—her big old one-eyed cat. He hauled back and flung it hard as he could into the woods. We heard it go like a live animal running through dead leaves. We heard it hit.

Duncan commenced to giggle, this time sobs in it. He threw down the sling and fell on his stomach, quiet for a while, sulking. Now and again you'd hear that giggle.

Nobody said nothing for the longest. Then here come Will shrieking. *Whip*poor*will! Whip*poor*will! Whip*poor*will!* Duncan put his hands over his ears. Loren he got up and taken a burning club out of the fire and walked toward the cry. *Whip*poor*will!* inside your head. It had moved. It was in the dead tree. Loren took his bearings and flung the lit wood. The bird hushed. The stick of wood caught up there in the crotch of the tree. For a minute it smoldered, then burst back into flame. Tree'd been split by lightning. The top had broke off and fell to lie so rotten and claimed by moss and fungus it was more like one long mole tunnel running toward the woods than like a treetrunk. Then a little crackle and the flame disappeared. The burning wood had fallen into the hollow at the broken top. We could see the glow of it, then the flame licked higher and we could see that too. The tree was a torch.

Loren said, "It'll go out."

But a dead vine was climbing the tree and pretty soon the vine caught at the top and we watched the fire move slow then shoot ever which way the vine went. I wrenched the bottle away from Duncan and the fire shot through me too ever which way, through all my veins that branch and divide and branch.

"It'll go out," Loren said.

"I hope it don't," I said.

"Set before you fall," he said.

Hedy come out on the porch again. Duncan shot up and set staring at her. We all looked at her. I sat down.

"You'd think they don't know the meaning of justice," Tige said. "Think they never heard the word."

"Ain't a woman's word," Loren said. "They don't have no truck with it."

"Don't know ere thing about it," Tige said. "Never did, never will. One a their lacks." He hooted. *"One* a them."

"Pester you to death," Gem said, weaving up the yard to stand unsteady, waving the jar at the house. "They'll spoil the one to death then turn right around and despise the more deserving. Don't talk to me. I see it all the time."

Hedy was still there on the porch, watching the fired tree. We were all watching it. Except Duncan. Long as she stood there, Duncan looked at her. "Were you with Emile?" I asked Tuckahoe.

Someone coming down the path. "Ain't nobody asleep tonight," Tige said.

It was Eustace. In the light of the tree-torch, we could see him stop where the path spilled out of her yam patch, hair standing over his forehead like a beak, looking toward the house. She'd gone in off the porch, but in a minute here come another one out to look. The vine's thick trunk had caught. I started to call Eustace but I didn't. Nobody else did either. We were all looking at him.

After a little, he walked toward us, stopped for a look up at the burning tree, then come on over and squatted across the fire from us. Looked strange. Something in the way his eyes was open. Round. Wide. And over them, dark triangle hollows full of shadow.

"Hell," Tige said, spitting into the fire. "Pa used to tell about a man done some awful crime. They took and first they hung him and second th'own him in his own hoglot and left him overnight. Said he never seen nothing like it —like what it was in the morning."

I was on my feet and had him up by his shirtfront before I knew I'd moved, his eyes on me full of terror, and my other arm back far enough to knock him into the next valley when Eustace said, "Earl." I let him go. Off-balance, legs wheeling him backward till he come up against a sweet gum where he leaned, shorter than he is, legs splayed out in front of him, eyes full of fear fast clouding with anger. He could a kilt me. He'd a been welcome to try. I turned my back on him.

"You needn't a done that on account of me," Eustace said.

I spun on him and yelled, "I never done it for you!"

"Hell," Tige said, still leaning where he'd landed, against the tree, "I might as well go back to Texies."

Gem said, "You just come from there."

"I ain't got a home," he said. "When'd I ever have a home? I don't belong no place."

Loren said, "Just hush up that."

They all stared up at the burning tree, faces lit by it. Loren said, "It's out of the woods. It won't go no place."

Where the bark caught from the vine trunk, it commenced to smolder, then here and there combust. But hardly a sound, flames like cat tongues.

Tuckahoe said, "How come you did it?"

We all turned and looked at him, all but Duncan, who looked asleep.

Kate appeared at the edge of the potato patch. She never paused but walked on toward the house. Eustace's eye followed her till she'd disappeared inside.

Then Duncan said, "I'm tared thinking about it. He's dead, ain't he? Nothing would a come of him. Mama's boy. I mind the time I took him swimming. Bothered me the way he done nothing but tail her. Big boy like that. He wouldn't a made a man if he'd lived to be a hunderd. Old as he'd ever a got, no matter when he died. So it don't matter when it happened, does it? That's how I look at it and I'm tared thinking about it."

Tige said angrily, "Now he's dead, she can carry on. Would she a wanted him sleeping in the house with her, after what he done?"

Duncan—faced away, you could hardly hear him—said, "She could a built her a cage to keep him in." And giggled.

Tige said, "Alive, they didn't want him around. Claimed he'd mark their unborn. Dead, he's their favorite. Weaken, they set down on top of you. How they love you! Ay-God, don't it almost make you want to lay down and take his place?"

Duncan said, "All dressed up in lace like a baby, coffin too short for him, a crib. They had to lay him on his side and double his knees to make him fit." And the giggle.

Loren said, "Dry up. You kill a killer. All they is to it." He got up and walked over to the tree to inspect it.

"Don't know how we found him," Gem said.

Loren looking up at the tree said, "You got to be what you hunt—especially the weakness. There's the part'll put him in your sights, the part you're killing—looklike you can see it when you bring him down, lying in that pitiful punctured skin. The cunning, the wary, they ain't there. You feel strong again, you're shut of him."

Georgia took out the outsized handkerchief she'd been honking into all night and honked again. "This smoke is ruining my eyes." Held the handkerchief up by her fingertips. It wasn't a handkerchief. Some piece of clothing. "I had this dream—woke out of it, so remembered it—something about my old chest. Some treasure put away in that old trunk."

Eustace said, "I never set store by dreams."

"Last night I climbed up to the loft and rummaged." She held it up. "This here's what it was." She laughed. "Some treasure! I'd swear I never saw it before. But must of. Packed that trunk myself in Carolina. Nothing but old clothes I needn't a brought along."

Eustace said, "I class them with heat lightning."

She took and held it by her fingertips again, a little apron or pinafore a child might wear. Holding it up, she laughed and, rising, ungainly, held it like an apron, and it no more than a loincloth, and danced a jig about as graceful as her Rufus, and giddied, set down and, looking at the little dress in her lap, asked no one in particular, "Who you reckon it belonged to?" Then laughed and blew her nose in it and balled it up. "*I'd* a hung him for killing the girl if I'd a been next-of-kin."

"I never minded dreams," Eustace said.

Mister Hite come stumbling over clods through her salad, uncouth and ravaged. No sooner stumbled up than he reached for the jar. Loren give it to him. We all sat watching him drink and shudder and drink and cough and drink and break out sweating. Done all of us one better just the little time he stood there in front of us drinking. Then said sternly to Gem, "You are wanted at home."

She sighed and took the bottle out of his hand and handed it to me, then taken one of his wrists and bent over in front of him and give his wrist a jerk that pulled him off balance. He fell like a timber across her back. Grunting, she took and hoisted him higher. We watched her stagger off. Then, bent square, she paused and turned. "Would someone hand that here?"

I picked up the little apron and carried it over to her.

"Just put it in his pocket," she said.

I done it. She trudged off homeward under the weight of him. The tree burning steady now, flames shooting maybe two foot out of the hollow top, give quite a light.

Eustace said, "Heat lightning." Loren offered him the jar. He shook his head. "I never been one to ponder does He exist or don't He. Always seemed to me one way or the other not to matter. I recall I was angry with her over some trifle, I forget what. It was her wedding day. I never believed in dreams, and anyway, I heard her safe with her mother in the kitchen. That one shocked me straight up in bed though. But I went back to sleep. Heat lightning. Saw her running through the deadening. I was stumbling after her, calling—" He stopped, had to bring himself to it, then cried, "Eily! Eily." Had to stop again before he went on. "And the same time seemed like it was me she was running *to*. There was some reason I couldn't save her. Like in a children's tale. Like Lot's wife and you mustn't look back. Yes, I remember. I mustn't see whatever was after her, wanting to . . . I see now it was Isaac. If dreams mean anything."

"How do you see that?" Tuck asked in a small voice.

"I remember whoever it was chased her because he loved her and didn't want her to leave him. Like Isaac. It was her wedding day." Fell silent for a time. Then, squatting across from us, looking at the fire, "I thought when I hung him that'd be the end of it." He sighed. "I didn't do it in anger. That wore out long ago. Wasn't for justice. There ain't none ceptin restitution. Couldn't a been restitution. Wasn't for hate. When I done it I loved him. He might a been part of me. Wasn't he something! All that way." Looked up at the tree.

Duncan sat straight up and yelled, "Sonabitch! I'm tared thinking about it!"

I sat there saying to myself over and over what I'd in other times defined to myself: *We all of us followed Eustace, for Eustace is a man fills out his space. You can trust Eustace. You can trust Eustace.* Then told myself quit thinking *Eustace,* try and think *Earl,* but only felt hot with anger, felt like Duncan felt, tired thinking about it. Felt like I felt standing there looking at him with the noose round his neck and Eustace lifting the lines to slap the mule, and me saying to him to myself: *You ain't nothing! Don't know nothing! Who are you? Ain't nobody! Not even a name but Isaac! And causing us all this!* I hated him. *Hated* him. Wanted to get it over and done with.

Kate stepped out of the house and, pulling her shawl about her, come on down the steps. She never looked at us but did look up once at the tree. When she'd almost crossed the potato patch, Eustace got up and went with his head bowed following her. The woods and the dark swallowed them but we went right on watching where they'd disappeared.

Tuckahoe, smiling his twist of smile, said, "Yes, well, I see, but only him you never kilt is dead." Then flung back his head and laughed, stretching that awful mask of a face.

"Were you with Emile?" I asked him again.

"You all rode off last night and left me to make a meal of water."

Nobody said nothing till I said, "Where you been all this time?"

"Why," he said, "I was detained by a sick friend now dead and in the grave I made him."

I watched his strange face some time before I said, "Emile?"

He nodded. "I stayed at your noisy spring. By and by a sound you can't mistake, a horse munching whole apples. When the moon rose, I found the old man's pony, unsaddled, trailing his reins, and finally found him under the church. He was all night dying. At sunup I buried him and fell asleep. I just woke up." Nobody let on like they heard. He reached for the jar. He turned it up. Empty. We'd run dry. And dark still stretching ahead of us.

Eustace Jurdin

Here in a fiction of sleep that mocks death, beside her a stiff except for the part that would not stand for a lady tonight. I guess I'm done. Others can talk, it never happened to me.

"Are you all right?"

I know you despised me, running off after justice, leaving you alone to wash her and dress her and follow her to the bed of her long night and witness her wed to the dirt flung on top of her.

"Eustace?"

Despised me because I turned and run. There may be good reasons for not staying and facing. Because you can't is not one of them.

"Are you awake?"

Despised me again today. And now—they can talk, it never happened to me before. The first time.

The first time since the first time.

She was a handsome woman with russet hair. I see her yet. A handsome woman with russet hair. When I told you, you thought I'd married you for the color of your hair.

Just a boy, not yet sixteen, driving a six-ox team alone to Charleston when, overtaken by dark near a well-to-do farm, I went in to ask could I sleep in the barn that night. And she, a woman of middle age, her husband gone to market some cows—and her sons, all older than I was then, grown and married with farms of their own—she was alone and said she'd be glad for company. So I went to unharness and bed my father's team while she heated a supper. Then she sat with me in the candle's light while I ate, and questioned me about myself. It was so cheerful to come in off the lonely road out of the dark to a lighted room and a pleasant lovely sort of woman, rust in her hair. When I'd eaten, I drew her a bucket of water for the dishes. She heated it on her big cookstove and poured me a panful and gave me a towel and sent me out to the porch to wash myself. I enjoyed the mothering. And while I stood shirtless at the bench, my galluses down my thighs, she came out to empty the dishpan and looked at me and said my mother must be proud of such a sturdy son. I heated, not for the praise but for the sudden forwardness against my drawers at being seen like that. She never looked but I'd swear she saw. Then, buttoned into my shirt again, I went in. She showed me a bed and left me, taking the lamp so the light went out with her, and I undressed and lay rigid in the dark because she also inhabited it. And when she came back without the lamp, I knew it wasn't a dream when she laid her hand along my cheek. A handsome woman with russet hair, the mother of sons my senior. And asked was it the first time. I lied. And when she'd drawn her gown off at her shoulders, I pillowed myself the length of her and I felt rich. In the pale lamp of a waning moon, in the luxury of bodies touching, I saw you smile. You guided me, gentled me. Relaxed in your certainty, I took my time, *all the time in the world* ran in my mind, fainting to feel your hands gently down my back, till I felt you gasp and open and swallow me deep. I never felt so strong, and stroking felt I grew again inside you till I thought I opened virgin depths and heard your small bird sounds of pleasure as your pulse commenced to suck, to pull, and finally to milk this member in a moment maintained out of time.

"Eustace?"

Where are you now? Old, grey your russet hair, no, must be dead, your body, the first that housed me, moldering. I've circled my round. Left mother to bed wife loved daughter and buried her found wife again to cry upon my mother.

"Oh Eustace."

Earl

In the morning we straggled by the dripping spring. Some of us plunged our whole head in and went on, dripping, up the hill to wait. I never offered to bear the pall. It was Gem and Nab brought it, unmatched pair of scarecrows, thrown together, Gem pale and hollow-eyed. She come behind them, followed it up front, never sat, stood there like she might a been waiting her turn to get over a footbridge, that's all. When she passed, I looked at her face and seen something new in it. Always meek and feared, and that still there. But anger?

Last, Mister Hite. Except for the well his eyes looked out of, he was trim, coat brushed, hair maybe clipped a little. Pale where Gem'd shaved him. And stood up there, head bowed, eyes closed. Never the whole time looked out at us on the pine benches.

"O Lord, don't speak to me, speak th'oo me." And sighed, getting his breath, faced us, eyes closed.

"Now listen. I'll tell you. No man has ever died. I ain't a-saying what you think I'm saying. Ain't talking about your hereafter or your immortal soul. Let that alone. Lay it down. Listen. No man who ever lived ever died." Stood there with his eyes closed like in spite of addressing us he wasn't talking to us, more to hisself, saying his thoughts instead of thinking them, finding them in words. "No man ever lived ever died. Men don't die. Men live. That's all.

No man has ever *done* it. Died. It is something you will never do. Can't be done. Just a word. All it is. A man commences to live and he lives and that's all they is to it. He is and he ain't. He don't come out of nothing and go into nothing. Can't even say a thing like that, for nothing must be something to fill us with such dread. Nosir—man don't die and he don't go into this dreadful nothing." Pacing a little to the right, a little to the left, "You say you once seen a man dying? I say if he was dying he was living. If he's living how can he be dying? You say you known a man now dead? I say no man can *be,* dead. No. No man who ever lived ever died. It's a thing a man cain't do. Cain't be done. How can a man be dead? The answer is, he cain't. Dead, no man can be. So no use to say he is. Dead, he ain't. That's all they is to it. Ain't. All you can say is a man lives, then that he has lived, and that's all, all in the world they is to the matter. It ain't a fearful thing."

While he was saying it, I caught a hold of it, a slippery hold. I couldn't hang onto it. Even when I caught it, it was sliding away from me. But I had it a minute there, while he was saying it. It went, but it left me knowing I'd had a holt of it, for a minute. And if I'd grasped it, then I'd known it too, this that he was saying that one way can't be said a-tall and the other way is a word game. But couldn't keep it, couldn't hang onto it.

He would a walked on out then, but one of the women hit a note and give it to the rest and they sang. And finally, they was still singing, Nab and Gem they got him and carried him out. I don't know who dug the grave, but there it was, shovel stuck up in the mound beside Emile's fresh grave next to Eily. Tuck was standing there all hunched into hisself, eyes narrowed against the smoke from his acrid Indian weed that mixed with the smell of

261

woodsmoke from the burning tree. I never knew had he been inside. We stood around and two nearly grown ridge boys held ropes across it and they set it on them and they played out the ropes. We watched it go down. Bottom must of been uneven. It settled at an angle. Nobody done nothing about it. I kept knowing Isaac was in that box and then see just the box.

Mister Hite went and stood at the head and though he never closed his eyes he never looked at anybody. And never raised his voice. Said it again, "No man ever lived ever died." But by then I'd lost it. By then I couldn't make fish, fowl, hide nor hair of it. Said to myself, *Ain't we this minute burying Isaac? Ain't Emile lying down there, dirt on his face?* He said: "It ain't a fearful thing. But if you can't see it that away, if you're saying in your heart I'm afraid, and I'm sick to death O Lord, sick sick sick to death O Lord my Lord of living in this world of sin sin sin, then I say to you, don't th'ow it out, oh don't revile it. This is the Jesus world."

The Tuckahoe

You said as soon as you feel, nothing's the same. But where is feeling now beneath one mound of three and all the same—so wide, so long, so deep, same sun, same earth, same matter, same elements, finally same dust? Old Frenchman talented in love, you kept each wife and the last love planted here beside you distinct in a memory that while it conjured them expired. But there they were and here they are in a green gauze sun. Emile lolls on the bank of a rilly stream, fishing, smoking his calumet. The boy with trousers rolled wades after crawdads, and the girl prone in a yellow dress along the trunk of a willow growing out over the water, faced away. In words that floated up from you, a picture you took a last look at and left with me? No matter. She lifts toward me as my vision fails a face I'll never see that dying chased them by its lack to fill it with another lack, and you another. Old man, which love's dying killed you most? Isaac's the one led you here, as you went all that way along to fetch him so he wouldn't be alone. Did you mean to keep him company this far back? You'll prove my point. Worms tunneling through will know you're all one earth. This grave will integrate you faster than my mind.

Toliver Pullen

There was a pumpkin moon so we never stopped for night, just when we had to rest the animals. But too late. Knew it soon as we pulled up in the churchyard and looked at them. Three. I guess I'd expected two. I got down off Beth, Tuttle off Enoch. He stood there at a loss after we'd hurried so, then took off his hat. I walked over to the bluff, no prayer in me nor no curse either, just a weight suspended in my chest, hung by the cords of my throat, and the remains of a flare of anger, that old expectation of reward for effort, for my exhaustion, marrow-deep, and all a waste.

It was along about sundown. I stood looking over Culloden valley, each house pointed out by the finger of smoke from its chimney—the Hites' place, Eustace's, McElroys'. No smoke thread from Emile. The third must be Emile. Eily, Isaac, Emile. No smoke from your own chimney, Lazarus. She's gone.

Lottie Petrie walked out with us to that other crest, arms crossed under her shawl. She'd argued, but I'd waked out of the fever crying "Isaac!" She squinted with thread and needle half the night over my old shirt. Made a bat out of cotton fresh from the boll, still full of seeds, backed it with outing and quilted it like a vest into my rag of shirt to protect my chest, grumbling, "Always in a hurry." But I sat still and content in her rocker, feet crossed on the fender, pleasuring in her, in the fire.

At sunup she walked us out to the bluff, and looking at that broad valley corridor I stood shimmering with weakness but with light, with air, dry odors of leaves, woodsmoke, the horses, my own damp flesh. Such distance in air blue as innocence, our view channeled by comely low hills, the only straight line the horizon and that in the eye as time in the thought. I felt presence. Not *a* presence, not my presence. Presence. Where light fell on bare earth, colors of flesh shimmering. Alive, all of it.

When I'd finished looking at her, I climbed on Beth. Holding onto my stirrup strap, she walked me to the head of her road. "Turtle," she said, "you the only man I ever saw'll wear out his shoes riding a mule."

Tuttle said, "Lottie Petrie good-bye."

Turned in my saddle, I watched her there long as I

could make her out. Now on this ridge too. One of those feelings that budding into thought dies.

Walking, leading our horses, we descended into yellow of hickory, chestnut, poplar, gold maples, sweet gum, red oak, and black gum. Shumate all gone. Pastern-deep humus of colored leaves. Strangely light, walking, after riding so long.

And into my lane where no wheel had turned leaves, no smoke marked a hearth. The stone in me, sadness. Then saw you, your back to me, walking toward the house.

You heard footsteps. You stopped and stood a moment before turning. At that distance, in that light, I couldn't see your face but could see the child in you riding high. Nature, you beggar, you'll accept anything. All that striving to complete a beginning. Such confusion of feelings, each canceling another. What were yours as you stood there, wind stirring your shawl, and one of those giant leaves you see only on seedlings turning, reaching, expiring against your dress?

You said, "Toliver." I couldn't touch you, neither did you find any simple form. I gave Beth to Tuttle and walked with you to the kitchen house. You lifted the chimney, lit the lamp, I stirred the embers in your banked fire and laid on wood. As we looked at each other, a kingfisher rattled the silence I didn't have to fill.

"I told myself long as Tuttle's not back. When I heard you, I was afraid if I turned I'd see only Tuttle."

Standing a little off from me, almost as tall as me, dark hair rich where the light fell into it, grave face, no mask. I once asked when you first knew you loved me. You said, "One day at home I dried my face on a towel you'd used," confusing me, too plain for the marvel I'd made you into.

"Are you hungry?"

I nodded. You dipped your chin, turned toward the sideboard, grey eyes under those dark brows. When I couldn't see your face, I watched your hands, long fingers blunt-ended.

You poured a little glass of wine and, turning, held it out to me. Your shawl slid down your arm. Reaching awkwardly across your breast, your free hand tugged it back in place. I couldn't look at your face for looking at your hand. It was shaking. And the glass, the reflected lamplight, those fingers, wine redder than ruby, cherry wine, all trembling. And in the clear wine the loom behind you threaded with some bright stuff, the kegs of staples, coffee mill on the wall, fire in your stove, all upside down in the red wine trembling, shattering in fragments to reform between your fingers in the glass you offered me while your other hand grasped the shawl.

71 72 73 10 9 8 7 6 5 4 3 2 1

Boston Public Library

Copley Square

PZ4
.D27LI

04245340

The Date Due Card in the pocket indi-
cates the date on or before which this
book should be returned to the Library.

Please do not remove cards from this
pocket.